Lucienne Diver writes the story beautifully giving you enough information from other books so you're not lost if this is the first one you have read. It also motivates you to read whatever you have missed! The investigations and people surrounding Tori are a blast to read, and you will enjoy every moment of it. I look forward to the next book in the series and following the antics of Tori and Apollo. *Blood Hunt* is an excitement-filled mystery with great characters and a good twist at the end.

FRESH FICTION

DISAPPEARED

DISAPPEARED

LUCIENNE DIVER

WFP
WORDFIRE PRESS

EBook ISBN: 978-1-68057-120-2
Trade Paperback ISBN: 978-1-68057-119-6
Hardcover ISBN: 978-1-68057-121-9
Cover design by Janet McDonald
Cover artwork images by Adobe Stock
Kevin J. Anderson, Art Director
Published by
WordFire Press, LLC
PO Box 1840
Monument CO 80132
Kevin J. Anderson & Rebecca Moesta, Publishers
WordFire Press eBook Edition 2020
WordFire Press Trade Paperback Edition 2020
WordFire Press Hardcover Edition 2020

Printed in the USA
Join our WordFire Press Readers Group for
sneak previews, updates, new projects, and giveaways.
Sign up at wordfirepress.com

✿ Created with Vellum

ONE

Friday morning

Emily

EMILY TUGGED her sleeve down into place, but she could still see the cut. It was thick, red, and angry. Not thin and healing like some of the others. Probably she should have used butterfly Band-Aids or derma glue or something when she realized how deep it was, but there hadn't been any in the house, and she didn't dare tell anyone about it. At least she'd gotten the bleeding to stop and flushed the bloody paper towels down the toilet before anyone could stumble on the evidence.

The fabric of her sleeve was scratchy against the cut, and she was afraid the irritation might open it up again. She was going to have to bandage it. And change. Long sleeves. Three-quarter-length at the very least. Nothing else was going to hide it.

The temperatures had been stupidly, unseasonably warm for New York in April. Someone would remark on the long sleeves.

Then again, maybe not. With Mom gone ... it wasn't like Dad or Jared paid any attention. Her brother was too busy being angry and Dad was gone more than home. As always. Probably, she could go slowly mad and no one would notice. She wasn't so sure it wasn't happening already.

But maybe tonight some kind of sanity would return. Mom was coming back for her and Jared for the first time since she'd left after that horrible final fight with Dad, when Jared had hustled her off to the neighbor's house before she could step between them like she always did. Or tried to. Sometimes the door was slammed in her face. Sometimes she saw ...

Nothing.

Fighting. People fought. Sometimes they got a little emotional. Things were thrown. Fists. Other things. It happened ... right?

No, wrong. Absolutely wrong.

Her cut throbbed, the pain bringing her back to now. Like it always did. The pain centered her. She knew that was messed up. She knew she'd be in trouble if anyone found out. She knew she had to stop.

The bathroom door jumped in its frame as someone pounded on it, and Emily jumped with it.

"Em, enough already!" Jared called from the other side. "I need to get in there too."

Had she locked the door? She was sure she had.

"Crap," she said under her breath. Then, "Hold your horses. I'll be right there."

She grabbed her make-up and rushed to the door before he could open it and catch her, just in case ...

It *had* been locked, but it didn't make any difference now. She turned the lock and yanked open the door, glaring at him. Things had been so much easier when she was still in middle school and had an extra hour to herself in the morning.

"Here," she said, "you happy?"

"Ecstatic," he answered.

"Ooh, big word."

"I learned it from you," he said, standing aside so she could head out and leave the bathroom to him.

But he watched her go, like he knew something was up. Was it her imagination, or was he looking at her left arm? She tugged self-consciously at her sleeve and double-timed it to her room.

She had Band-Aids in her sock drawer, so she took care of her cut before picking out a long-sleeved t-shirt in basic black and the ivory scarf her mother had given her with Emily Dickinson poems printed on it. Mom said she was named for the Emilys—Dickinson and Brontë—which was both cool, because they were seriously awesome and edgy for their times, and a burden. Like she carried the weight of expectation.

She shook it off and headed for the kitchen, hoping to have it to herself, but surprised to find Dad still there. He stood in the breakfast nook staring out the sliding glass doors onto their concrete slab patio with the phone pressed to his ear. Mom used to call Dad her bear. Backlit as he was, Emily could almost see it. Only instead of a teddy bear right now, he looked more like a grizzly, big and bristling.

"We'll talk about it tonight," he said into the phone. It was his angry voice, like his breath was being forced out through clenched teeth.

Emily wondered whether she should head back to her room, give him some privacy, but she couldn't quite bring herself to walk away. It had to be Mom on the other end of the phone. She was the only person Dad talked to like that. And sometimes Jared. Hardly ever Emily. Mom and Dad must have loved each other once to make each other so crazy now. If only they could remember that.

But whatever Mom said, Dad exploded. "Diane, I said we'll talk tonight. I'm not getting into this over the phone when I have Jared and Emily to get out the door and off to school by myself because *you left*. And I have to get myself to work. You know, that thing that keeps the roof over our heads."

He listened for half a second before spitting out, "*Goodbye, Diane,*" and mashing his finger down on the hang-up button.

Emily flinched as Dad whirled around before she could retreat, arm raised as though he was ready to throw the phone across the room. He stopped when he spotted her staring. Her eyes were probably as big as dinner plates. That was how they felt.

"Um, hey," she said lamely.

Dad's face transformed, the rage on it falling away like he'd dropped a curtain. So fast she couldn't be sure she'd seen it at all. Or that it had been as high-intensity as she'd thought if he could shut it down so quickly.

"Oh, honey," he said in an entirely different voice than the one he'd just used on Mom. Gentle, sad. "I'm sorry you had to hear that."

He took a step toward her and Emily didn't move. Part of her wanted the hug it looked like he was about to give. He'd hugged her less and less recently, like it was weird now that she had boobs. Like that somehow made her untouchable. Part of her missed being Daddy's little girl. Another part yelled at her to grow up.

"What are you going to talk about later?" she asked, unable to help herself. He already knew she'd overheard him. There was no use pretending.

The question stopped Dad in his tracks, and Emily missed the hug she'd headed off. She wrapped her arms around herself instead. It would have felt disloyal to Mom to hug Dad now anyway.

He wouldn't meet her gaze as he answered, "Adult stuff."

"You always say that, but if it's about me and Jared, we have the right to know."

"It's not about you," he said. "You need to grab something to eat and start getting ready for school. Do you want me to toast you a waffle?"

Did she? Like the hug, it felt disloyal to Mom to accept

anything from him, like saying everything was okay, like the way he talked to Mom.

On the other, he was the only parent she had right now.

Torn, Emily just shrugged. Let him make of that whatever he wanted.

"Syrup and strawberry jelly?" he asked.

She was surprised that he'd noticed. And touched enough to nod. It was just a waffle. It wasn't anything like taking sides.

Friday morning

Jared

Jared stood under the water of the shower longer than he should have, knowing he was wasting water. But getting out meant getting on with the day, and that seemed especially rough this morning. He reminded himself that at least he'd see Aaliyah at school if not over the weekend, because ... Mom.

He was excited to see her tonight, and angry at himself for being excited. She'd left them. For good reason, maybe, but he couldn't help feeling that she should have fought harder to stay. Or taken them with her. He knew that wasn't fair, that she'd left in the heat of the moment, without even a plan about where to go. But nothing he told himself made him feel any better.

He kept looking for Mom, expecting her in the mornings when he got up or when he arrived home. It hurt every time he remembered she was gone, and not just at the library where she worked a few days a week. Dad he never expected and didn't necessarily want. When he was home, he was busy finding fault with everything Jared did. He'd yell about homework, but never actually offer to help. He'd rant about Jared's messy room with no idea that between track, homework and his girlfriend, Jared hardly ever got to bed before midnight, even though he had to be up and out by seven for school. *Mom* knew, because she was the one driving him everywhere or, for the past few months since he got his permit, teaching him to drive. And now she was gone.

But she was coming tonight. And taking them away for the whole weekend, which meant no Aaliyah, and …

Screw it.

Jared struck the shower handle to shut off the flow of water and let his forehead fall against the wall. He gave himself a few seconds of pity. Three, two, one. Then he bucked himself off the wall, threw open the shower curtain and grabbed for the towel. He raked it through his short hair, leaving it sticking up at all angles, and then wiped down his body, wrapping the towel around his waist.

He hit the fan on his way out of the bathroom so that the condensation would clear by the time he was dressed and back to shave, though given how he was feeling, maybe it was best not to try to shave today. It wasn't like anyone would notice. His friend Danny had a whole almost-beard already, but all Jared had were a few stragglers, hardly enough for a goatee, which was okay, really, because he was certainly no hipster, and hair was friction.

When he got to the kitchen, dressed and shaved despite himself with only a single nick, he was surprised to find Dad still home, and Emily with a stack of half-eaten waffles. There was another stack in front of his usual place at the table, even though Jared didn't eat waffles, unless he was carb-loading before a race. They burned off too quickly, leaving him asleep at his desk. Not that Dad could be expected to know that.

He looked at his father. "What's this?"

His father glanced at his plate and then up at him, a smile on his face. *A smile.* "Smart guy like you, I'd think you'd know waffles when you see them."

The urge to smile back tugged at him, but he resisted. Something was up. "I mean, why are they here?"

"Breakfast," Dad answered, the smile falling off his face.

Good. It had looked odd there. "I made some for Emily, and thought I'd make you some as well."

"Thanks?" Jared said. He didn't know what else to say. He'd have to grab one of his protein bars on the way out to actually hold him over, but he supposed a few waffles wouldn't hurt anyone, even though Dad was acting strange. Maybe he was honestly trying to be a good parent, give them a sense of normalcy. Or maybe he was just trying to score some points before they had Mom back to compare him to.

When Danny's parents got divorced last year, they'd played that game. The *Who's Best* game, complete with presents and pizza, ice cream and outings. Danny and his brothers had milked it.

Jared sat down at his place at the table, which also, miraculously, had orange juice waiting, and reached for the butter, hoping the waffles were still hot enough to melt it. He hated when butter sat congealed in the pockets. But there was always the microwave to give things a boost. His father watched him while he doctored his waffles until he couldn't take it anymore.

"What?" he asked, putting down his knife and staring back at his Dad.

"I just can't get over what a young man you've become."

Jared bit back the first remark that wanted to rise up, that if his father paid more attention it wouldn't be such a shock. He didn't trust the new, *dadlier* Dad, but he was afraid to say anything and shut down whatever this was. Dad might use it as an excuse never to try again. "Uh, thanks?" he said again, for lack of anything better.

Then he cut a big bite and shoved waffles into his mouth so he couldn't be expected to make more conversation. Emily kicked him under the table, as if telling him to be nice. Like *kicking* was nice.

"What time is Mom coming tonight?" she asked Dad.

The look on Dad's face made it hard to believe Jared had ever seen a smile on it at all. "Around two thirty when you both get home from school, but she won't be taking you off right away, so you'll have time to pack. She and I have a few things to discuss, so we're going to do that over dinner. Gran is going to watch you while we're out."

Gran? Jared stared at his father in disbelief. "Dad, I'm almost sixteen; Emily's fourteen. We don't need a babysitter."

"Oh no? What if something happens? I want a driver in the house."

"Dad, nothing's going to happen, and if it does, we'll call 911. We've known that since we were kids."

Dad gave him that look that dared him to say another word. Just dared him. "It's already done. I want you back here after school."

Jared looked away, because he knew that if he looked at Dad, he'd glare, and that was as good—or as bad—as challenging him outright. At least in Dad's eyes.

"There's no practice on Fridays anyway," he mumbled.

Then he shoveled the last of the waffles into his mouth, downed the last of the juice, and threw his dishes in the sink.

His father half rose from the table, about to get on him, he knew, for not rinsing and putting things right into the dishwasher.

"I'll take care of it when I get home," he said over his shoulder, as he jammed his feet into the untied sneakers he had ready by the door and grabbed his backpack. He was out of the house before his father could make an issue of it. Leaving Emily behind. Not that she'd be long behind. They both had a bus to catch. Anyway, she didn't have the same trouble with Dad that he did. Maybe it was because she was a girl, though that didn't seem to matter in Mom's case. Maybe it was because she was the good kid. The one who got the grades and pretty much did what she was asked without arguing. He couldn't quite manage the same thing.

Whatever. In a couple more years he'd be eighteen and out of there.

He stopped a block away and set down his backpack to tie his shoes. It wasn't good for his feet or ankles for him to go around with his shoes untied. He didn't want to risk tripping or otherwise screwing himself up. Track and Aaliyah were his only excuses to get out of the house, and Dad didn't always find his girlfriend an acceptable excuse. Dad used her more like the carrot and the stick. *You want to see your girlfriend, you'll make sure this room is clean.*

Or *If I see one more missing homework, there are no more date nights for you. I have to feed and clothe you, but I'm not obligated to drive you anywhere or give you money you're old enough to start making for yourself. Speaking of which, I don't want to see another B. Not a single one. No excuses. I don't have money to pay for college, especially with this damned divorce, so if you're going—and you don't have any other options, because you're not staying here forever and you can't live on minimum wage—you're going to need a scholarship. That means all As, all the time.*

Because, yeah, he really needed to be *more* terrified about the future. Already he didn't know how bad things would get with the divorce. Would they have to sell the house to divide assets? Would he and Emily be shuttled back and forth between apartments? Would they have to deal with ... urg, he couldn't even think about his parents actually dating again. The custody crap was going to play hell with his job prospects and his time with Aaliyah, even if and when he got his license and his own wheels.

Mom had just moved out of Aunt Aggie's one-bedroom apartment, where she'd been crashing on the couch, into her own place nearby, which was still forty-five minutes away from them. According to Emily, anyway. Jared hadn't been able to bring himself to talk to Mom since she'd left.

Abandoned them.

He got it. She'd had to go. He knew that in his head. His heart wasn't so easily convinced, especially when in a deep-down part of himself he didn't even want to admit to, he was more than hurt, he was jealous. Mom had gotten out. He was stuck at home where nothing he did or said was right. Nothing.

But maybe ... Well, they'd find out this weekend. Maybe Mom would come back to town and sue for full-time custody and he and Emily wouldn't have to worry about living in limbo, leaving half of their lives behind everywhere they went. But he didn't really believe it. Mom hadn't worked more than a part-time job since Emily was born. He had no idea how she'd support herself, let alone them. The fear and uncertainty of the situation ate at him worse than pre-race jitters, gnawing at his belly, poking holes for the acid to rush in. It pooled like hot lava in the pit of his stomach.

TWO

Friday afternoon

Emily

EMILY HADN'T SEEN Jared get on the bus. She could have missed him, maybe while she was distracted by Taylor Dean and the way he looked in his distressed jeans, but she didn't think so. Dad was going to be pissed. Not that she would tell him. Maybe he'd never find out. Surely Jared would beat him home. Definitely, if he knew what was good for him.

She kept an eye out for him on the walk home from the bus stop. Maybe he'd gotten a ride with Aaliyah. Maybe—

She stopped in her tracks at the sight of Mom's car in their driveway. She was here! Already!

She started to jog and quickly accelerated into a run, her backpack banging painfully against her shoulder blades. A half block away, she shrugged it off and ran unencumbered. She'd go back for it. No one wanted her ratty schoolbooks anyway.

She didn't slow as she got to the car and saw that no one was in it, but veered for the front door, sure Mom would be inside.

She pounded on the door when she realized she couldn't let herself in because her keys were in the backpack she'd dropped. Her mother must have been waiting right there by the door, because it swung open as she hauled back for another pounding, and instead she flung herself into her mother's arms.

"Mom!" she said.

Mom folded her up, hugging Emily for all she was worth. Emily soaked up two weeks' worth of missed hugs, ignoring the flare of pain in her bandaged shoulder. Mom was back. All was right with the world.

She was *not* crying.

"Emily," her mother said, kissing the top of her head over and over. "Oh, my girl. I missed you so much."

Finally, Mom let her go and held her back to look at her. Her Mom's eyes glistened at the corners. "I'd swear you've grown just since I've been gone."

Emily laughed. "Wouldn't that be nice."

Mom looked past her, which was easy given her lack of height. "Where's Jared?"

Emily bit her lip. She hadn't thought as far as what to say to Mom. "Um, probably right behind me. I think he got a ride home."

There. Not a lie.

And at that moment, a neon blue Hyundai pulled up to their mailbox. Aaliyah's car. They both watched as the passenger side popped open, but no Jared immediately appeared. At least, no more than his foot to the curb, the rest of him still in the car, probably kissing his girlfriend good-bye.

"I'd better go grab my backpack," Emily said, leaving Mom and Jared to their reunion and taking off down the street.

She didn't know how it would go. Jared seemed so angry lately. He didn't dare unleash it on Dad. She hoped he'd hold himself back with Mom.

When she grabbed her backpack and turned around, Mom was over on the driver's side of the car, chatting with Aaliyah, but it didn't last long. Aaliyah drove off, waving an arm out the window at Emily, as she trudged back with her overstuffed backpack.

It left Mom and Jared staring at each other on the front walkway.

"Hi, Jared," Mom said. To Emily it sounded restrained. Cautious, like she was afraid to have it thrown back in her face. "I've missed you."

Mom said it every time she called, and Emily passed it on to Jared every time. He never did more than grunt in response.

"I—" he didn't seem to know how to go on, so he didn't. He just stopped and then circled around her, headed for the house.

"I'm hungry," he tossed over his shoulder. "Long day. Long week."

Almost a speech for him these days. Mom looked helplessly at Emily and followed Jared in. She took up the rear.

"I'll make you something," Mom said as she passed through the doorway.

"I've got it," Jared responded. "I've gotten good at that."

Mom missed a step like she felt his words physically, but then she kept going. "It was good to see Aaliyah."

"*I'm* fine, Mom, thanks for asking."

Mom's face closed off, the way it did when Dad went at her. "I can't say anything right, can I?" It was as though someone had squashed her voice flat.

Jared didn't answer.

"Oh!" Mom said, forcing life back into her voice, "I almost forgot. I brought you presents!"

"And so it begins," Jared muttered.

Emily wanted to kick him like she had that morning, but there was no way he'd let her get away with it twice. And anyway, she wasn't close enough to be subtle about it.

So, she made up for her brother, pumping enthusiasm into her voice as she asked, "Ooh, what?"

She didn't really *need* a present, but a fancy new notebook, a really nice fountain pen … No, Mom didn't have that kind of money. It would probably be something small. Would Jared's gift be enough to win him over? Could he be won?

"Let me get them."

Mom retreated to the foyer, and Emily shot her brother a hard look. "You could be nicer," she said. "Mom's trying. I'm sad she's gone too, but maybe it's for the best. Maybe they'll even realize how much they miss each other. You saw how they were."

"I saw." He had the peanut butter out and was focused on slathering it thickly on a slice of bread, putting her hard look to waste.

"So …" she prompted.

"So, what?"

"So you could understand. You could try. Even Dad is trying." That morning. At breakfast. And Jared hadn't given him half the crap he gave Mom.

Jared slapped the bread down on the plate. "Whatever, all right? You're the perfect one. You've got this. Mom and Dad both love you. You love them. One big happy family. Well, I'm not happy, okay? You can't tell me not to feel what I'm feeling or to just get over it. I'm trying. If you can't see it, that's not my problem."

He stood there practically seething, and Emily took a step back.

"You think I'm happy?" she asked. If only he knew. "Well, screw you. I'm just trying not to make everyone feel worse."

Jared glared so hard that if he had laser vision, she'd be dead. She glared back, even though her glare was starting to get a little watery around the edges. Oh, hell. She couldn't cry. He'd pass it off as her being an emotional little girl. Only fourteen months between them and he acted like it was everything.

He whirled around suddenly and stomped off toward his room, leaving Emily and his sandwich behind.

When she turned away from staring after him, Mom was right there with tears in her eyes.

"I'm so sorry," Mom said, like it was her fault. "I never meant for any of this to happen."

"He'll get over it," Emily said, finding it weird that she sounded like the parent. She didn't really know what Jared would or wouldn't do. He'd never confided in her, and lately he'd been a stranger.

"So, what did you bring me?" Emily asked. She didn't so much care anymore, but it was a distraction, and they both needed that.

Mom went to the counter and grabbed a few napkins to wipe away the tears. She didn't touch Jared's plate. Neither did Emily. She doubted he'd be back for it, but she didn't dare assume. When she turned back around, Mom had pasted a smile on her face and held up the bag she'd gone to the foyer to grab.

"It's right here," she said, pulling out a nail polish kit, the kind with rainbow colors and stencils.

Emily hadn't realized she was excited for the present until her heart sank. It was like in two weeks, Mom had forgotten everything she knew about her daughter. Nail polish lasted all of five seconds on her nails before she picked or chewed it off. She couldn't remember the last time she'd bothered to apply any.

"Great," she said, forcing enthusiasm.

Her mother laughed. "I know it's not exactly your thing, but it's nail *art*. Look, it's got stencils and gems and a dozen different colors. I figured it was something we could do together. Like when you were a kid. You can do my nails, and I can mangle yours, and we can laugh. You'll dismantle my disasterpieces before they can embarrass you anyway."

Now Emily did smile. *Disasterpieces.* She loved it. That's what they would be, too. Mom couldn't even braid hair.

"It sounds like fun."

"Really?" her mother asked.

"Really. Tell me you got the same thing for Jared."

Mom laughed, and it made Emily laugh too.

"Sorry, no."

＊

Mom's laughter went right through Jared. He was in his room, but the walls weren't nearly as thick as they should be. He felt crappy in every way it was possible to feel crappy. Emily was both right and wrong. He *was* lashing out, but he couldn't help himself. He was angry and upset and sad and missing Mom and hurt all at once. The jumble of emotions made his brain feel too big for his skull, like it was bruised from bumping up against the bone casing.

He wanted to go back out there and be part of everything, but he didn't feel any differently than he had when he got home, and so he didn't see how things would go any better. He might snap at Mom again, and he didn't want that. He didn't want to be Dad, and her comment about not being able to say anything right went straight through him.

His phone buzzed, and he pulled it from his pocket to see that a text had come in.

How's it going?

It was Aaliyah. Would she worry if he didn't answer, or assume he was busy with the family?

How did he respond to that? He couldn't lie to her and say it was going great, but he couldn't say why not. Because he was an ass? Because Emily had called him on his shit?

Okay, I guess, he sent finally.

So what are you doing writing to me then? Go have fun. Be familial!

To Jared's shock, a smile started to crack his face. Aaliyah had that kind of effect. You never knew how a conversation was going to go. You thought you were gone one place and then —*boom*—you were at another entirely. He liked that. It kept him on his toes.

Sounds like an order, he texted back.

Damned straight.

How would you like it if I gave you an order?

You could try. (smiley face, raspberry face)

Jared sent back a raspberry and a kissy face and googly eyes and half a dozen other emojis and then waited for a response.

Stop stalling, she said. *Go.*

Jared stuck his tongue out at the phone. Not that Aaliyah could see him. If she was here, she'd tell him there were better things to do with that tongue and they'd roll around on his bed kissing.

Or maybe not.

No doubt she'd be pushing him back toward the living room. He looked to his door. Aaliyah would probably grill him on Monday, and he'd have to lie if he hid out in his room. Now that he was calmer, it seemed like that—hiding, rather than deescalating or whatever his psych teacher would call it.

He sighed and forced himself up off his bed. If he was going to do this, he might as well get it over with.

Jared opened the door and started back down the hall slowly, like he was going to his own execution. He smelled the nail polish before he even hit the kitchen. Good, they'd be busy. They might hardly notice him going for the sandwich he'd left behind. He was almost sure that was a good thing and that he wasn't hurt they'd moved on without him, doing something that shut him out.

He hardly spared them a glance as he got to the peanut butter bread and flipped one side over to make it a half sandwich. With no jelly, it was going to be dry, so he helped himself to some milk and took it all to the breakfast bar, since his mother and sister had taken over the kitchen table.

No one said anything, but the air was heavy with more than the reek of nail polish.

Mom was painting Emily's nails. Or, really, had already painted them white and was now doing something with the tiniest brush he'd ever seen with red polish pooling at the end like a blood droplet. The red had already hit some of the nails, making them look like the Japanese flag or something—a scarlet circle on a field of white.

"What's that supposed to be?" he asked, careful to keep his voice neutral. He didn't want to sound too critical or too inviting, like he was over everything.

Mom held up Emily's half-finished hand. "Ladybugs," she said. "I figured even I couldn't screw them up. Red body, black spots, right?"

"Uh," he started.

Mom smiled at him, "It's okay, you can say it. I'm hopeless."

Emily laughed. "Maybe you'd better let me take over while you give Jared his present."

"I thought you'd never ask." Mom put the red brush back into the small glass bottle and pushed it toward Emily. Then she stood up and headed for the kitchen island and a bag she had there. She brought it over to Jared and put it down on the counter beside his plate. "Here. I hope you like it."

She was trying to catch his gaze, but he wasn't ready for that yet.

Jared pushed his now-empty plate aside and pulled the bag into the void left behind. He reached in and pulled out ... a runner's backpack, complete with hydration bladder and drinking tube. Then he did look at his mother. "I have one of these," he said, thinking even as he did that he sounded like an ungrateful kid at Christmas.

Despite that, she smiled at him. "I know. You have one for here. I thought I'd get you a backpack you could keep at my apartment so that you always have one handy."

A million emotions bounced around his brain, but he couldn't catch hold of any of them. He didn't want to be touched by the thoughtfulness or upset at the significance or anything else he might be feeling.

"Thanks," he said, knowing that was the right answer at least.

"You're welcome," she said. She came around the breakfast bar to hug him, and he allowed it, even if he didn't hug her back. He wanted to. He just had this feeling that if he opened up, everything in the world was going to come spilling out and he wouldn't know how to bottle it again. He did lean in, though, and he couldn't help noticing that she smelled the same, like lavender. She'd taken her shower stuff with her or bought more once she was out. At least something felt familiar. Unchanged. It unclenched something in his gut, and he pulled away before it could spread.

Mom gave him a last squeeze before letting go. Then she looked back and forth between Jared and Emily, "So, what should we do until your father comes home?" Her face contorted when she said *your father*, but weirdly, like she was trying not to let it and the effort was too much for her. "He wants to go out and talk about things tonight, so I guess we'll officially be off in the morning, but that doesn't mean we can't start our time together now. Game? Movie? Ice cream?"

"Yes!" Emily answered instantly.

Mom laughed. "Yes to which?"

"Any of it. All of it. Jared, what do you think?" Emily looked at him so hopefully. He wasn't in the mood for a game and all that interaction, but he could probably sit through a movie, as long as they could decide on one, and ice cream sounded pretty good, maybe a Coke float to combine sugar *and* caffeine.

"Sure, ice cream and a movie would be good. As long as you don't choose a chick flick. Then you're on your own."

"Got it," Mom said. "Something brimming with testosterone. Maybe explosions. But ice cream first."

THREE

JARED JUMPED SO HARD in his sleep, he almost fell out of bed. He lay there, disoriented, sweating, tangled in his sheets, his heart beating so hard it was knocking on his ribs. There was a hard crash and a muffled sound—a cry?—that seemed like it had come from the kitchen, if not farther. The garage? Wherever, it couldn't have been the first crash, because something had already snapped Jared awake.

He tried to listen over the pounding of his heart and rushing in his ears. Was their house being broken into? Had Dad come home or was it still just Gran in the house, babysitting even though they were too old for it? Gran was half deaf, and Emily could sleep through a nuclear explosion. If it was only them, then it was up to Jared to protect the house, protect them. But if Dad was home ...

He didn't hear anything else. Did that mean there were no intruders or that the breaking part was done and they were now entering? Jared had an aluminum bat in his closet from his little league days, but it wouldn't do anything against guns except maybe get him killed.

He had to decide what to do—and fast, if he was going to get the jump on them.

He had one foot on the floor, apparently already decided, when he heard the door from the garage into the house swing open and a muffled curse. It sounded like his father. Had he come back angry from his dinner with Mom? Drunk? Both? Whatever, there was no way Jared was going out there now. He pulled his foot back under the covers and strained to listen. He heard the water go on in the kitchen and stay on for a while. Shortly after it shut off, he heard footsteps coming down the hall.

He could have opened his door and asked his father what all the noise was about, but some instinct made him close his eyes and pretend to be asleep instead. Maybe self-preservation. If Dad had come home angry and Jared questioned him ... He didn't know exactly what would happen, only that the thought made his heart beat so hard he was afraid it would give him away if his father opened his door. *The Telltale Heart*, like the story they'd read in language arts. Only that heartbeat had come from beyond the grave.

The footsteps stopped right outside his door, and Jared did his best to calm his breathing. In through his nose, out through his mouth. Deep, long, slow breaths. He felt like they weren't getting him any air, but he couldn't help that. His knob turned. His door opened. He snapped his eyelids shut, made his breathing as regular as he could. Nothing to see here. Sleeping. Just sleeping. His father stood there for a minute. Jared could sense him watching, but he didn't know why.

The feeling of not getting enough air was heightening. Any moment now he was going to gasp like a fish out of water, desperate for oxygen. Then his Dad would wonder why he pretended. *He* wondered why he pretended, but he couldn't seem to stop himself. If he had to, he could mimic waking up to see his father standing there. *And then what?*

But he didn't do it. An instant before he would have blown the whole thing, his father backed out of the room and closed the door behind him. Jared pulled the blankets up over his face and exhaled hard, then gulped in air and more air. So hard he almost choked on it.

He had to get a grip. What was it he thought he'd heard? If not a break-in, then what? His father letting off steam, slamming things around? Something toppling off one of the storage shelves in the garage? He'd have to check in the morning. There was no way he was getting out of bed now. Not with the weird vibe his Dad was giving off and his own crazy reaction.

He froze as he heard the door to the garage open again. Maybe Dad was going out to clean up whatever had fallen? But then he heard the automatic door open and a minute later close. Had Dad taken the car back out? He wasn't sure. Dad's new Beamer was so quiet. Maybe he was just running something out to Mom, but why hadn't he left the garage door open if he was coming right back?

It didn't make any sense, not Jared's reaction and not the fact that he listened for his father's return for an hour or more, which was how long it took his heart to settle down and the fight or flight response to drain out of him. He never heard Dad come back. Maybe he'd missed it. Maybe he'd fallen asleep and hadn't realized it. He could walk down the hall and peek into his father's room, see for himself. But he didn't. His father was as light a sleeper as he was, and if Jared checked on him, he might wake up. He'd want to know why Jared was in his room. And Jared wouldn't have an answer.

He lay there forever more, waiting and listening, but it was hard to keep up the vigilance when there was nothing to hear and his brain kept spinning on nothing at all. *Weird.* That was the word that kept going around and around in his head. Everything—the night, his reaction, Dad checking on him. Not the others, who slept like rocks. Just him. *Weird.* And eerie.

Finally, he pulled his phone off the charger and texted Aaliyah, *You up?* Sometimes she was. She had insomnia on a pretty regular basis. But there was no response.

He turned on his TV, hoping a plotline or something would supplant the non-thoughts buzzing his brain like bees.

Eventually, it must have happened, because he woke in the morning to silence. Either the cable box had automatically shut off after a time or someone had shut it off for him.

FOUR

Saturday Morning

Emily

EMILY SAT IN THE KITCHEN, trying to tune out Gran's whistle-snore, which was the only sound in the otherwise silent house. She didn't know what time Mom was coming for them, but she was going to make the most of the quiet to get her assignments done so she wouldn't have to do anything at Mom's but enjoy. They had a lot of lost time to make up for.

Specifically, she had to get through the poetry assignment due Monday. She'd had weeks, but the unit had started right when Mom left, and she hadn't exactly been inspired. She couldn't wait for inspiration now. It was down to the wire. She couldn't let her grades slip or give Mom and Dad one more thing to stress over. To fight over. She'd seen how Dad went after Jared for his grades, even though they weren't exactly in the toilet. Didn't matter. Anything less than an A was failure in his eyes.

She blew her strawberry-blonde hair out of her face, got up, grabbed a scrunchie out of the basket on the counter where odds and ends collected, and pulled her hair back mercilessly. She didn't recognize the scrunchie—one of Mom's, probably, though she tended more toward neutrals than the jewel tones, and this one was bright red. Maybe Aaliyah's? Anyway, it was hers for now. Hair contained, she returned to the kitchen table, and flipped open her notebook, tapping her pen against her teeth as she stared at the blank page. She consulted her worksheet again for the millionth time. She *really* couldn't wait until her creative writing class moved on to short stories. For now, she was stuck with poetry. Haiku, Quatrain, Sonnet, Refrain, Limerick … She had to pick five out of the ten options listed and create her own.

Almost without her thinking about it her pen started to move across the page.

Screw you; there's your haiku.

Damn, too many syllables to start. And Ms. Castillo would *not* be amused.

She crossed out the line and stuck her pen in her mouth, nibbling on the already well-chewed end. Probably a good thing Mom hadn't gotten her fancy pens. She liked to think she wouldn't gnaw them as she did her regular pens, pencils and fingernails, but she was probably fooling herself.

Inspiration struck again suddenly, and she jumped to get everything down before the flow stopped. Or someone woke up and interrupted her.

A poem is like a slash to the wrist.
Bleed out on the page,
Smear it with your effusions.
Do it on command.
Because they say.
Because they are owed.
Tick tock, assignment due.

Surely you have blood to spare.
You'll be judged on the patterns of your pain.
Pools and whirls,
Eddies and absences.
Quick before it clots.
But it's the surface pain
That leaks out upon the page.
The deepest cuts leave no artist to appreciate.

The pen paused once or twice, nearly made it to her teeth before moving again across the page. Like the poem had always been inside of her and had leapt at the chance to escape.

She read it over. Probably it needed work. *Effusions?* That didn't seem a very poetical word. On the other hand, it wasn't a poetical poem. Not in the beautiful, Robert Frost kind of way. *Nature's first green is gold, Her hardest hue to hold.* No, this was an in-your-face poem. A shock poem. Too revealing? Maybe. Probably.

She turned her notebook to a new, blank page. She'd hold onto the poem. Turn it in only if nothing else presented itself. Maybe work on those last lines.

But she seemed to have burnt herself out. She started and stopped a half dozen more poems before finally squeaking out a haiku, and not even a very good one. Passable at best. "Get it down, then get it right," that was what Ms. Castillo was always telling them. *Don't get hung up on perfect. You can't revise what isn't there.*

Sure. But that only went so far. A rotten apple was never going to make an award-winning pie, no matter how well you worked it.

She was ready to throw her pen across the room when Jared lumbered into the kitchen, something like a zombie, headed straight for the refrigerator.

"Hi," she said, since she was sure he hadn't seen her.

Jared nearly jumped out of his skin. His head swung around,

and he focused on her with wide eyes. "You scared me," he accused.

"All I said was 'hi.'"

"Still."

"Whatever, *sorry*."

But he looked spooked, and instead of continuing on to the refrigerator, he changed course and headed for her. Jared pulled out the chair across from her, unusually careful not to scrape it noisily along the floor, and sat, staring her down so intently she couldn't look away. What on Earth was his deal?

"Did you hear anything last night?" he asked.

She wanted to laugh, but couldn't. He was too intense. "You're kidding, right? You know me—once I'm out, a herd of elephants couldn't wake me. Why, did you hear something?"

Jared looked off toward the hallway, as though to make sure no one was coming. Weird. Weirder even than usual for him.

"I don't know," he said miserably.

"You must have heard something, if you asked. Was it like a car alarm or a crash or …?"

"I said I don't know," Jared snapped. Then his lips twisted, like he regretted it, though he didn't apologize. "It's just … something woke me up. I couldn't get back to sleep."

"Probably Dad coming home. You could ask him, if it bothers you."

"Ask who what?" Dad asked, coming into the kitchen.

Jared jerked as though he'd been struck. Or caught at something. He twisted in his seat to stare at Dad, who looked terrible. Like he'd had the same trouble Jared had sleeping. More even. The bags under his eyes looked like they were packed for vacation and not just an overnight. His sandy hair was all rucked up on one side, and he had crease lines on his face. He flexed and fisted his right hand, like it had fallen asleep and he was trying to wake it, only it didn't look pale and bloodless as she thought it should in that case. Was it her imagination or were the knuckles dark, maybe even a little bruised? She looked closer.

The knuckles were definitely swollen, one even cracked open. If things had gotten heated last night with him and Mom, he might have punched a wall ... again. That was probably what Jared had heard. She glanced at her brother, ready to signal him about Dad's hand, but he wasn't looking at her.

Yeah, Jared wasn't going to ask Dad about the noise. She didn't blame him.

"Nothing," she said. "School stuff."

Dad lost interest. He started puttering in the kitchen, putting on coffee, making a whole pot, even though he was now the only one who drank it. Gran wasn't supposed to have anything but decaf, if that.

"What time is Mom coming?" Emily asked. She caught sight of her latest poetry attempt, and turned her notebook over on the table to make sure no one got curious. She didn't think Jared could read upside down, but she wasn't taking any chances.

Dad didn't answer. When she looked up to see what the problem was, she found him frozen in the middle of the kitchen, like someone had hit his pause button.

But then he snapped out of it and headed for the refrigerator, not sparing Emily a glance. "I'm not so sure she is. We got into another fight last night. She ... said she needed time."

"Time for what?" Jared asked. He sounded suspicious enough for the both of them.

Emily realized she was holding her breath waiting on the answer.

"I don't know," Dad said, raking a hand through his hair and rucking up the other side as well. "I'm not a mind-reader. Time to figure out what she wants, I guess. I told her this wouldn't work—two households, towns apart. You both have school, commitments, meets, and practices. She can't tear you out of your routines. Maybe she'll change her mind once she cools down."

Emily went cold. Heart-stoppingly, mind-numbingly cold.

She had a horrible thought building to the point where it was going to burst out of her.

"You chased her off," she said. Like the poem, the words just poured out.

Dad turned slowly as he closed the refrigerator door, and Emily was afraid about how he'd react, but his voice was calm, quiet, as he said, "Why would I do that?"

Emily had no answer.

"So you think Mom will call?" she pushed. Jared coughed suddenly, as though warning her to stop.

"Or text or something," her father said, not at all concerned. "Look, you have your schedules cleared for the day. Why don't we do something together, just the three of us? When was the last time we did that?"

Emily had no idea. Maybe never. She and Jared exchanged a look.

"We could go to a movie, maybe that new superhero film. Go out for pizza."

"It's a little early for pizza," Jared said.

"Now, maybe, but not after the movie. The early show probably starts around ten or eleven."

She couldn't believe her father was acting like all this was nothing. Like he hadn't just brought their world to a screaming halt. *Mom was gone,* and he was talking about pizza?

And then a really terrible thought occurred to her. Worse than her last. It *had* been a wall Dad had hit last night, hadn't it?

"I'm going to call Mom," she announced. At that moment, she didn't care what Dad thought or what he'd do.

She grabbed her cell phone out of her pocket and told it to dial Mom, pushing the button for speakerphone so they could all hear.

There wasn't a single ring before it went straight to voicemail, and Mom's cheerful greeting sliced through the silence, the same one she'd had forever. "Hello, you're reached Diane. You know what to do. Talk with you soon!" *With*, not *to*, because one way was a dialogue and the other a speech, so said her mother.

The pain nearly knocked her out of her seat. She looked at her father and brother, one staring at the phone, face locked down like a vault, the other, also staring at the phone, looking ... she couldn't think of a word for it but vulnerable. Her tough, sometimes intimidating brother looked like she felt.

She couldn't take it anymore. She jabbed the button to take it off speaker and ran with the phone to her room, pressing it to her face as she ran. "Mom, it's Emily." Her voice cracked with emotion. "Dad says you're not coming, but—"

She slammed her door behind her, shutting the rest of them out.

※

Jared stared after his sister in shock. She was always the peace-maker. The people-pleaser. For her to challenge their father ... Nothing about any of this was right. And now Dad was looking at him, waiting. For what, he had no idea.

It seemed like the moment of truth. He could ask Dad about the noise. Part of him desperately wanted to so Dad could explain it away. He didn't even know what he was worried about, and that was part of the problem. Dad would ask. And he'd get worked up about whatever answer Jared might give. Jared could tell by his lowered brow that Dad was worked up already, either by Mom's disappearing act or Emily's behavior. Dad had been so calm so far ... with Emily. Would the same extend to him?

"What about you?" Dad said, studying him.

"What about me?" he asked, baffled.

"Pizza and a movie? Or we can go out and shoot some hoops. There must be something you want to do today."

Spend it with Mom.

"Sleep," he said, getting up from the table.

He hadn't eaten breakfast, but he didn't have the stomach for it. He couldn't believe his father. Acting like it was nothing, like parents were interchangeable. Like he and Emily could be bribed by the miracle of time with their father. Or maybe it was the pizza and movie that were supposed to be the draw. Whatever. They weren't kids to be won over with treats.

He felt sick. Empty. He'd been so stupid, refusing to talk to Mom after she moved out, holding it against her like it was her fault. Punishing her. His gut twisted. Maybe if he hadn't, she'd have known how much she was needed. Loved. She wouldn't have let the fight with Dad chase her off.

He went back to his room and grabbed his phone off the charger where he'd left it. He added his voice to Emily's, leaving yet another voicemail. "Mom, when you get this, please call. Please, please. I'm so sorry for how I've been. I love you. And miss you. Emily is beside herself. We both are. Please come back."

He immediately followed it up with a text, just in case. *I love you. Please call.*

He held the phone in his hands for a full five minutes that seemed like a year, waiting for a response, even though it seemed his mother's phone must be off. If she had thinking to do, she probably wouldn't want them interrupting or adding their needs to hers, but damn, she had to know how they felt. How much they cared. Maybe it would help with the thinking process. Maybe she was already on her way back and just couldn't use the phone while driving.

He wished he believed it.

He heard Gran get up and go to the bathroom. He heard all kinds of strange noises coming from there and vowed he wouldn't use it for at least a half hour. But he was waiting for her in the hall as she came out.

"Jared!" she said, loudly. The sound bounced around the hallway, and Jared knew he couldn't ask Gran about the noise, even if there was a chance it had woken her too. Dad would hear everything. "I was afraid I'd missed seeing you and Emily off."

He froze. "I, uh—"

Emily flew out of her room and into Gran's arms. Gran stumbled back a step as she caught her.

"Mom's gone," Emily said, sobbing, barely understandable. "She and Dad got into another fight, and she's not coming for us."

"What?" Gran looked up at Jared for confirmation.

"That's what Dad says," he answered.

And suddenly Dad was there at the end of the hallway where it opened onto the rest of the house.

"Diane's not coming," he confirmed.

Emily's sobs got louder, and Gran's arms tightened around her.

"Mom, why don't I make you breakfast and we can talk?" Dad said.

Jared wondered if Gran would get something better than frozen waffles. It was a stupid thought, pointless in the face of everything else, but he didn't think Dad knew how to cook. It was always Mom. Or cereal. Or Gran if they were over at her house.

Gran bent to kiss the top of Emily's head. Not that she had to bend a lot. Gran had always been small and slight. A little wisp of a woman with blowy dandelion hair.

"Come on," she said to Emily. "I bet you haven't eaten either. I'll make you some hot chocolate while your Dad fries up some eggs. I taught him that much, anyway. Bet he still remembers." She caught Jared up in her look. "You too, young man. You need to eat. Your mother will come around. Meanwhile, you need to feed those muscles of yours."

Jared still didn't want to eat, but he didn't have anything better to do. Not until Mom answered. Or Aaliyah woke up. She still hadn't responded to him from last night.

He nodded and led the way into the kitchen, since he was in the way where he was.

He got out plates and stuff while Gran made them hot cocoa using heated up milk instead of microwaved water. Dad cooked eggs and Emily made toast after blowing her nose half a dozen times and washing her face and hands. They all pretended it was perfectly normal. No one talked about Mom, at least not after Gran pulled Dad aside to ask what was going on in what she thought was a whisper. He flashed a glance at Jared and Emily and promised they'd talk in the car when he dropped her home. Because Gran's car was in the shop due to what she called "a little fender bender." And after all the fuss Dad made about having a driver in the house. She didn't look satisfied with being put off, but she didn't push it. People generally didn't with Dad.

It was all so pretend-fine that he wanted to scream.

It wasn't fifteen minutes after they left that his and Emily's phones lit up.

FIVE

Sunday morning

Jared

JARED WAS STILL STARING at his phone when Emily came rushing in from the kitchen.

"Did you see it?" she asked.

It was a text from Mom: *I'm so sorry. I need to get away for a while to think. Be in touch when I can. I love you.*

But it didn't feel right. All while Mom had been gone, she'd called. Why text now? Afraid they'd talk her out of leaving?

"I saw," Jared answered. "Hold up."

He hit the button to dial Mom.

"We know her phone is on," he said to Emily as it rang. "Let's try her. Maybe if she knows Dad is out ..."

But it went to voicemail, just like when Emily had tried earlier. Mom really didn't want to talk. Or maybe didn't want to be found. Phones had GPS. There were ways to turn it off without turning off your phone, but Mom might not know them. Did she think they were going to track her down?

He hung up without leaving a message. Emily looked like she was going to cry again, and Jared couldn't blame her. He wanted to rip Mom a new one for what she was doing to Emily, and was immediately ashamed of it. Wasn't that the same thing he'd done when Mom moved out? Default to anger. What the hell was wrong with him?

"Text her back," Jared said, afraid of what he might type. "If that's how she wants to communicate, text her."

Emily sat down next to him on the living room couch and started typing feverishly. When she hit send, she looked up, spearing him with her gaze. "Now you," she said.

Jared felt hot and cold all at the same time. A message that would bring Mom back and not drive her away. It seemed impossible.

"I don't know what to say."

"Tell her how much we miss her. Tell her about school. Say anything. Make her want us."

Her voice cracked, and Jared's hands tightened on his phone, as if he could take out all of his aggressions on it.

"I'll try," he said.

He stared at his phone for a full minute before typing, *Mom, you have to come home. Dad's not even here right now. You can come and go without seeing him. Emily is in tears. She's so hurt. She doesn't understand. Neither of us does. Explain it to us.*

They both sat there waiting for an answer, ignoring the TV Jared had paused in the background. Seconds felt like minutes that felt like hours. No response came.

"At least we know she's okay," Jared said. He did feel better about that. Some knotted up part of him released.

Emily sniffled.

He held one arm out to her, and she skootched along the couch to settle under it. They weren't a really touchy-feely family. They probably hadn't cuddled up together since they were kids, falling asleep on each other in the backseat of a car during road trips. Happier times. But he hugged her now and she hugged back. He kissed the top of her head like Gran had done and reached for the TV remote, ignoring the fact that things looked a little blurry, like he had tears gathering in his own eyes. He tried to wipe them away with a shrug of his shoulder, but he only had one free, and it didn't work very well.

He hit the play button on the remote to reanimate the Simpsons, and sat there watching with Emily until their father came home. Emily hopped up to show Dad the text, but Jared didn't move. He felt like he was made of lead and couldn't imagine what it would take to get him off the couch. Mom was gone. Nothing else seemed important.

His phone lit up again in his lap and pinged with the sound of an incoming text, and his heart gave a leap. For the first time since he'd known her, he was disappointed to see it was just Aaliyah. He'd never before thought "just" and Aaliyah in the same sentence.

Hey, you. Sorry, I slept in. Hope you got back to sleep. How's your morning going? You at your Mom's? Is it nice?

Jared's heart turned into a brick and sank like one. He started to type back, but just couldn't. He couldn't say his mother had left them. It felt too raw and yet still didn't feel real. Gran said Mom would come around, but then what? Were he and Emily supposed to just forget being abandoned and open themselves up for that kind of hurt and rejection the next time things got tough? What was the alternative? No more Mom? Things didn't work like that, even if he wanted them to, and he didn't, despite everything. What he *wanted* was for all of this to never have happened—his parents not to have fought like honey badgers, his Mom not to have moved out. Not to be gone.

But wanting was useless. Wishing was useless. Things were what they were. He was mature enough to face up to that.

"I'm going running," he announced, forcing himself up from the couch.

He still felt like lead. His heart still felt like a brick, too hard and stiff to pump the blood he needed, but he'd had crappy days before where he didn't feel like running. The trick was doing it anyway. Sucked for the first mile or so, but then the endorphins kicked in.

Jared went to his room to change before anyone could protest. Not that they would. He changed into a tracksuit, grabbed his earbuds and hydration backpack—the one for here, not the one his mother had given him for the apartment he'd never even seen. He wished he could get out without facing anyone, but he had to stop in the kitchen to fill his hydration bladder from the filtered water tap.

It was okay. No one tried to talk to him.

He finished with the bladder and was out on the street in no time, looking up and down it for inspiration. He no longer felt like running, not in either direction. He realized what he was really looking for was his mother's car. Or maybe some sign that she'd been there. Tire marks from peeling out or ... He had no idea. But he spotted nothing in either direction except Mr. Meyers sculpting his hedges. The annoying sound of the trimmer decided Jared.

He started running in the other direction, jogging at first, getting his body and his muscles warmed up. Maybe the temperature would go up later in the day, but for now, it seemed their warm snap was over. The air was brisk. The morning fog hadn't yet burned off, giving the whole world a semi-surreal quality.

It took a monumental effort to keep pace. Worse than usual. But after a few blocks, his body didn't feel quite so heavy—as if he was made of clay, not lead, and it fractured away with the force of each footstep. Like stomping off muddy boots. Another block and he took the turn toward Edger Addison Park. He was moving faster now, more smoothly. His stride not even broken when he had to hop off the sidewalk to avoid a woman with a stroller, her friend walking alongside so that he couldn't pass. He dodged a shaggy dog on a leash who lunged for him. He'd met the dog before, Stanley. If he was at the end of his run, he might pause and let Stanley jump up for face licks and ear ruffling, but he wasn't. Momentum kept him going. A day like today if he stopped he might never start again.

He ran through the park—overly warm now, though he knew better than to remove his jacket—around the lake, dodging obstacles with Linkin Park and Five Finger Death Punch and Three Days Grace fueling him. Linkin Park's "Numb" was pounding through his head, skirting the thoughts he was trying to outrun. He wanted to be numb, instead of what he was. Angry. Hurt.

Green Day came on as he hit the end of the park, which signaled his cool down. He'd started to slow when the music suddenly cut out for a ping that said he had a text coming in, and it stopped him cold. It could be Mom. Hope beat out anger and pain for a second as he freed the phone from his armband holster. He pressed his finger against the sensor to unlock the phone.

His heart dropped.

Aaliyah again. *Hey, you there? Checking in.*

Right, he'd never answered. He'd done that before, or she had—in a movie, in the shower, whatever, but he'd never gone the day without saying something. Damn. He had to keep moving, but he had to text Aaliyah. He hit the button for his microphone to do voice-to-text and started jogging in place.

"Sorry so silent. Stuff to work out. No Mom. Running to clear my head. I'll call when I'm back."

He hit send without actually checking the readout, so he hoped voice-to-text got things right for once. Then he slid his phone back into his holder and kept going, slowing even further as he hit his neighborhood from the other end, stopping at the Meyers' fence to stretch out, since he no longer heard the sound of the trimmer or saw any sign of their neighbor. Not that he was a bad guy, but Jared didn't want to talk, and Mr. Meyers could be … not so much a talker as a questioner, as in, "How is your sister? Your parents doing well?" Not questions he wanted to answer today. He wondered how his son Andrew survived the constant surveillance.

He was stretching his quads when Mr. Meyers' head popped up above the fence. Not finished, apparently; just bagging the clippings.

"Young Mr. Graham," he said cheerily, pushing his black-framed glasses back up where sweat had slid them down, leaving behind a smudge from his gardening gloves. "It's good to see you. I wish I had your drive."

Damn. He'd nearly made it home, free and clear.

"Hi, Mr. Meyers," he said, hoping his real feelings didn't show. "Good to see you. Hope you don't mind me hanging onto your fence while I stretch."

Mr. Meyers waved that away. They'd had this conversation before. It had never been an issue.

"How's your mother? I was so sorry to hear she'd moved out." Mr. Meyers' glasses made his eyes look big, owlish.

The endorphins that had flooded Jared's system seemed to wash out in one great wave. "Fine," he said tightly. "I have to get home."

He skipped the other quad. He'd have to finish stretching at home or on the way before he tightened up, but he needed to not be having this conversation. If he didn't want to talk to Aaliyah, he sure as hell didn't want to talk to Mr. Meyers, who already knew too much. It had been his house he and Emily had run to the night of his parents' final fight. Or maybe not so final.

He started off again, but Mr. Meyers paced him along the fence. "Jared," he said, slowing him up, since he was too polite to just walk on. "Tell your mother that Carla and I are here if she needs to talk, okay? She has our number."

Jared really looked at him now. Sean and Carla had been close to his parents. "Sorry to hear" that his mother moved out implied she hadn't talked to them directly. Probably not since she'd left. Certainly not last night, when she was upset enough to leave and not come back, but apparently not too emotional to drive. Not so devastated that she sought out a sympathetic ear or a shoulder to cry on.

On the other hand, if Mom couldn't be bothered to stay part of his and Emily's lives, it would have been crushing if the Meyers had made the cut.

To confirm, Jared asked, "So she hasn't talked to you at all since she left? You didn't hear from her last night, maybe?"

Mr. Meyers gave him a sharp look. "No," he answered slowly. "Why?"

"No reason." He was to the end of the fence now and starting to speed up again.

"I'll check in with Carla," Mr. Meyers called after him.

He waved but didn't look back. He hit his yard at a power walk and stretched out on his front porch rather than go inside just yet. Lunges, hip flexors, calf stretches, back. The sweat was starting to dry, and the shade of the porch made the cool-down a bit too literal. He finished up fast and went in for a shower, keeping the earbuds in until he got to the bathroom so no one would try to talk to him.

He took the shower as hot as he could stand it to wash away the grime. If only his excess emotions would sluice off as easily as the sweat.

When he got out, he called Aaliyah, as promised.

SIX

Sunday morning

Emily

EMILY WAS the one who answered the phone when Aunt Aggie called Sunday morning. She was back at work on her poems, but they were all coming out like overblown crap, and she was glad to throw down her pen and go for the phone.

"Oh my god, Emily? Where are you?" her aunt sounded borderline frantic. "No, scratch that, I know where you are. You've just answered the phone, but why are you there? You're supposed to be with your mother. You were supposed to have met me half an hour ago for breakfast."

Emily was totally confused. "If you didn't think we'd be here, why did you call?"

Aunt Aggie took a deep breath and let it out slowly, as if counting. "Emily," she said fake-calmly, "can you answer my questions, honey?"

Aunt Aggie hadn't answered *hers*, but she supposed her aunt had asked first. Her heart was starting to squeeze. If her mother had reached out to anyone or gone anywhere but her new apartment, it would have been to her only sister.

"Mom came Friday, but then she and Dad had a fight and she left," Emily said. "She didn't call you?"

It was clear enough, but she had to be sure. Now she was really, really worried about Mom. More scared even than hurt. She hadn't felt right since yesterday. After the relief of hearing from Mom, the pain had swamped her. Dad hadn't made it up. Mom really had left them. She wouldn't even call or text them back. And despite her begging, Dad said he wouldn't chase Mom down, even if he knew where to look. She hadn't given him her new address.

"She didn't call," Aunt Aggie said. "She didn't answer any of my texts, not even to confirm breakfast this morning. I just figured she was busy with you and Jared and that I'd see you at the restaurant, but none of you showed, and now you tell me you never even left...." Her voice was starting to go sharp. "Emily, please put your father on the phone."

Emily's heart started to flutter. "Aunt Aggie, what's wrong? Something's going on, isn't it? I know you don't want to worry me, but I'm already worried."

"Please, let me talk to your father. Maybe we can figure this out."

The sick feeling in the pit of her stomach grew to swallow her whole. She'd heard Dad moving around in his room, but he hadn't yet come out. He wasn't going to like being disturbed for this. Not that it mattered. Mom came first.

"Emily?" her aunt asked.

"Just a minute."

She brought the cordless phone to Dad's door and used it to tap, forgetting it would hurt Aunt Aggie's ears.

"What?" he asked, and not happily.

"Aunt Aggie's on the phone. She's looking for Mom."

"Tell her your mother's not here," he called through the door.

"I told her that. She's worried. Mom was supposed to meet Aunt Aggie for breakfast this morning. With us."

Dad growled, and she took two steps away from his door. She heard Jared's door open behind her and knew he was there too, listening to everything.

Dad was suddenly looming in his doorway, reaching out one big paw for the phone. "I'll talk to her," he said, grabbing the phone out of Emily's hand and shutting the door between them.

Emily glanced back at Jared. "What do we do?" she asked.

"We listen," he said quietly.

Her heart jerked in fear. "What if he catches us?"

Jared's eyes burned. "I'll listen. You go to your room or something. I'll fill you in."

Emily was frozen with indecision. She wanted to hear, even though she knew Dad wouldn't like it. She couldn't let Jared take the brunt of things. But he would anyway, wouldn't he? He always did. But ... Too many buts.

"No, I'm in."

Jared shrugged, and they both approached Dad's door, silently pressing ears to it.

"All I know is she's not here," Dad growled, but quietly. So quietly Emily stopped breathing to hear. She tried to time her breaths for his pauses.

"You tell *me*. Where would she go? Did you check her place?"

Pause.

"And?" Dad asked.

There was a longer pause this time, before he said, "I don't know, maybe she's got a boyfriend socked away somewhere. Maybe she's off with him. Or a girlfriend. Who knows?"

Emily's chest squeezed until she couldn't have taken a breath even if she wanted to. A boyfriend? But Dad couldn't be right. She wouldn't have chosen some guy over them. Or girl. She just wouldn't.

"No, I don't think that. Look, an adult has to be gone for, what—twenty-four or forty-eight hours before they can be considered missing? She's missed one breakfast. I don't think we should call out a search party just yet."

Emily gasped when her air ran out, and Jared threw a hand over her mouth and backpedaled her away from the door. It seemed extreme, but she didn't want to kick up a fuss Dad would hear.

"Quick," he whispered, letting go of her mouth but grabbing for her hand and making a run for the kitchen.

They'd just hit it when Dad's door opened. Emily's heart was pounding so hard she thought it would explode.

"Do something," Jared whispered.

Emily went for her notebook, which she'd left on the kitchen counter, and Jared headed for the fridge.

Dad came quietly after them and replaced the phone in the cradle on the wall. He didn't say a word, but stood there breathing, watching the phone like it might do something interesting.

Emily wanted to ask a million questions—wasn't he worried? Shouldn't they do something, like maybe call the police?

But she didn't dare let on that they'd heard.

"What's going on?" Jared asked, and Emily blessed him silently.

"Nothing," Dad answered, turning back toward them and making eye contact with each in turn. "Your aunt is all worked up because your mother didn't tell her she was taking off. It will blow over."

"Aren't you worried?" Jared asked. "If no one's heard from her—"

"You heard from her," Dad cut in. "Yesterday. Emily showed me the text."

Jared bit his lip. To keep from saying something else, Emily thought. He cut a glance toward her, but she couldn't interpret it. Was he afraid to say something that would get Dad worked up or did he have something to say he didn't want her to hear?

SEVEN

Sunday morning

Jared

JARED ALMOST DIDN'T GET out of the house. Dad didn't like Aaliyah at the best of times. He suspected it was a secret racism his father wouldn't admit to, maybe even to himself. He certainly wasn't happy today with Jared "ditching" the family when they were in need.

But Jared had already arranged things, and he'd go crazy if he had to sit around the house waiting for his mother to appear or text or call. He had a bad, bad feeling in the pit of his stomach, a pressure behind his eyes and a tightness in his chest. Aaliyah would take his mind off all that. And she'd help. He had some ideas. She'd for sure tell him if they were stupid.

Instead of honking, which had set his father off the one time she'd done it, Aaliyah texted to let Jared know she was outside in the car. She was a full five months older than Jared *and* had gotten her learner's permit before he had, hence the reason she was driving and he wasn't. He tried not to care. He knew it was sexist, and Aaliyah teased him about the fact, but it still felt wrong that she was doing all the driving.

Dad warned him to be back by dinnertime and glared at his retreating back. Jared could feel it all the way to the door, but he didn't look back to confirm.

He waved at Aaliyah as soon as he was out, his heart lightening already. He wouldn't have thought he had any smiles to give, but apparently he was wrong. As soon as he got into the car, she leaned in for a kiss, and he didn't disappoint her. Aaliyah's lips were ... awesome. The kind of lips women got those injections to puff up, only hers were natural. Firm and soft and hotter than hell, just like her.

When they broke off, the tension behind his eyes was gone.

"I needed that," he said, drinking her in. He was playing way out of his league, and knew it. Smartest girl in school—one of them, anyway—beautiful, confident. Her dark skin was nearly flawless. Her hair was pulled back into a small ponytail at the nape of her neck, showing off her amazing cheekbones. Her dark-framed glasses emphasized eyes that gleamed with intelligence and amusement, like life was a puzzle she'd already solved. Like she saw more than everyone else.

If so, he had no idea what she was doing with him. He had a mirror. He knew he was no slouch. Track kept him in good shape, and girls loved to run their hands through his thick dark hair and tease him about his golden-green eyes. He got his share of attention. But where Aaliyah had everything figured out, knew what she wanted to do and where she wanted to go in life —and had the drive to get there—Jared had no idea. Not a one.

"There's more where that came from," Aaliyah said, drawing his mind back to that kiss.

"Awesome," he said, but then his gaze wandered back toward his house and the warm feeling vanished. "Do me a favor? Drive. Before Dad thinks up some reason I have to stay."

Aaliyah didn't need to be asked twice. She was off like a shot. "My parents are home," she warned, "but we can go to my place."

Jared nodded, not untensing until *his* place disappeared from the rearview mirror.

"What's up?" Aaliyah asked, taking her attention off the road momentarily to look at him. "You've told me hardly anything, and you're acting like you just escaped from Alcatraz."

"I feel like it."

Jared filled her in on everything from seeing his mother on Friday through Aunt Aggie's call that morning. Well, almost everything.

"You're leaving something out," she said.

"What?" Jared asked.

"You tell me. I just know that if you'd told me everything, you'd be relieved at getting it off of your chest, but you're as tense as a kitten in a dog park."

Then there was the flipside of having a smart, perceptive girlfriend.

He debated with himself, but if he didn't tell her, she'd think it was bigger than it was. Maybe she'd tell him he was crazy or … There was no maybe about it. Aaliyah would come up with some logical explanation.

"It's stupid," he said.

"Let me be the judge of that."

"Really, it's nothing."

"Who are you trying to convince—me or yourself?"

So he told her. All of it. Not that there was much to tell. He didn't know what had caused the noise that woke him up. None of the explanations he came up with himself were shiny and happy.

When he finished, she stayed silent, pressing her lips together. "Hmm," she said.

"Hmm, what?"

Aaliyah reached over to squeeze his knee, but she didn't look away from the road this time. "That's weird," she said when she uncompressed her lips.

It was as if she'd squeezed his heart instead.

"In what way?" he asked. He really hoped she'd put it all into some perfectly normal perspective.

"Did you ask your Dad about it?" she asked instead of answering.

"No," he admitted. Did not asking make him seem like a coward?

"It could clear things up," she said, pulling onto her street. "There must be a reason you don't want to ask. What do you think happened?"

That was the million-dollar question. What did he think? He didn't even know. Just that it all seemed very suspicious, especially with his mother vanishing the way she had. That text ... He wanted it to be comforting, but it wasn't. Stupid Dugan had once gotten hold of his phone and sent Aaliyah all kinds of crazy texts supposedly from him that luckily she was too smart to believe. Anyone could have texted from Mom's phone. But if she'd lost it, why hadn't she come looking? Even if she thought she'd left it somewhere else, it didn't explain her not finding a way to contact them. When she'd first taken off, left Dad, she'd called *every day*. This wasn't like her, but he couldn't put his worry into words. That would make it too real.

Aaliyah waited for an answer. They'd hit her house and were now sitting in the driveway, but she made no move to open her door and neither did he.

"I don't know," Jared said. "But I think we have to find out."

"You said the sound probably came from the garage. Have you checked it?"

"Dad's hardly been out of the house."

"So the next time he is ..."

"Yeah," Jared said, feeling sick about it. What did he expect to find and what would he do if he found it? "In the meantime, I thought you might help me with something."

"What?" she asked.

"Breaking into Mom's e-mails."

Aaliyah blinked at him. *"What?"*

"So, here's the thing, she's not using her phone, right? Maybe she doesn't know how to turn off the GPS. Maybe she's afraid we can track her down when it pings off cell towers, and she's not ready to be found. But what if she's in trouble? There's got to be some clue that will help us track her. Maybe in her e-mail. If nothing else, she'll have given someone her new address, and we can start there."

"You want to break into her place?"

Heat went through him. He hadn't thought of it that way. He was just going on instinct. "I didn't say that. But we could drive there if she doesn't turn up. Check it out. See if her car's there, maybe catch her coming and going. If she doesn't want to see me and Emily—" his breath stopped. He couldn't say "that's fine" because it wasn't. He went with, "That's her call. But at least I'll know she's all right, that she didn't get into an accident on the way home because she was upset or anything like that."

"Have you checked accident reports?" Aaliyah asked. "Hospitals?"

"Not yet."

Aaliyah's mother pushed a curtain aside in the front window and looked out at them still sitting in the car. Jared's face went hot, even though they weren't doing anything.

Aaliyah waved, blew her a kiss, and opened her car door. Jared started to climb out of the car as well.

As they walked toward the house, Aaliyah said, "Mom and Dad are not going to let us retreat to my room, so we're going to have to do all of this in the dining room or somewhere like that. You've got your laptop?"

Jared patted his backpack.

"Good. When we get in, let me talk to Mom, and you set up the laptop so the screen faces the window. That ought to do it. She's not nosy, only worried about us doing the nasty. She's not even going to consider a little light hacking."

Even with everything going on, Jared smiled. *Doing the nasty* sounded way better than what he had in mind. Way, *way* better. So far they'd only gotten to a little under the clothes action.

Aaliyah saw the smile and gave him a playful swat to the arm. "Down, boy," she said.

"Hey, I can dream."

Her mother answered the door as they reached it, "Hello, Jared. Nice to see you."

Aaliyah's parents liked him okay, he thought. But they always watched him like he was out to defile their daughter. Probably Dad would be watching the guys Emily brought home the same way, if and when she ever brought anyone. She hadn't shown any interest so far ... that he knew of.

"Hi, Mrs. Persad. Nice to see you too."

So polite. Gah, how long would he have to date Aaliyah before they could just smile at each other and he could call her Mrs. P or something like that?

She stood aside to let them pass, her bright orange, red and black patterned dress clashing with his mood. In contrast to Aaliyah's simple style, her mother had her hair twined in ropes woven into a braid at the back of her head. She was only an inch taller than Aaliyah in flats, but she was almost Jared's height at the moment, which meant she was wearing heels, which meant she was probably going out. Jared could hope, especially with Aaliyah's comment still swirling around in his head.

Jared followed Aaliyah into the kitchen, where she asked if she could get him anything.

"Soda would be great," he said.

She nodded. "Mom, how about you?"

Mrs. P smiled and put a hand to Aaliyah's cheek. Jared's heart twisted and he glanced away.

"So sweet," she said. "I'm meeting friends for brunch. Your father is working in his office if you need anything," she gave Jared a significant look. Clearly this was meant to remind them they weren't alone and there should be no funny business.

"Thanks, Mrs. P." He tried it out. She snorted, and he figured he'd miscalculated. Clearly now was not the time.

"You kids have fun," she said. "There's frozen pizza in the icebox if you get hungry."

"Thanks, Mom," Aaliyah said this time. "We'll be fine."

Mrs. P didn't look so sure of that, but she grabbed a fringed shawl off the kitchen counter that picked up the red in her dress and was out the door with only one or two backward glances.

"Well, that was easier than I thought," Aaliyah said. "If Dad's working on something, we might not see him at all. Unless Mom left instructions to check on us every hour or something … which she probably did."

Jared's eyes rolled, as if he never even considered doing anything that needed to be checked up on.

"Gotcha, hands to myself."

"Well, maybe not entirely."

He grabbed one of her hands and pulled her to him. She went willingly, and he backed up against the counter, hands on her hips while hers were locked around his neck. She met him halfway when he went in for the kiss, and he just kept himself from groaning. She felt *so good* pressed up against him. He was pretty sure she could tell *how* good she felt.

A voice cleared behind them, and they jumped apart, Aaliyah smoothing her hair down as though he'd messed it up. Jared was glad the kitchen island half hid him from Aaliyah's father. He was in no condition to meet him full on.

"Dad!" Aaliyah said brightly. "Jared's here."

"I can see that," her father answered, eying Jared like he knew what he was hiding.

"I heard the door and wanted to say 'hello.'"

"Uh, hello," Jared said. Smooth.

He made himself step forward and reach across the island to shake Mr. Persad's hand, as he knew was expected.

Aaliyah's father took the offered hand, slowly enough to let Jared know he could as easily *not* shake, that the acceptance was a privilege, not a right.

"What do you two have planned today?" he asked pointedly.

"Research," Jared said, shrugging off his backpack and holding it up as proof. He hoped Aaliyah's father would assume it was for school and not push for details.

"We figure we'll set up in the dining room," Aaliyah said, furthering their innocence. Well trafficked area, no chance for funny business … unless Mr. P remembered that he'd just caught them up against the kitchen counter, so there were no guarantees.

"I'll be checking in," he warned with a hard look at Jared.

He only nodded. What else could he do?

Aaliyah waited until her father turned his back to roll her eyes. "Sure you don't want to take this somewhere else?" she asked Jared softly.

"You mean somewhere public, like the library?" he asked. "No thanks."

"Okay then, I'll get you that Coke and we'll get to it."

Jared proceeded to the dining room to set up like Aaliyah had suggested, with his back to the wall so his computer screen would be facing that way as well. He booted up his laptop and had his browser open by the time Aaliyah came back. He knew his mother's e-mail address, of course, but not her password, though he did know the PIN on her phone, because she'd given it to him once so he could answer for her when she was elbow deep in dishes. And it wasn't hard to remember, since it was the month and date of his birth.

Aaliyah skootched her chair over next to his as he tried his birthday as her Gmail password. No luck. He tried Emily's birthday. Still nothing. Then he tried his name with his birthday following, Emily's name and birthday, his parents' anniversary. Nothing, nothing, nothing.

"You're going to get locked out," Aaliyah said helpfully.

"Any ideas?"

"You could reset the password."

"Except the program would probably ask me a whole bunch of questions I can't answer or text the code to her cell phone, which I don't have. And if she has it and I'm worried for nothing, she'll know someone's trying to break into her e-mail."

"Okay then, what does she love?"

"Us, I would have said ... up until a few days ago."

Aaliyah let that go by.

"It could be anything," she said, "any combination of your names or dates or both. Let's see if we can think of something else."

Jared raked his hands through his hair. "I don't know. She loves food shows. Good Eats, Food Porn, Hell's Kitchen, all that kind of thing. She likes travel shows too. She's always dreamed of going places. Dad always promised trips we never got around to taking. Too busy at work or a downturn in the market ..."

"Travel?" she asked.

"Don't get any ideas. Mom doesn't even have a passport. And she'd never take off on us ... Not like that."

"I'm just thinking about passwords," Aaliyah said.

But Jared wasn't so sure. Now that she'd put it into his head, he couldn't stop thinking about it. Would he know if Mom had gotten a passport? She'd always wanted to see Paris. What if she'd been squirreling away money? What if her fight with Dad was the last straw and she'd had it with all of them and wanted to completely start over somewhere else?

"Wait," he said. He typed desperately, feeling like this was a last-ditch effort, not only to get the password right, but to prove Mom wouldn't have taken off. That she loved them.

jaredemsmom

He hoped she was too lazy a typist to throw in capitals, because he was at the end of his attempts.

He held his breath as he clicked Enter and let it out in a gust as a loading bar appeared instead of a lockout screen.

Aaliyah clapped him on the shoulders. "Good going! What did you type?"

Oh, right, because the screen showed asterisks as he typed, not the keystrokes of the password. He told her.

"How did you know to use Em and not Emily?"

"Mom always shortens it. I figured she'd use the same shortcut in typing."

"Go, you!"

Yeah, only now that Mom's e-mails had loaded onto the screen, he felt a little sick. Was he really going to do this, snoop through her messages? He could mark them as unread, so hopefully she'd never know, but ... It was still a violation.

He was torn between frustration and relief when what came up was a lot of crap—credit card and insurance offers, special deals, sales fliers.

"No one uses e-mail anymore," Aaliyah said with a sigh. "It's all about texting."

Which gave Jared an idea. Mom had complained that Facebook kept trying to integrate her messages so that her texts and everything went through their Messenger program. He could only hope she hadn't fixed the problem.

He clicked onto Facebook and logged out from the account he'd created but never used. He tried to log onto his mother's account, but the password wasn't the same as for her e-mail. Dammit.

Aaliyah was out of her seat and standing behind him, either for the view or because she couldn't sit still.

"Reset her password," she said.

Jared craned his neck to look up at her. "But she'll know."

The sad look Aaliyah shot him went straight to his heart.

"She's already gone. Are you more worried about upsetting or finding her?"

He typed in lieu of a response, answering the security questions Facebook threw his way and hoping for the best.

It was the longest half minute of his life waiting for the reset code and instructions to be delivered to Mom's e-mail, but once he had those, he set a new password, the same as for her e-mail, and was in. He clicked over to her messages, and his heart seized.

There were messages, but not nearly as many as there would have been if Mom's texts were still integrated. Nothing from him or Emily. However, there were five listed as unread, all from a man he'd never heard of, a man with two first names—Richard Travis. His icon in Messenger was too small to see more than that it was some guy crouched down next to a dog. Jared clicked on the messages, the one at the bottom, the latest, asked, *Everything okay? I haven't heard from you. Worried.*

Well, that makes two, Jared thought. He looked back at Aaliyah, who was signing at him to scroll up, but he was only a few messages in when he had to get up and move away from the screen, afraid of what was coming next.

"I can't read it," he said, as Aaliyah started to ask. "I just—it sounds—"

"Like they started a friendship," Aaliyah finished for him. "That's all. You don't know that it went anywhere romantic."

"And I don't want to find out. If it did ... If she left us to go to *him*—"

"Then he wouldn't be asking whether everything was okay. He'd know, because they'd be together. This message was sent early this morning. The others were Friday and Saturday. So, he hasn't been in touch with her all weekend."

Again, that horrible rush of emotion that made Jared feel like he had a fever. If Mom *was* with this guy, then at least she was okay, but if not ... "Would you—" Jared swallowed. He couldn't ask his girlfriend to read through his mother's possibly illicit messages to her boyfriend. That was too much. "Never mind."

He forced himself to sit back down and start skimming. Mom and this Richard guy met at the Italian cooking class Mom had taken in the spring, the one Dad hardly ever let her cook from, because he said his cholesterol would skyrocket. From there, she and *Dick* became Facebook friends, but from what he could tell, while it got a little flirty, mostly food puns, it didn't go beyond that. They shared recipes. There'd been a request on Dick's part for them to get together, but if it happened, they didn't talk about it on Facebook. Did the fact that they used Messenger at all mean they'd never progressed to the swapping of phone numbers?

"Maybe you should send him a message," Aaliyah said. "Ask him to let you know if he hears from your mom and to encourage her to call if he does?"

Did he want to do that? His head agreed that it was a good idea, but his heart wanted nothing to do with it.

"Jared?" Aaliyah asked when he didn't move or respond.

"Just trying to figure out what to say."

He got as far as, *Hi, this is Diane's son* before freezing up. The next logical thing was *My mother is missing*, but he hadn't even admitted it to himself. And what if she wasn't. They had yet to go by her house—Jared didn't even know her new address. She could be hiding out. Aunt Aggie would surely have checked it, but if Mom was quiet or sleeping or in the shower ...

He hit the backspace button to erase his message, but as he did a notification popped up: *Richard is typing....*

Damn, had he seen that "Diane Graham" was online? Jared only went on Facebook when something he wanted to see had a Facebook page rather than a normal web address. He hadn't really thought about that feature, though now that he was aware, he noticed a bar down the right-hand side of the screen with green lights indicating which of his mom's friends were online.

Then the new message popped up. *Diane, I've been so worried. You okay? Did he hurt you?*

Jared's blood ran cold. He looked at Aaliyah, to see if she'd seen, and she was staring back at him, her eyes wide. Jared hadn't told Aaliyah how bad it had gotten. She knew about Mom and Dad's fights, but not that they'd turned physical. He didn't want anyone to know, but especially not Aaliyah. What if she worried he'd follow in his father's footsteps?

What if he was afraid of it sometimes himself? Not that he ever wanted to hurt anyone, but anger seemed to be his default. Like with Mom. So far, he'd only expressed himself with words or silences. Or once throwing a game controller at the wall, but … what if that was how it started? What if he was like Dad?

Then a thought nearly as bad occurred to him. He hadn't seen anything about Dad being abusive in their messages above, which meant that this Richard guy must communicate with Mom outside of Messenger. Maybe even in person.

Who the hell are you? Jared typed, before he could help himself. *Stay out of our business.* He jammed his finger on the Send button, instantly regretting it. But it was too late. The message had gone out.

Richard is typing….

Who is this? he asked.

Jared logged out of Facebook and slammed down the lid of his laptop.

Aaliyah jerked back like he'd thrust it at her. "What was that all about?" she asked, her voice tight.

"What?"

"That. All of it. Him asking whether your father had hurt your mother. You flying off the handle."

"Wouldn't *you* be upset if someone said that about your family?"

She studied him, her dark eyes hard, not molten or sparkling or any of the ways she usually looked at him. He felt cold in his core. But maybe that had come earlier, when he first saw the five waiting messages to his mother from a man he didn't know.

"That's not an answer. It's deflection."

"I know," he said, glancing at her. Maybe the tortured look he was sure he wore would tell her everything he couldn't put into words. Getting defensive and shutting her out would only drive her away. He couldn't lose Aaliyah like he'd lost his mother.

"Oh, honey." Aaliyah opened her arms and Jared leaned into her, his face pressed into her stomach so that his nose filled with her amazing ginger and whatever body wash. She wrapped her arms around him, finger-combing his hair with one hand.

He hugged her back, but far more gently than he wanted, feeling too childlike in that position and worried about seeming too needy.

They heard footsteps coming their way, intentionally heavy-footed, he thought, so that they'd know Mr. Persad was coming and cease whatever it was they were up to. Jared let Aaliyah go, reluctantly, and she sat back down in her seat to stare at the entrance to the dining room where her father appeared.

"Hi, Dad," she said wryly.

"Hi, kids," he answered, emphasizing the *kids*. "How's the research coming?"

"We're all done," Aaliyah said, indicating Jared's closed computer. "We were just going to put on a movie. Wanna join us?"

Please say no, please say no, Jared chanted in his head.

"Thanks, but I've still got a bit of work to do, and I don't want to cramp your style," he said, though the last part was clearly a lie. "Have fun."

Jared tried a smile he was sure failed spectacularly, but Mr. Persad was already turning away and never noticed.

"Assuming you want to watch a movie," Aaliyah said when he was gone. "I thought maybe something to take your mind off things …"

That sounded awesome, if probably impossible.

"Sure," Jared answered. "Maybe something stupid funny. Lots of action and no redeeming social value."

"Like?"

"Anything."

"Let's raid our collection."

For the next two hours, they watched Kevin Hart make his "oh crap!" face. Jared surprised himself by mostly forgetting himself and even laughing along.

The police were waiting when he got home.

EIGHT

Sunday afternoon

Emily

EMILY FROZE when she opened the door and saw two police officers standing on their front porch. Her heart started to pound.

"Mom?" she asked, before they could even talk. All she could think was that Mom had gotten into an accident and *that* was why she hadn't called.

"I'm sorry?" asked the taller officer, taken aback.

"Did something happen to Mom? Is that why you're here?"

He shared a look with his partner, but neither one answered directly. "Is your father at home?" he asked.

"Dad!" Emily shouted into the house. "Dad, the police are here!"

She turned back around. "Please, uh, come in."

They crowded into the foyer, and she retreated before them, feeling very small. Even the shorter officer—a lean woman with dark hair, dark eyes, and bags underneath them even though she couldn't have been more than twenty-five—was about Jared's height. Like five-nine. The other officer, big, blonde and bulky, was almost as tall as Dad, who came into the picture just then to make her feel even smaller.

He looked down at Emily, and for a second she wondered if she shouldn't have let them in, but they were *the police*. What else was she supposed to do? Maybe she should have asked to see badges first or waited for Dad to take care of that.

But then he passed right over her to the officers, a smile starting on his face. They didn't echo it.

"Officers," he said, holding out a hand to the man to shake. "I'm Drew Graham." After the guy had shaken, he held his hand out to the woman. "What's this about?"

"I'm Officer Villarreal," she said, "and this is Officer VanWyck. We're here about your wife. Your sister-in-law reported her missing."

Dad glanced down at Emily again, and she was afraid he was going to send her to her room. Like she didn't already know something was wrong. Like she wasn't crazy-worried. She hugged herself, pressing her fingers hard into her still-healing cut to focus away from the present pain. She hid a wince and forced herself to ease off before she went too far and had to explain the bleeding.

Before Mom left, her greatest fear had been that someone would find out about the cutting and she'd be committed. One of Jared's friends had been sent away for a mandatory seventy-two hour watch last year after he'd tried to hurt himself. He'd said it was hell, and the whole school wouldn't shut up about it. In his case, it was his wrists he'd cut, and his intent had been … different. She wasn't sure the police or her father would get the distinction. She didn't want to end anything but her pain. Yet if she ever cut too deeply … maybe there wasn't as much difference as she wanted to believe.

But Dad was saying something to the officers, and she had to focus back in. "I was afraid this would happen," he said, his voice gone weary and sad like it did when he was disappointed in her. "Aggie was really concerned when Diane didn't meet her this morning. I told her—I'm sorry, I don't mean to keep you standing here. Maybe you want to come in? I can make coffee or something. I'm sure you have to ask your questions."

"Yes, sir, we do," the taller officer, VanWyck, said, but Emily thought she saw his shoulders drop just a little bit, his tension easing at the lack of confrontation. It must be tough to be a police officer and never know what you were walking into.

Dad led the officers into the kitchen, hugging Emily to his side along the way, surprising a gasp out of her when his hand pressed against the wound on her shoulder. He either pretended not to notice or really didn't, and she breathed a sigh of relief. He signaled the officers to seats at the kitchen table, but only VanWyck took him up on it. Officer Villarreal stayed standing, her back up against the wall of the breakfast nook, gaze sweeping the house. She held her hands loosely at her sides, like she might have to go for her gun at any time. Her nails were as bitten down as Emily's, and she felt a weird kinship. If she were writing a story, Officer Villarreal would be the hero. But this was real life, and she couldn't get lost in fantasy.

"Emily, why don't you see if the officers would like anything to drink," Dad said.

Because she was a girl and lived to serve (not) or because she'd stayed standing, unsure of her welcome? It didn't matter, both officers declined.

Emily got herself something instead, to give herself a reason to stay in the kitchen, as if worry over her mother wasn't enough. She grabbed a bottle of soda out of the refrigerator and poured herself a cup as quietly as she could manage, then stayed there leaning against the counter, out of Dad's eyesight.

"As I told Aggie," Dad said, leaning confidentially toward officer VanWyck, who was sitting across from him, poised with a notebook and pen, "Diane and I got into a fight Friday night. It got a little heated, and she left, saying she couldn't handle things right now. She needed to get herself centered before she could be anything to anyone else. Then she took off. She was supposed to have the kids this weekend, but she left them behind."

Officer Villarreal shot Emily a look, and her heart sped up an extra few beats. The look was more than just sympathy. There was speculation there, and Emily had no idea what she was thinking. She hoped it wasn't that this conversation would be better held without her. She was relieved when the officer focused back on her father.

"Heated how?" she asked.

Did Villarreal know about the previous call out to their house? No charges had been filed, so surely there wouldn't be anything on record. Emily was suddenly afraid for her father. What if the police thought he'd done something more than just drive Mom away?

"Don't get the wrong idea," her father said. "It was just words. We were in a public restaurant."

"Which one?"

"Vespucci's."

Officer VanWyck was taking it all down.

"What time was that?" he asked, looking up from his notepad.

"I don't know, around six thirty or seven."

"And when you left?"

"Maybe close to ten."

"Long dinner."

"We had a lot to iron out," Dad said.

"And then?"

"I paid the bill; we went our separate ways."

"And you haven't heard from her since?" Officer Villarreal asked. Emily didn't like the way she was looking at Dad.

"I've heard from her!" Emily jumped in. "She texted me and Jared yesterday."

"Can we see the text?" the officer asked, shrugging away from the wall.

Emily fought her phone out of her pocket, unlocked it, and swiped over to her texts. She opened the conversation with Mom and scrolled up so the cop could see Mom's text rather than just Emily's pleas for her to come back. Then she held her phone out to them, screen first.

"May I?" Officer Villarreal asked, already reaching for the phone.

Emily nodded.

She took the phone from Emily's hand and bent forward with it so that her partner could see as well. Without asking, she scrolled down. Then she scrolled up. She stopped at a certain point, scrolled down again. Stopped.

She and Officer VanWyck shared a look.

"What?" Emily asked.

"Nothing," she answered unconvincingly. "Can you screenshot and send me this?"

"Sure," she answered. But there were butterflies with razor wings fluttering through her stomach. What had they seen? Was she doing a good thing or bad sending them the texts?

"Great. Mr. Graham, do you mind if I look around the house while my partner asks you a few more questions?" Officer Villarreal asked, handing Emily's phone back along with her card.

"What are you hoping to find?" An edge was creeping into Dad's voice now, like he too sensed there was something the police weren't telling them. "For that matter, why are you taking this so seriously? My wife isn't missing. She's just clearing her head."

"Sir, are you denying me permission to look around?" Officer Villarreal asked. Wow, biting her nails might indicate nerves, but Emily thought they were made of steel.

Dad looked surprised. "Not at all. Look anywhere you want. I'll show you around myself." He started to rise, but the officer motioned him down. "That won't be necessary."

"Mr. Graham," said her partner, capturing his attention,

"maybe your daughter would like to go to her room? She doesn't need to hear all of this."

Emily tensed. She'd suspected it was coming. Now she had to decide what to do about it. She didn't want to go, partly because she needed to hear what was being said and partly, as crazy as it was, because she felt Dad needed someone in his corner. It was two against one, and Dad didn't always make the best impression.

Inspiration struck. "Let me try Mom one more time first. Maybe she just wasn't in the mood to talk yesterday. Maybe she's back today and everything's fine." Surely, if Mom knew the police were looking for her, and questioning Dad, she'd have to respond.

She didn't wait for anyone's approval, but hit the button to dial Mom. The call went straight to voicemail just like yesterday. "Mom," Emily said, hating the quiver in her voice. "Mom, everyone's really worried. The police are here looking for you. Please call to say you're okay." *Even if you don't love us anymore.* She wouldn't say it in front of everyone, but the thought hit her with a wave of tears. She bit them back and apologized to the rest of them, like it was her fault she hadn't gotten an answer. Then she went off to her room like they wanted, taking the phone with her in case of a call she knew wouldn't come.

Door closed, she forced her thoughts away from the dark path they wanted to take involving her razor and relief that was only temporary. The shame and self-loathing were more lasting. And if anyone came to check on her the consequences would be huge. To distract herself, she sat on her bed and scrolled through her texts, trying to figure out what the police had been so interested in. She froze when she found it.

Jared

Aaliyah pulled in right beside the police car and looked at Jared, her eyes wide. "Do you want me to come in?" she asked. "In case ... I don't even know what."

Jared felt like he'd taken a hurdle to the chest. Fear flashed through him that the police were there about the hacking, but that was ridiculous. No way he'd have been found out so quickly. And if Mom *had* seen and suspected and reported him, then that meant she was okay. Nothing to worry about.

Jared just shook his head, his mouth too dry to even answer Aaliyah. He bolted out of the car, yanking his keys out of his backpack on the way, but when he got to his front door, the knob turned in his hand. His first thought was that someone was going to get in trouble for leaving the door unlocked. But then, with the police there, he guessed it didn't matter.

He burst into the entryway and came nearly face to face with a policewoman on the other side of the door. She pulled it out of his hand and looked past him at Aaliyah's car, which was still sitting there in the driveway. He knew Aaliyah would decide for herself whether or not he needed backup. His head shake wouldn't discourage her if she didn't want to be discouraged, but as he looked back, she started to pull out. The officer watched for a second, as though memorizing the car, and then closed the door before turning to Jared.

"You must be the son," she said.

"What's going on?" he asked. "Is Mom all right?"

She studied him as he studied her. "That does seem to be the question," she said. "Why don't you come in?"

"I'm in," he said. "Just tell me."

"Jared," Dad called from the kitchen. "We're in here."

Clearly, "we" weren't *all* there, since Jared and the police officer were standing in the foyer. He couldn't see into the kitchen with the half wall in place and Dad, he was guessing, sitting beyond it at the eat-in table.

"Why do you think something has happened to your mom?" the officer asked.

It was a valid question. He didn't know what she made of his hesitation.

"Well, police don't usually come around for nothing, do they? What happened?"

He started to go around her, toward Dad. If she wouldn't tell him, surely his father would. The officer stepped into his path. "If you answer my question, I'll answer yours."

"I just told you. You're here. That must mean something. And I only left Dad and Emily a few hours ago, so I figure they're all right."

"When did you last see your mother?"

Jared shook his head. "That's another question, and you haven't answered mine."

He took another step. The officer was going to have to get out of his way or lay her hands on him. He didn't think she was going to do that, and she didn't. She backed out of his way and let him continue on to his Dad, who was sitting at the kitchen table with another officer, a guy this time, like they were having coffee, only neither of them had anything in front of them.

"Dad, what's going on?" he asked.

His father didn't look at either of the cops, only at Jared. "Your aunt reported your mother missing. It's nothing to worry about."

"Nothing to worry about? Dad, there are *police in our house.*"

The other cop had followed Jared into the kitchen, and now her partner asked her, "Did you find anything?"

"Nothing certain," she said.

"Nothing certain?" Jared repeated. "What does that mean?"

"I'll show you. I'd like to get your take on it."

She started in the direction of the garage, and her partner rose to follow her. Jared's heart seized. The garage. Where he'd heard the strange noises that had woken him up Friday night. What had she found?

Since he was already standing, he followed along after them, and sensed his father doing the same. He wondered where

Emily was, and hoped she was with a friend and had missed all of this. She was already worried. The police showing up would blow that into full-on hysteria. He got that. He felt a little hysteria coming on himself. Or at least light-headedness, like all the air had been sucked out of the house.

The female cop opened the door to the garage and motioned her partner through, then held up her hand for Jared and his father to stay behind, but she left the door open. Jared pressed into the entryway, Dad at his back.

He let out a breath he didn't realize he'd been holding when she showed her partner to a hole in the drywall to the side of the door at about head height.

"That's where Dad punched the wall a few weeks ago," he said, before they could make anything else of it. "That's nothing."

The female officer turned her gaze on his father, "Is that true, sir? Why did you punch the wall?"

"What does that have to do with my wife?"

"You tell me."

Jared watched his father, willing him to hold it together. He could not lose it with the officers like he did with Mom, like he did sometimes with him.

He looked around for something to distract or diffuse the situation, and stopped on the car. There was a new dent in the hood, as though something had landed on it. Or maybe bounced off. Surely Dad hadn't gone from hitting the wall to hitting the car. He'd bust his wrist.

But he couldn't say any of that.

He glanced away quickly before anyone could follow the direction of his gaze and get suspicious, assuming the officer *hadn't* seen the dent. And really he didn't know how she could miss it.

"It has nothing to do with her," Dad was saying, his voice tight as though the effort to contain himself had locked his jaw. "Look, I'm really sorry that Diane is missing, but she chose this path. If I thought something had happened to her, I'd be the first person out looking. She's the mother of my kids, and I still love her, despite everything. That's why I took her to dinner on Friday night, to try to work things out."

Jared watched his father. Was that true? *Could* things even be worked out after ... everything? Was there enough therapy in the world? Or anger management classes? Or—

"But you haven't shown me any evidence that anything is wrong," his father went on, "and you're upsetting my kids. They have enough to deal with already without you putting new worries into their heads. I'm afraid I'm going to have to ask you to leave."

Jared sucked in a breath. He was no expert, but he didn't think that was going to leave the police with the best impression.

Still, his father started to move out of the doorway to the garage, and motioned Jared out of the way as well. He held the door for the officers, showing them with an outstretched arm the way out.

The female officer—he still hadn't gotten her name ... *either* of their names—sighed heavily and shook her head. "You're not helping yourself, sir. This would look a lot better if you were cooperative." Just as Jared thought.

"I've been cooperative. I let you search the house. I let you question me. And now we're done," his dad responded. To his credit, he kept any anger in check.

But he followed the officers to the front door, as though afraid they'd get lost on the way. Jared watched it all, his heart feeling like it was twisted up into knots.

The male officer pulled two cards out of his pocket as Dad yanked the door open to show them out. He handed one to each of them. "If you hear from Mrs. Graham, or if there's anything you need to get off your chests, call us." He gave Dad an intense look, filled with significance, then shifted his gaze to Jared. "Any time."

He felt Dad's gaze on him as well, but didn't look back at

either of them. What did they think he might know? A noise that he couldn't identify? As far as Dad knew he'd been asleep. And anyway, he wasn't sure what he'd heard. Certainly not sure enough to open his mouth and risk his father being carted away in handcuffs.

He jumped when the door closed hard behind the officers, and he was left there with Dad. Finally, he glanced up, afraid of what he'd see, but more afraid not to see something coming so that he could prepare.

Dad ran his hand hard down his face, stretching his skin. It almost seemed to stay drooped, like Dad was exhausted down to the cellular level. Maybe Mom's disappearance was weighing on him more than he let on. Was it possible he really was worried and was only pretending to stay strong for them?

"I need a drink," he said. "Jared, do you want to order that pizza I promised your sister? I'd mentioned going out, but I don't think any of us is up to that right now."

That was it? They weren't going to talk about this? They were going to pretend everything was normal?

He was half-relieved. He'd been braced for worse—Dad to rant and rave or punch something again. But ... Mom was missing. They should be calling all her friends or out looking for her or ... something. Denial wasn't going to help anyone. But did he dare push it?

"I'll go see what she wants," Jared said, even though Emily always wanted the same thing—plain cheese. He needed the time to think.

Dad just nodded and headed for the liquor cabinet above the refrigerator.

Jared took off down the hall to his sister's room and tapped on the door.

"Who is it?" Emily asked.

"Jared."

"Are they gone?"

"Yes."

"Okay," she said, "come in."

He did, and found Emily sitting on her bed, her phone in her hand, tissues scattered around on her comforter, tear tracks down her face. It was so sad his brick heart felt like it would break. He sat down on the edge of her bed, making sure to avoid the snotty tissues.

"You all right?" he asked.

She gave him a look full of scorn. "Are you?"

"Okay, dumb question. But Emily, the police are on it. They'll find Mom. And anyway, she's missing by choice, right?" Now who was in denial? Maybe it was instinctive when trying to protect someone, and Emily looked so fragile right then. Jared reached out to take the hand that wasn't clutching her used tissues.

"I don't think so," Emily said so quietly Jared had to lean in to hear.

"What?" Not because he hadn't heard, but because he couldn't process. He had all kind of doubts he couldn't name, but his sister shouldn't have to shoulder any of them. Imagine her being the first to drop the pretense that everything was alright.

Emily took her hand back from Jared and did something with her phone before handing it over to him. It was open to her text conversation with Mom. "Look through this. Tell me if you see anything odd."

Jared took the phone, scrolled up and up, reading messages. It was a lot of routine stuff. *How was your day? Can't wait to see you. Miss you.*

"No," he admitted. "What am I supposed to be seeing?"

"Look at how Mom says 'I love you.'"

But he knew already. Mom always wrote it with the <3 sign so that it formed a heart, reading I ♡ U.

Wait a minute.

He scrolled down again, to the last message they'd gotten from Mom. Yesterday. The one that told them she was okay.

I love you.

All written out.

Oh, holy hell. He looked at Emily in horror. He couldn't protect her from this. She'd seen it first.

But what did it mean?

Emily nodded. "Mom didn't write that," she said, voice still quiet, and eerily calm, as though she'd gone numb or was retreating into shock.

"You don't know that," he said. "She could have been doing voice to text. Or she could have been driving and had someone type it for her. It could be anything."

Emily had tears in her eyes again. "You really believe that?"

"I have to," he said honestly. "Don't you?"

Emily hurled herself at him, sobbing. He caught her and pulled her into his lap, holding her like he used to when they were little and she fell on the playground or someone had been mean to her. She hadn't gone through her growth spurt yet, so it wasn't all that different. She cried so hard she shook, and he held her and stroked her hair and pretended not to notice she was soaking his shirt. He hoped just with tears, but the tissues said it might be otherwise.

He realized he was whispering, "Shhh, shhh," like that was at all comforting, but he couldn't seem to stop until he laid his cheek down on the top of her head and just let her be, trying to keep back tears of his own.

She pulled away after a bit to grab a wad of tissues and wipe at her face. She blew her nose so hard he made a crappy little joke from when they were kids.

"Wow, did you blow your brains right out?"

She gave a hysterical half-laugh at that. "What brains?"

"Exactly," he said, but with a smile so she'd know he didn't mean it.

Emily gave a tremulous smile back, but it didn't last long.

"Jared," she said, looking up at him through red, puffy eyes, "don't ever leave me, okay? I mean *ever*."

Now wasn't the time to point out that someday in the not-too-distant future he'd be going off to college and a place of his own. It wasn't what she meant.

"I won't," he promised, his heart squeezing.

She started to gather up all the tissues on her bed.

"Dad wants to know what kind of pizza you want," he added lamely.

Emily's gaze flicked up at him.

"Cheese, right?" he said when she didn't answer beyond that.

"Like I can think about food right now."

"I know, but Dad seems to want—" How did he say this? *To pretend everything is normal.* "Dad, I think, wants everything to be as normal as possible. He's sure Mom will come back when she's ready."

"I hope so," Emily said, "but—"

Yeah, but. Those buts were going to kill them.

NINE

Monday morning

Emily

EMILY'S HEART fluttered at the sound of the doorbell. Hope and terror clashing with each other until she thought she'd be sick. Mom? The police again? Or just the pizza they'd called for, though it seemed a little soon for that.

She wouldn't know until she opened the door. She threw down the limerick she'd been working on, which sucked anyway, because it wasn't funny or dirty.

> There once was a girl so sad
> Her poetry all turned out bad
> When attempting a verse
> She was under a curse
> The resultant rhymes sullied the pad.

Eww, gross. It sounded like she was talking about a menstrual pad. And would the teacher realize she was using "bad" instead of "badly" on purpose to demonstrate the awfulness of her verse or would she think Emily didn't know how to use the English language? She tossed the notebook aside and went for the door.

She beat Jared to it, but only by a few steps. She could have fallen back when she realized he was going for it, but she didn't. Her heart was pounding, and she had to know. They had a peephole in their front door, but she was too short to use it, so she just took a chance and opened the door.

Ms. Carla stood there in a form-fitting red dress with no jacket, a matching red scarf over her long, dark hair to protect it from the wind, which was blowing like a storm was whipping up. She was holding a casserole. Or at least, something in a casserole dish with foil over it that smelled cheesy and delicious when a gust of wind blew her way. Fresh from the oven then. Probably still hot enough to have kept her warm on the short walk over. It would be a cold walk back.

"This is for you," Ms. Carla said. "I ... heard about your mother, and I thought you might like a nice, hot meal."

But she didn't hold the casserole out for Emily to take. Which was okay, because suddenly she was so heartsick she didn't know if she could hold on to it. The tears were starting up again. She dug her fingernails into the palms of her hands to redirect the pain.

"Oh, honey," Ms. Carla said, at the sight of Emily's tears. "This is hot, so maybe it's best if I bring this inside for you?"

Emily noticed now that Ms. Carla had towels in each hand, using them to hold onto the glass dish. She tried to clear tears from her throat so she could talk, but Jared gently moved her aside and took over.

"Come in," he said. "And thank you."

But we have pizza coming, came Emily's incongruous thought. And really, in the face of everything, it was so small and stupid, but she wanted comfort food. She didn't want some home cooked meal from someone else's mother.

Jared and Emily followed Ms. Carla into the kitchen, where she set the casserole down on the counter. Then she turned and reached out to Emily, and before Emily could even decide if she *wanted* a hug, she was enveloped in one. It was about the least comfortable thing ever, because, with her lack of height, Ms. Carla's heels, and her impressive chest, she was all but cheek to boob.

"You poor dear," Ms. Carla said.

Emily pulled back as quickly as she could, and Ms. Carla released her in stages, going from arms around her back to hands on her shoulders, rubbing up and down in what was probably supposed to be comfort. She stopped when she hit the oversized Band-Aid hiding beneath her shirt.

"But what is this?" she asked, reaching for Emily's sleeve like she would pull it up. "Have you hurt yourself?"

Emily yanked out of her grip entirely and moved away, "Nothing," she said. "Monster zit gone wrong." All the while she was thinking *what the hell*.

"Maybe I should take a look. It could be infected." She was watching Emily too closely, almost like she could see right through the lie. Or her sleeve. Maybe she sensed that something wrong. Maternal instincts or something.

"I'm fine," Emily said a little sharply, but at this point rudeness seemed the only way to get some space.

Dad's door opened down the hall, and they all heard him before they saw him. "I heard the doorbell," he said.

Ms. Carla's attention went immediately to the hallway, and Emily blessed her father for the rescue.

His eyes lit up as he smelled the casserole and spotted Ms. Carla, who was taking the scarf from her hair and fluffing it, as if she would stay awhile. "Ah, Carla, you brought food. That was kind of you."

"Of course. When I heard about Diane ... Well, I wanted to do *something*. And to let you know that we're here if you or the kids need anything. I'm here," which Emily thought was a strange addition, since she was already part of "we," as in her and Mr. Meyers ... and their son Andrew, she guessed, though he was a senior and already seemed to have one foot out the door.

"Thank you, the kids and I are fine," Dad said, and there was something hard in his voice, like that was the last word. *Fine. Accept it and move on.* Like Emily's zit explanation.

"Oh, I'm so relieved. After the police—"

"Have they talked to you?" Dad cut in.

Jared, who'd been taking the casserole to the refrigerator, froze in place and glanced back sharply.

Carla looked taken aback. "Yes, a few questions. We don't know anything, of course. We haven't heard from Diane. I think they may have talked to a few people on the street."

Dad cursed in a way he would have given them hell for.

"Maybe I should walk you home," he said.

Carla's eyes were big now. "Do you think that's wise?"

Because neighbors would talk about seeing Dad and Ms. Carla together in broad daylight with Mom out of the picture? Had things gotten that bad that fast? Mom was only just gone and ... The police. That made it so much worse. What were people thinking or saying about them having the police at their place? Asking questions up and down the block? She felt panic start to rise and dug her fingernails into her palms again. There was nothing she could do about it. What was that serenity prayer? *God grant me the serenity to accept the things I cannot change....* She didn't know if she believed in God, but serenity seemed so far out of the realm of possibility that it might as well be myth.

"If people want to talk, they'll find something to talk about," Dad said, which was probably true.

Emily tried to let it ease her. If Dad wasn't worried ...

He gave Carla an "after you" sort of gesture, and let her lead the way to the door. Emily went to the couch and watched them through the front window, possibly like some of the neighbors were doing. She didn't know why. There was just something funny about it all. It looked like they were arguing. But why would they do that? If they were going to be the new neighborhood gossip, that would only give people something to speculate about. And if people were going to turn against them—or Dad, anyway—they couldn't afford to offend any allies.

This whole thing was so wrong.

"Emily, come away from the window," Jared said gently.

"They're fighting," she said, not moving a muscle.

Instead of insisting, Jared came up beside her and peered through the slit she'd made in the curtains.

"I wouldn't call it *fighting*," he said when they were out of eyesight.

Maybe not. Not if the standard for that was Mom and Dad.

"Fine, disagreeing then," Emily said. "I wonder what about."

Jared had no answers for her.

✳

The bus stop the next morning was beyond uncomfortable. There wasn't usually a lot of chatter in the morning with everyone still waking up. Most people were glued to their phones or tuned into whatever was coming through their earbuds. Today was different. There was talk, but she and Jared were left out of it except for sly glances darted their way.

She and Jared usually ignored each other, as though they weren't even related, but today he stuck close, and she could see him bristling, seeming almost to grow with every heavy breath he took in. Like Dad did sometimes. His nostrils flared like Dad's too. He wasn't just darting glances back at the kids, he was glaring them down. Siobhan and Katie looked away and hushed right up. Marshall and Kian and Stacy, though, didn't seem to notice.

Jared started in their direction, and Emily put a hand on his arm, which was almost as hard and veined as granite. Only granite didn't quiver as though barely constrained. "Don't," she said.

He made an effort. Another deep breath, which he let out slowly, as though maybe counting to five. Then Stacy laughed, an explosive thing, and he ripped his arm out of her hand.

"What?" he said, starting forward. "What's so funny?"

Everyone else went silent and stared, waiting to see what would happen. Marshall easily had five inches on Jared, and a linebacker's build. Kian was leaner, softer but not soft, and was about his height. It was three against one if Stacy jumped in. Or three against two, she guessed, since she'd have to defend her brother. But she hadn't gotten into a fight since she and Shara had tussled over the slide back in elementary school.

"Nothing," Marshall said. "Jeez, man. Chill." He held two hands out in a no-harm-no-foul sort of way, but Jared didn't stop until he was right up in Marshall's personal space.

"Say it," he said. "Whatever you have to say to everyone else, say it to me."

Marshall was not going to back down. She could see it.

He and Jared were bristling like wild dogs trying to scare each other off a kill.

"I said—"

A big, shaggy golden retriever burst in on whatever he was about to say, its leash trailing it, the plastic of its retractable handle clattering loudly on the sidewalk. It bounded right up to Jared and reared up on its hind legs so it could land its front paws on his shoulders and proceed to give him a tongue bath.

A woman came running up, her face as red as her jacket, calling, "Stanley! Stanley, get down!"

Stanley didn't listen to her until she jiggled her pocket. *That* got Stanley's attention, and he dropped to all fours to nuzzle her jacket instead of Jared. Probably where she kept his treats.

"So sorry about that. Sometimes he just gets away from me," she said, in a way that made Emily think she wasn't sorry at all and that maybe she'd even let Stanley loose on purpose to defuse the situation.

It had worked, too, because now the bus was here, and there was no more time for trouble.

As everyone else looked to the bus, Emily looked to the woman. "Thank you," she mouthed.

The woman winked back, and she and Stanley continued on their way. She saw the lady slip him a treat as they went.

It hadn't gotten any better from there. It was horrible enough that Mom was gone without it being everyone else's business. There were whispers, sidelong glances, sympathetic looks from the teachers. Only Shara and Tammany asked her how she was doing with anything approaching understanding rather than a desire for good gossip.

By third period she was ready to lose it. She hoped Jared was doing better and that he hadn't hit anyone.

When she reached language arts, Ms. Castillo tried to pull her aside, and she shook her head and mouthed "Please." One more expression of sympathy and she was going to break down. She did *not* want to lose it in front of the class. She didn't want to lose it at all. The other night when the tears had started, she was afraid they'd never stop. She'd tried self-soothing methods she'd read about online—yelling into a pillow, tearing something up, trying to use the shock of ice in place of pain. She'd tried a rubber band around the wrist, snapping it to cause pain instead of cutting. It helped a little. Enough that she didn't do more. Not then. But all of this … the pressure was building again, and she didn't know what she was going to do. If Mom was around, she might have reached out, but that was the problem, wasn't it?

Ms. Castillo seemed to understand. She didn't insist, but nodded Emily to her seat, which Emily took without making eye contact with anyone but Shara, who sat two rows over and several seats behind her. Assigned seating, otherwise they'd have been right next to each other and Emily would have at least some support.

"Take out your poetry packets," Ms. Castillo said, her gaze sweeping around the classroom to make sure that everyone had something to show. "Now, as we've talked about, poetry exists to make you feel, to evoke an emotion or a scene. Art is only part creation. The other part is interpretation. You know what your work means to you. Today you'll find out whether you've conveyed your meaning. I want you each to share your work with someone else. Read, critique. Be honest, but *kind*. Remember you're not critiquing to show off how clever you are, but to be helpful. Remember that the feedback you receive is about your work and not you. Also remember that art is subjective. Not everything said will resonate with you, and that's okay. Just listen with an open mind."

Emily paused with her packet only half out of her backpack. Share her work? Oh, no, no, no. It was bad enough the teacher was going to see it.

Emily started to raise her hand, to ask to be excused, suddenly sick, but Ms. Castillo didn't pick on her. She continued on. "With the understanding that your writing can be deeply personal, today I'll let you pick your partners."

Her hand went down, and she glanced immediately to Shara. If she could get her friend … Shara was nodding right back at her. Thank goodness. She was still tense, but at least this would be survivable.

"Partners?" asked a voice from her right. She almost hyperventilated. Josh sat there. *Josh.* No way was she sharing her work with him.

She turned in her seat, meeting his ridiculously long-lashed golden-brown gaze. He'd hit *his* growth spurt over the summer, and where they'd been practically nose to nose growing up, now they were more like nose to chin. And something else had changed too. She couldn't say what, only that it tied her up in knots to talk to him. "Sorry, I'm working with Shara." She felt sorry for a second, when he actually looked disappointed. But she was more relieved than anything.

"Switch seats?" Shara said, coming up and looming over them. "I think Terry needs a partner." She nodded back to the girl who sat behind her, who was leaning forward in her seat watching them. Or, more accurately, watching Josh.

"Um, sure." He gathered his stuff and stood, but stopped next to Emily's desk to lean down. Her heart stuttered as his mouth got close to her ear. So stupid. "Maybe we can talk later?" he said.

She was so stunned she couldn't even answer. There was no way Josh was interested in her. No way. And not NOW. With everything going on. She made herself tilt her head up, to nod at least, but he was already moving on, maybe assuming her answer. Everyone wanted to talk to Josh. Why wouldn't she?

"Ooh," Shara said, slipping into Josh's seat. "What was that about?"

Emily blinked over at her. "I have no idea. He said he wants to talk."

"Talking's a good start."

Emily threw her a *look*. "Don't, okay? It's not *that*."

"How do you know?"

"I just do. Let's get this over with."

They pulled their desks together, as others were doing across the room, making her head hurt momentarily until the noise subsided. Even then.

"Be gentle with me," Shara said, handing her packet over. "I don't think I'm cut out for poetry."

Emily exchanged her own poems for Shara's. "I hear you."

Silence followed, during which Ms. Castillo walked the room, stopping by each set of desks, reading over shoulders, making everyone uncomfortable. Teachers were good at that. She dreaded their turn for scrutiny.

Five minutes into it, Shara looked up at her, making Emily break from her own reading. "You suck," Shara said.

It was like an arrow to the heart. She'd said that about her own writing, but it wasn't until she heard it from Shara that she realized she secretly thought otherwise. She'd actually thought a couple of her poems were pretty good. "What?" she asked, trying to keep the pain out of her voice. "Ms. Castillo said to be constructive."

"You suck because these are awesome, and there you were pretending to feel my pain."

The turn-around was so abrupt she felt like she had whiplash. "What?"

"Well, maybe not the mad/sad poem, because probably half the class used those rhymes, but everything else."

"Oh ... thanks?"

"But—"

Oh, here it comes, Emily thought. She was starting to regret exchanging with Shara. Her friend wouldn't mince words. She never did. And Emily was so stupid fragile right now. And so angry at herself for it.

"But this one—" Shara pulled out her first poem.

> A poem is like a slash to the wrist.
> Bleed out on the page,
> Smear it with your effusions....

"Em, it's amazing. And scary. I honestly don't know whether I should be impressed or worried about you."

Ms. Castillo was standing over them now, reading over Shara's shoulder. Emily was as tense as a drawn bowstring. Neither of them spoke for a second, while Ms. Castillo finished. Then she flashed a glance at Emily. "Wow," she said.

She'd gotten a "wow" from Ms. Castillo. For a second, she thought her literary forbearers might be proud. And then Ms. C ruined it.

"Can I read this for the class?"

"What? No!" Couldn't she tell this was personal? What was she thinking?

"Are you sure? It's very deep. A little aggressive, maybe, but that's a good thing. It's coming from an authentic place."

That was the whole problem.

"I'm sure." She held out her hand to take the poem back, ready to swipe it if Ms. C didn't hand it right over.

Luckily, she didn't have to worry. Ms. Castillo surrendered her work and moved on. Emily was used to being a people-pleaser, yet she'd managed to disappoint two people in the space of a few minutes. Go her. But there was no way the class was getting to deconstruct her work.

A few tables later, Ms. C read a pastoral about baby goats and life and springtime from Cindy Mannerlee, who actually lived on a farm. It was way more upbeat than Emily's piece. And then, to her shock, Ms. C held up a poem by Josh, who stared at his desk the whole time she read it.

The clock has a face that doth never change
Hands spinning their eternal loop, and yet
We mortals, granted the free will to range
Rarely stray from the common path we're set.
Are we no more than rank mechanics then,
Ticking and tocking in a measured pace?
The road of expectations paved by men.
No thought, no step out of ordained place....

Emily's mouth dropped open, and she closed it immediately. It was *good*. No, more than good. It was pretty damned amazing. *And* he'd somehow managed to do it in rhyme and constrained to ten syllables a line. A sonnet, very Shakespearean. Emily had avoided that form like the plague. But it was the subject that really got to her.

Was that what Mom had done? Broken away from the expectations of everyone around her—Dad's that Mom would fall into line, Emily's that she'd be loved and cared for, Jared's that Mom would accept the punishment he heaped on her for leaving and keep coming back for more until he ran himself out. Had she chucked it all and decided on a different path, one that didn't include them, where she could be anyone, do anything, go anywhere. No ties to hold her back.

Emily bit back a sob, but Shara must have heard, because she reached out a hand to rub her back. Gently, comfortingly ... which made holding back the tears even harder.

"Don't," Emily said quietly, not daring to look at Shara to see whether there was hurt or understanding in her eyes. If there was sympathy or, worse, pity, she'd lose it.

Her hands were clenched so hard that if her nails were longer, they'd have drawn blood from her palms. Wouldn't *that* give everyone something to talk about.

Everyone was silent for a second when Ms. Castillo stopped reading, probably in awe. Until one of the boys in the back of the class scoffed, "Doth? Who says that?"

"Adam, that's enough. Or maybe you'd like me to read yours next."

Adam shut up.

"Great work, Josh," Ms. Castillo said, patting him on the shoulder.

She went back to the front of the class, declining to make anyone follow Josh's poem.

"Spend the rest of the class workshopping and critiquing. I want your revised efforts in by the end of the week."

"I'll catch up with you," Emily told Shara after class.

Shara gave her a knowing look, which was valid, because they *always* walked to lunch together.

"Shut it," Emily said, before Shara could say anything. "I just want to hear what he has to say."

"Okay, but you'd better report right back to me."

Emily rolled her eyes. "Whatever."

"And for that, I want a cookie. No, make it two. That'll teach you to roll your eyes at your best friend."

"Would you just go?" she asked desperately. Josh was almost

to his desk, and Emily definitely didn't want to talk to him with an audience.

You owe me, Shara mouthed as she swung her backpack up onto her shoulder. Emily rolled her eyes again. If she was going to owe cookies, she was going to get her money's worth.

Josh stopped at his now deserted desk and asked, "Is now a good time?"

"Um, sure." The class was clearing out around them, Terry sending Josh a backwards glance. "Here?"

He glanced over at Ms. Castillo, pretending not to watch them, and pulled her toward the back of the classroom, saying, "This is probably more private than the hallway."

Her stomach was starting to feel like it might fly away, even though she couldn't think that he meant to talk to her about anything like what Shara was thinking. She and Josh had barely spoken ten words to each other all semester. But the anticipation was killing her all the same. Once they had the back of the room to themselves, he seemed to struggle. They wouldn't be alone— or nearly alone—for long before kids from the next period class started to straggle in.

Someone had to say something, so she started. "I liked your poem," she said. Lame. "It was pretty amazing."

"Oh, um, thanks," he said, not meeting her gaze. Clearly poetry was the last thing on his mind. "Um, look, it's about your mother."

That was about the last thing in the world she expected him to say, and the way he'd said it, it wasn't anything good. "What about her?"

"Word is she took off on you?" he looked up at her briefly as he said it, as though to confirm.

Emily's stomach no longer fluttered. The butterflies withered and died. "Yeah," she answered. If this was about sympathy, she had lunch to get to. Or to skip. She didn't want to face food or Shara right now.

"Look, I don't know if this helps—and I'd never have said

anything if things were cool—but my family and I were out to dinner last week, and we saw her with a guy. Well, I saw her, and I'm pretty sure Mom did too."

"A guy?" she asked. "Are you sure? I mean, are you sure it was her? I guess you know a guy when you see one."

Josh gave a feeble smile. More than it deserved, especially since she hadn't meant to be funny.

"I'm sure. It hasn't been *that* long since we hung out together. She doesn't look any different."

Emily felt sick. Had Mom been seeing some guy in the two weeks she'd stayed away from them? Getting settled, she'd said. Maybe he'd been helping with that?

"What did he look like?" she asked.

Maybe it was a friend, someone they knew. Maybe she and Dad had even met secretly, trying to work things out. She and Josh had hung out when they were kids, so probably he knew her father by sight, but Dad worked a lot. It was *possible* Josh had never met or barely remembered him.

"One of those guys with a young face and old hair. You know, gray before his time, but still kind of good looking. Like from a commercial."

Definitely not Dad, whose hair was still red-blonde, like hers.

"Did they—"

Kids were starting to file in, and she felt really self-conscious whispering in the back of class, but she had to know. "Did they look … cozy?"

"You mean like dating? They didn't kiss or anything—at least, not while I was watching—but yeah, if I didn't know she was your mother, I'd have said they were on a date."

Emily's heart wanted to fall right out of her chest.

"Why are you telling me now?" she asked.

"I don't know, I thought that maybe if you knew anyone like that, you could start there. You know, maybe she's with this guy?"

"Thanks," she said faintly. "I don't. Would you know him if you saw him again?"

"I think so."

"Will you call me if you do?"

"If you give me your number."

"Oooh!" Jay Radcliffe said, sliding into a seat in the back row. "Getting digits! I'll take some of that action!"

Emily gave him a look that should have melted him to slag there in his seat. She gave Josh her number quickly, quietly, hoping he caught it, then took off before she could self-destruct. That hot, horrible pressure was building up again, and there was nothing she could do about it.

TEN

Monday

Jared

SCHOOL SUCKED, as always. Though today was a special level of suckage. The math sheet they were assigned in class didn't make any sense to him. It might as well have been written in gibberish. If he could focus, he might have been able to muddle through, but as it was all he could think about was Mom. Had she really left them? With nothing but a single text?

Really?

But what was the alternative? His mind stuttered and stopped at that question every time. He wanted to think she'd been in an accident somewhere and that they'd find her relatively unharmed, although he couldn't think of an accident that would put her out of touch for two days and still be okay. So maybe she'd been hurt, like a concussion or something, and couldn't remember who she was or where she was supposed to be.

Or how to use a phone? His brain taunted him. *And what about ID? She'd have her purse with her; she'd be found and identified.* Maybe she'd left her purse somewhere with her phone inside. Maybe it had been stolen. It happened.

But if she didn't have her phone, then someone else had sent that text, just like Emily thought, and he couldn't see why anyone besides Mom would text to say she was okay and that she loved them. Unless maybe Mom had asked them to so that she could leave her phone in one place and be in another if anyone tried to track her that way. Maybe she really, *really* didn't want to be found.

Maybe. It was the only thing that even sort of made sense. Either Mom had truly decided to drop off the face of the earth and out of their lives or ...

There was no *or*. The *or* was unthinkable.

And yet ... And yet he thought it.

Or she was dead.

Dead. Dead. Dead. The thought bounced around in his head as though his skull didn't want to let it go and release it out into the world. As if that might make it true. It stayed inside, growing in strength until it edged everything else out. He tried to tame it back, but now that the thought was free, it wouldn't be caged.

Desperately, his hand shot up, waving for the teacher's attention. He had to get out of there. To the bathroom. To the nurse's office. It didn't really matter. But maybe a change of scenery would change his thoughts. Distract him.

The bell rang just then. He hadn't realized the time.

He headed to the nurse's office instead of his next class and pleaded a headache. He wasn't lying. His head was pounding now, throbbing behind the eyes as though there was no room for them with the dark thoughts crowding them out. Mrs. Kowalski gave him two Ibuprofen and a cool cloth for his forehead and sent him to lie down in a dark, quiet room. He was *not* about to call his Dad for a pick up.

A dark, quiet room turned out to be absolutely the worst thing for him. There were no distractions. Nothing to do but think, and his thoughts wanted to eat him alive.

He grabbed his phone from the pocket of his backpack and checked it for the fifty-seventh time that day. Just in case Mom had called or Dad or Aunt Aggie sent word saying they'd heard something.

There was a text from Aunt Aggie. Mom hadn't shown up to her new job this morning. And she hadn't called in. His aunt needed to talk to him.

He went cold. Like his heart, his whole body had flash frozen. The idea that Mom had run off seemed more and more unlikely. She'd left for the night once before when she and Dad got into a really bad fight. Jared hadn't seen what happened then. He'd already been in bed. But he saw the aftermath, when Mom returned home the next day after Dad left for work, a scarf around her neck and oversized sunglasses not actually hiding the big bruise on her swollen cheek. She didn't talk much that day, and when she did, she sounded funny. Quiet, like she was afraid Dad might hear them, even though he was long gone. Or like—his brain kept shying away from it, but the thought kept creeping back anyway—or like her throat was hurt. Combined with the scarf ...

He asked. He wasn't going to be *that guy*, the one who didn't know because he didn't want to know. If Mom was hurt—no, that was stupid. *Of course* she was hurt. But how hurt? And what did he do about it?

Mom said her throat was just sore from the shouting match she'd had with Dad and that she'd be okay. He asked about her cheek. She said she'd bumped into the door in her hurry to leave the night before.

She lied.

He knew it then, but he didn't know what to do. Convince Mom to press charges against his own dad? If she lied to Jared, she'd probably lie to the police. Was she doing it to protect them? Keep them from losing their father? Who was protecting her?

He wished now he'd pushed harder. Done more.

He tried not to examine why he was thinking about this all now, but the answer wouldn't stay down.

He was afraid his father had done something to his mother. He was afraid she was never coming back. And he was tormented at the thought that he'd heard the whole thing. That his mother lay dying while he pretended to sleep, and he hadn't done a thing to save her.

Jared texted back to Aunt Aggie promising to call soon and asking for Mom's address, and sent a message to Aaliyah. *You free after school?*

They never got together on Mondays. For one, he had track. He was religious about practices, almost as much as his coach. But this was a special case. He could miss one practice, especially with a headache and clinic visit as alibis.

Yeah, why? Aaliyah responded a second later.

Free enough for a road trip? he asked.

No response. He had to remember that she was in class. He was amazed she'd answered at all.

"You okay in there?" the nurse asked. Probably she saw the glow of his phone screen in the dark room. Maybe she even thought he was using the headache as an excuse to get out of class.

"Feel awful," he answered honestly.

"Trying to read with a headache probably isn't helping, especially on a tiny, backlit screen."

"Yeah." He didn't know what else to say. He couldn't promise to stop. Not yet.

Need to see my aunt and check out my mother's place. 45 mins away. Hate to ask, he sent.

Almost an hour there, at least another checking things out and talking to Aunt Aggie, a third back. How was she going to explain to her parents being out so long on a school night? And

with all the homework he knew she had for her advanced place-
ment classes? Maybe he should scrap the whole thing.

But he couldn't. One way or another, he had to get out there.
In theory, he could just call his aunt. Or ask her to come to him.
But really, he *couldn't*. She might discourage him, and he *had* to
see his mother's place. He had to know for himself she wasn't
there.

He was still holding the phone when his aunt's text came in.
3562 Greenlake Ter, it said. *But I've already gone by. No one home. No
note.*

She hadn't given him the apartment number. Probably she'd
be suspicious if he asked. But surely he could find out on his
own. There'd be mailboxes. Or a directory. He just hoped Mom
wasn't so new she wasn't yet listed. If he had to, he'd ring all the
buzzers. But then what? He couldn't very well break into any
apartment with no answer. He'd figure it out. He couldn't get it
out of his head that this was the thing to do. Maybe Mom's
apartment would hold answers. If nothing else, he'd know for
good and all whether she'd packed up and taken off. If her
toothbrush was still in the holder ...

He swallowed hard.

If her toothbrush was still in the holder, then her laptop
ought to still be there. Surely all of her passwords—those he
hadn't changed on her—would be preprogrammed in. Why
wouldn't they be on her personal computer? If Dad wasn't the
one to ... do whatever had been done to Mom, there'd be some
other evidence of trouble—Mom complaining about a stalker or
telling someone to f—off. Maybe someone threatening Mom or
seducing her away from her family, telling her to leave everything behind; he'd buy her a whole new life.

Jared had to find the trail that would lead him to Mom. He
wanted it more than he wanted anything.

And if he found evidence that the person after Mom was his
own father?

She should never have come back to the house. Or gone out

with Dad to talk about the separation. Maybe Mom had felt safe in a public place. Or coming back to the house because Gran was there with the kids. She *should* have been safe.

The pain behind Jared's eyes flared and he cried out before he could stop himself, letting his arm drop to his side, his phone with it.

The nurse appeared at the door. "Maybe we should call your mother to come pick you up," she said kindly.

She didn't know. She was probably the only one who didn't at this point.

"Mom's ... not at home," he said, struggling to get the words out around the pain.

"Your father then?"

Jared started to shake his head and stopped when it threatened to explode. "No," he answered.

"Is there anyone else?"

That was the question, wasn't it? If his mother was gone and his father ... No, he wasn't finishing that thought again. What would happen to him and Emily? How did he protect her? He'd failed his mother. He couldn't fail Em too.

"No," he said.

Gran's car was still in the shop, and she was the only other person close enough to come get him. Even if she could, there was no way he could go home early from school and then take off with Aaliyah later. His father would blow a gasket. The thought sent shivers down his spine.

"I'm turning off my phone now. If I could just lay here for a bit longer. Until the medicine kicks in?"

She eyed him, and whatever she saw must have been convincing, because she nodded and backed out. Jared did as promised. He let his phone lie there beside him so he'd hear if it pinged, but he didn't pick it up again. Instead, he rolled to his side, closed his eyes, and tried to rest. His brain throbbed too much for that, but also for any more coherent thought, so he drifted in a haze of anxiety and pain until he was startled by the class bell and a ping from his phone a second later.

Aaliyah. *Okay,* she said. *I'll figure out a way. Parking lot after school.*

Thx, he texted back, and let his arm drop again.

The plan was in motion. Now his head needed to cooperate.

ELEVEN

Monday

Jared

JARED MET Aaliyah in the parking lot. She stood by the Hyundai that her parents said would be hers some day and waved at him as he approached. Like he could miss her in that bold blue dress just a few shades off from the car and the white cardigan she wore over it, because the school was terrified that the very sight of shoulders might send boys into paroxysms of lust.

"Hey," she said, when he reached her.

"Hey, yourself."

He pulled her in for a kiss ... started to, because she pulled him instead until she was leaning up against the car and he was pressed against her. She felt so amazing.

"Whoo hoo!" someone yelled from a row over.

"Get a room!" yelled someone else.

Jared heard them only vaguely and wasn't going to let it stop him, but Aaliyah froze up and pushed him away, gently but firmly. He went, glaring around to see who'd ruined everything, but no one met his gaze.

Cowards.

He sighed and backed off another step to look Aaliyah in the eye. "Thanks for taking me. I hope this is okay. I don't want to get you into any trouble."

Her father already wasn't too sure about him. Or about Aaliyah dating at all. He'd insisted she hold off until sixteen, and so he and Aaliyah had waited until then to make anything officially official.

"I told Dad we're picking up things for that artifact box I have to do for English."

"For English?"

"Yeah, we have to do a presentation of artifacts or evidence from one of the books on our reading list. I picked *Devil in the White City*. Piece of cake."

Aaliyah had told him about that book—non-fiction, but written like a novel, about the old Chicago World's Fair and that serial killer, H.H. Holmes, who operated during it. It had actually sounded pretty cool when she described it. Now, faced with his own mystery, not so much.

"So we have to come back with some kind of artifact? How are we going to manage that?"

"We stop off at the store on the way back. Shredded Wheat was introduced at the Fair. But I can get that near home. Better if we spot an antique or thrift store where I can find something to pass off as an old tonic bottle, since Holmes posed as a doctor, or some bones or a poker I can say he used to tend his personal crematorium or maybe an old skeleton key."

"Stop." He held up a hand for reinforcement. His head was pounding again, and after he'd beaten the headache back to a dull roar, miraculously falling asleep in the nurse's office after making the plan with Aaliyah.

"You okay?" She looked at him closely. "You don't look so good."

"Thanks."

"No, I mean—"

"I know what you mean. I have a headache. I think I'll feel better when we find my mother."

Now she looked *really* concerned. "You do understand that might take a while, right? Especially if she doesn't want to be found."

He didn't say any of what he was thinking, but just nodded and moved around to the passenger side of the car. If he was wrong—hell, he hoped he was wrong. He hoped and prayed.

He put the address his aunt had given him into the GPS, and they didn't talk for a while, letting the phone speak for them. After a minute or two of that, Aaliyah reached over to turn the radio on. Beyoncé's "Crazy in Love" came on, and Aaliyah sang along with more passion than skill. It made him smile for probably the first time that day, especially when she nudged him, trying to get him to join in. Like that was going to happen.

They made it in fifty minutes, most of it accompanied by Aaliyah's sing-along mix. Or, at least, that's what he figured it was. Beyoncé, Sia, Nicki Minaj, Jesse J, Ariana Grande, Taylor Swift, and Katy Perry. Every once in a while, there was a male voice in there. She sang along to every single song. He didn't.

He did, however, sit up straighter as they got to his mother's complex. There seemed to be three buildings, each resembling a three-level motel more than a block of apartments. The buildings themselves were putty-colored stucco with darker brown doors. Dirt Brown. A matching brown railing with narrowly spaced slats to keep people from falling through circled the second and third floors. Aaliyah's car bounced, canted, and resettled as they hit the craterlike potholes in the parking lot.

Building 3562 was the first one on the left. They pulled into a parking spot near the building. If it was reserved, there was nothing to indicate it. They were still early enough that most people were at work. They ought to be gone by the time most returned home.

The mailboxes for the place were all clustered together in front of the central building, outside rather than inside so that all the mail person had to do was pull up, open up the boxes, shove the mail in and be off.

Jared and Aaliyah headed for them, but they were no help at all. The only thing on the mailboxes was the unit number they represented. No names.

"What now?" Aaliyah asked.

"Reconnaissance."

She put her hands on her hips. "Seriously?"

"Yeah, why?"

Her face darkened, her good mood from singing along to the music gone now. She cocked her head at him, "If we go skulking around here without a plan, we're going to get into trouble."

He rolled his eyes. "No, we won't. We'll pretend we belong."

She chewed her lip and didn't look at all convinced, "This place isn't that big. Probably everyone knows each other." But she grabbed for his hand. "Maybe if we look like a couple out for a walk."

"Which we are," he said.

He could feel the tension in her grip, and he didn't get it. He stroked her hand with his thumb and walked her toward his mother's building. A couple of the dirt brown doors had something hanging on them—one a wreath with white and pink flowers, another a quilted "G," probably to symbolize the occupant's last name. He could rule those out.

Aaliyah pulled out her phone and started swiping and typing.

"What are you doing?" he asked.

"Making a list. We can cross off 1E and 2D."

Great minds thought alike. They strolled like they had no particular place to be, around the side of the building, then to the back where the same brown iron railing partitioned off the narrow balconies on the second and third floors, each just large enough for a couple of folding chairs and a single small table, which two of the units had, one on the first floor and another on the third. One unit had nothing but an ashtray precariously balanced on the railing. Others held clutter—children's bikes, toys, planters in various states, drying towels or laundry. Only two units had nothing at all.

He was betting on those.

"Great," he said, staring up. They'd stopped to gawk and so that Aaliyah could make her notes. He saw the vertical blinds on one of the sliding doors sway as though someone had just been there. It was the one with the ashtray as the sole accessory. "Well, we can narrow it down to two anyway, assuming she hasn't decorated yet."

"One, actually. 1E had the 'G' on the front door, so I'm guessing 2F is her unit. But what now? I should have thought of this sooner, but how does knowing help you?"

This was the part of the plan he didn't want to involve Aaliyah in. He didn't want to be involved himself, but he could see no other option.

"Now we knock," he said, hoping it would be as simple as that, but knowing it wouldn't be. "You can wait in the car if you want."

She gave him a *don't-be-stupid* look.

Sighing, he took her hand again and they finished their walk around the complex toward the front. Together, they climbed the stairs and stopped at the door to 2F. There was a bell, and he tried that first.

No answer. He hadn't expected one.

The apartment *felt* empty. He didn't know how that was possible, but he sensed it nonetheless.

He reached for his wallet and his school ID as Aaliyah tried the bell again.

"What are you going to do?" she asked.

"Watch."

He slid the ID into the tight space between the door and the frame and wiggled it downward. Aaliyah gasped and looked around.

"Don't do that," he hissed. "Just cover me. Look normal, like we're using a key."

Aaliyah let out a harsh breath. She moved in closer to cover him, but her body language was stiff.

He gave her a confident smile, but she was really worried and wasn't having any of it. He had to make the door thing work. He and his friend Cal had done it a couple of times at his place when he'd locked himself out, but that was no guarantee he could do it again on a strange door.

Ah ha! He felt the click and the give and whipped the door open, dashing inside with Aaliyah on his heels. She shut the door softly behind them, but then knocked him in the shoulder with unexpected force, surprising him an extra step forward.

"Did you even think?" she started on him. "Let's say the cops don't get called for a random white boy skulking around the neighborhood, but maybe you've noticed, I'm *black*. If I were a black boy or wearing a hoodie, the cops would be here by now."

Jared was stunned.

"What?" he said, brilliantly.

"Never mind," she hissed. "Do what you came here to do and let's get out. I have a bad feeling about this."

She turned away from him, looking around. He felt like Aaliyah had punched him in the gut. Was it really like that? He'd never considered—

He reached for her shoulder, and she shook him off.

"I'm sorry," he said, meaning it.

"Just get it done."

She'd shut him out, her back to him. He wanted to argue, but he knew it would only make things worse. So he did what he came to do, first scanning to see where to start. It didn't take long. The apartment opened straight into a living room with a small kitchen to the left behind a half wall that served as a breakfast bar. His mother had no other eating surface or even room for one. Maybe she could put a table in the living room, but it was really just big enough for the old couch he recognized from Aunt Aggie's basement and a small coffee table. The television was wall-mounted, so that didn't take up any space at all. Beyond the living room, also to the left, was a doorway he guessed led to the bed and bath.

"Do you want to take the living room and kitchen?" Jared asked. "I'll take the bedroom."

"Okay," she said, the word bitten off at the end like taffy. Or as though what she really wanted to bite off was his head.

He turned for the back of the apartment while she headed for the kitchen.

"What are we looking for?" she asked, her voice deadened.

It stopped him temporarily. "Anything with a schedule, addresses, phone numbers, passwords ... I don't know, really."

"Great," she said, though clearly it wasn't.

He hoped he could make things up to Aaliyah when this was all over. Nothing so terrible had happened ... yet ... but her sense of impending doom had infected him, spreading like a disease.

He hit the bathroom first, fixated on his toothbrush theory. His heart broke when he saw it slotted through one of those built-in ceramic holders with a depression for a cup in the center and holes for two brushes at the front. Her toothpaste lay across the top in place of a rinsing cup. He'd never taken an inventory of Mom's stuff, but if anything was missing, he couldn't see what. Deodorant, make up, a hairbrush, it was all lined up on the counter under the light switch. If she'd taken off, she hadn't stopped home first.

He tried not to make too much of that. None of this was irreplaceable. If Mom could leave her kids behind, surely she could leave her toothbrush.

He headed for the bedroom, where there was also nothing much. A metal frame and a mattress made up the single bed. He wondered where Mom had expected him and Emily to sleep.

Maybe one would take the couch, but the other? He kept looking. The closet held clothes, and a duffle bag with an air mattress inside, which solved one mystery. There was a dresser that had seen better days, probably another hand-me-down from Aunt Aggie, like the couch. He recognized the laptop sitting on top of the dresser. It was pretty distinctive with the Eiffel Tower sticker on the cover.

This was what he'd come for. He checked Mom's drawers in case they hid anything he hadn't thought of, feeling really creepy when he got to her underwear drawer, but there was nothing there. Or, nothing he didn't expect. Except lace. He tried not to see that. As far as he was concerned, Mom wore mom-panties. White. Cotton. Boring.

He didn't waste any more time on the bedroom, but brought the laptop to the kitchen. Maybe he could interest Aaliyah in the search, engage her intellectual curiosity, and she'd ease up. Maybe if they found something …

She did look toward him as he set the computer on the breakfast bar, but she didn't make eye contact. Her attention was all for the computer, but when he opened it and pushed the power button, she asked, "What are you doing? We can't go through it *here*. We've been here too long already."

She went to the window and slitted the blinds so that she could look through them. The second floor ought to have a pretty decent view of the parking lot.

"Anything?" he asked.

"No," she admitted. As though it wouldn't already be too late if there *was* anything.

The login screen appeared, and Jared typed in Mom's password, praying for the computer to boot quickly.

Before it finished whirring he clicked to open her e-mail program and her browser. He wanted to check those other unread Facebook messages and to see whether the cooking class guy had responded further. The wait for things to open nearly killed him. Aaliyah sat still and stiff at his side.

When Facebook came up, she gasped. He might have as well. Despite the fact that he could see at least two messages that hadn't been there before, neither were marked as unread.

There were *no* unread messages, according to Facebook ... which meant someone had been reading them.

A crazy hope rose up. Maybe it was Mom herself. He exchanged a glance with Aaliyah. She was looking at him now in shock.

She opened her mouth to say something, but was stopped by a pounding at the door that made them both jump.

"Police! Open up!"

But they were hardly given a chance to follow instructions before the door crashed open and two officers stood in the entryway, guns out and pointed straight for them.

TWELVE

Monday

Emily

THERE WAS a strange car waiting in the driveway when Emily got home. Jared hadn't been on the bus this afternoon, so she was alone as she approached. She looked around to be sure, but they lived the farthest from the bus stop, and everyone else had made it home. It was just her out on the street.

Maybe it was a detective or someone coming to ask more questions about Mom. They drove regular cars, right? Not police cruisers.

She slowed as she approached the car, trying to see in through the windows before getting close enough that someone could grab her. She didn't actually expect it to happen, but it was a possibility. Mom had drilled it into her since she was a kid— *don't talk to strangers, be aware of your surroundings, always be ready to run, yell, draw attention.* She didn't think anyone would try to kidnap her in broad daylight sitting in her driveway where all the neighbors could see if they happened to look, but she had a bad feeling nonetheless.

The car windows weren't tinted, but the way the sun was reflecting off them, she really couldn't see anything. So, she'd move fast, skirt widely around the car, outside grabbing range, and hope to get inside the house before anything could happen.

She was a few feet away from the back bumper when the driver's door opened, and she sped up as she saw a strange man get out of the car. She was behind it, speeding toward the other side when he unfolded to his full height and towered over the top of the car. He was at least six feet tall, a full foot or more taller than her, with dark glasses and dark hair that started too high on his head and then went a little wild. Not gray, so not the guy Josh had seen with her mother.

"Emily?" he said.

That stopped her, but only because she was on the far side of the car now. A safe distance.

"Yeah?" she said suspiciously. He knew her name. Maybe he had a message from Mom. Or knew something about her. She couldn't just bolt.

"I'm Jake Cassuary," he said, as if that should mean something. When he didn't see the reaction he was going for, he added, "Maybe your mother talked about me?"

She shook her head, her mouth too dry to speak.

"Oh, well," his face fell, "I, uh, don't suppose she's home?"

His hands were clenched on the roof of the car so hard that if he was Superman, he'd have dented the steel.

Well, hell. The brief flicker of hope that he might know something died a horrible death, leaving her cold despite her long sleeves.

"I don't know how to tell you this, but Mom's gone."

"Gone like to the store? I can wait," He said, shutting his door and starting toward her.

That bad feeling kicked into high gear, and she backed away, rifling in her backpack for the keys she should have had out and ready. Her father had been the one to drill that into her; she should have listened.

"I have to go," she said, still backing away. She didn't know why she felt the need to say anything—be polite, make an excuse. Probably the polite thing had been drilled into her as well. Not the best survival skill when a creepy guy appeared out of nowhere. And there was something seriously weird about this guy just showing up.

"But I'm not a stranger. I'm a friend of your mother's from high school. It's been awhile, but we reconnected online, and when she dropped out of touch, I got worried about her. Please tell me—gone where?"

Emily's brows scrunched together. Mom had gone to school in Connecticut. They lived in New York, which meant this guy probably hadn't come from across town. And he hadn't been invited or he'd have known Mom didn't live here anymore.

"Gone away," she said. Ah ha, found the keys. She started to run for the front door, flashing a look over her shoulder to keep him in sight.

"Please, wait!"

She squeaked as he started to run after her, his longer strides eating up the distance, his hand outstretched as though to grab her.

She instantly gave up on the idea of the front door. Fumbling the key into the lock would slow her down, maybe long enough for him to catch her and push her inside and … No!

The Meyers were just a few houses down. Ms. Carla had said to come to her if she needed anything. She bounced off the front stairs as she hit them and veered for their house, running full out and resisting the urge to look behind her again, knowing it would only slow her down. It wasn't until she was through the Meyers' gate and pounding on Ms. Carla's door that she had the chance to glance back. That Jake guy wasn't behind her anymore. He wasn't even in sight. With any luck, he'd taken off.

The door opened, and Emily was prepared to launch herself

at Ms. Carla, but stopped short at the sight of her son, Andrew, staring down at her in surprise, as though he'd opened the door to walk through and not because he heard her pounding. He was dressed for work in the donut shop polo shirt and khakis, his hair pulled into a man-bun at the back of his head, keys jangling in his hand.

"Erica," he said, "everything okay?" He looked beyond her, trying to see what had sent her running. Maybe it was her breathlessness. Or the tension she probably radiated.

"Emily," she corrected, trying not to be impatient that he didn't even know her name. Their parents were friends, but not them. Not even him and Jared, who was only a couple of years behind, but who he treated like a kid. "Can I come in?"

"Hang on. Mom," he yelled back into the house. "The Graham girl is here. I have to get to work."

The Graham girl. She huffed.

"Well, let her in!" Ms. Carla called. She appeared about a second later, as Andrew was excusing himself to squeeze past her and take off to work.

"Emily, what's wrong?" she asked, as soon as she saw her. Apparently, her upset could be seen from space.

"There was a guy at the house, asking about Mom. He … freaked me out."

It sounded so stupid now that she said it. He hadn't actually *done* anything, but was she supposed to wait until he made a move?

But Ms. Carla took her seriously enough. "A man? Wait here."

She took off, leaving Emily standing there on the doorstep, watching as she fast-walked down the block to check things out. Emily couldn't actually see her driveway from there, not past various shrubberies and fences. She half wanted the guy to be gone, hopefully for good, and half wanted someone else to see him, to validate her fear or to be able to say she was just being silly.

Ms. Carla reappeared a few seconds later, shaking her head. "He's long gone. Do you want to come in and tell me about it?"

Did she? Maybe. She certainly wasn't ready to go home to an empty house.

"Maybe just for a glass of water." She was so dry, she realized, now that the adrenaline was wearing away.

"I can do better than that. Andrew brought home some donuts last night. They may be a touch on the stale side, but I find that warming them in the microwave wrapped in a damp towel makes all the difference."

Stale donuts sounded surprisingly good. She suddenly craved sugar like a caffeine addict craved coffee.

"Thanks."

Ms. Carla lead her to the kitchen, a mirror image of their own, only with all-white cabinetry rather than their lighter wood and with a pressed metal backsplash as opposed to their tile. She liked it. It looked so clean.

Ms. Carla waved Emily to a seat at the breakfast bar as she grabbed a glass and clattered ice into it from the refrigerator, then hit the button for water.

She handed it over to Emily and watched her drink before prepping the donuts. Seconds later, she set a warm glazed donut in front of Emily, the frosting just a bit melted and sticky. She took a bite, and it was heaven. It practically melted in her mouth like cotton candy.

"So, tell me about this man," she asked when Emily had finished chewing. "He scared you?"

"No," she said. "I mean, *yes*, but he didn't actually do anything threatening. He just asked about Mom, and it seemed like he was going to follow me into the house to wait for her, which creeped me out, so I ran." She felt a little stupid now that it was all over, but still her heart raced just thinking of him coming toward her. If she had it to do over again, she'd probably run again. Better paranoid than dead.

Holy drama llama, Emily, she thought to herself. But no matter how much she beat herself up, she couldn't change how she felt. The guy had scared her. Maybe Mom's absence had her on high alert.

"You did the right thing," Ms. Carla said. "Do you want me to call your father?"

Emily shook her head no. Her father didn't even take her fears about her mother seriously. She didn't want him using this to downplay her other fears, like she flew off the handle at every little thing.

THIRTEEN

Jared

HOLY HELL IN A HANDBASKET.

Jared's hands went up. Aaliyah's too. She was going to kill him. Probably not the first thought he should have had, but there it was.

Second thought was that Dad was going to kill him more.

Oh hell no. Dad could *not* find out.

"Move away from the counter," one cop said.

Jared got awkwardly off his stool and moved away from his mother's laptop. "We didn't do anything wrong," he said. "This is my mother's place. She lives here."

He wanted to glance at Aaliyah, see how she was doing, but he couldn't make himself look away from the guns.

"Uh huh," the officer said. "You can tell us all about it down at the station. Turn around and put your hands behind your backs."

They were getting arrested? Oh no. No-no-no-no-no. His life was over.

"But—"

"Turn. Around." The cop bit off each word and his gun came up fractionally higher. Right at about heart level.

Would he really shoot an unarmed kid? Jared didn't want to find out. He sensed more than saw Aaliyah already turning around. He did the same, feeling like there was a target right between his shoulder blades. Blind to what was going on behind him and with his hands behind his back, he felt horribly vulnerable. And stupid. So, so stupid. They couldn't go to jail. Not for stupidity.

But for breaking and entering?

He hated the feel of the cold metal cuffs being snapped around his wrists. They felt like prison bars closing on him. Worse was the quick, brusque frisking, knowing it was his fault Aaliyah was going through it as well.

He risked a glance at Aaliyah, but she wouldn't look at him. She had her head held high, her chin up, her features frozen in place. Jared had seen her like that before, her jaw clenched to keep from crying. It was her defiant face, but behind it there was fear. Well, sure, people didn't defy what didn't stand against them, but in this case it was him and the police. And he was the one who put her in that position.

The cop frisking him had found and removed his wallet, flipped it open to his ID and was studying his learner's permit.

"Jared Graham, eh? Well, Jared, you have the right to remain silent. You too," he added, giving Aaliyah the side eye. "You have the right—"

He was reciting their Miranda warning. They were being arrested.

Really and truly arrested.

Like criminals.

"But I told you," Jared cut in, one last ditch effort. He hoped he was the only one who could hear the tremor in his voice. "I live here. Or anyway, I'm supposed to. Part time. My mother was supposed to come and get us—me and my sister—this weekend, and she didn't. Or, she did, but then she disappeared. My girlfriend and I only came over to check on her."

"And broke in," said the one cop, totally emotionless, as if that was all there was to the story. Over and done.

But the other cop, the one who'd held the gun while his partner had done the cuffing, said, "We can't talk to you. Not without a parent or advocate present."

"But you're not talking to me. I'm talking to you. I'm trying to tell you our side. We had to see—"

"My momma always told me 'you don't see with your hands,'" handcuff cop said. "And yet, you went right for her computer. Is that the problem? You a little too handsy with people's stuff, maybe with your mother herself? Is that why she left?"

Jared gaped. Wait, *what?*

Where would the police come up with something so disgusting? Sure, he and Aaliyah had broken in, but ... he never imagined how that might look. Hell, he never imagined they'd get caught, despite Aaliyah's warning. All he could think of was finding his mother. He knew her best. He cared the most. He had to do everything he could. Yeah, his aunt had filed a report, but with his mother a grown woman, he didn't know how seriously the police would take her disappearance. Certainly not as seriously as he did. How was he supposed to sit back and wait? What had he done that was so wrong?

To his surprise, Aaliyah came to his defense. "He's completely torn up about his mother, can't you see that? All he wants is to *find* evidence leading to her, not destroy it."

"So you broke in? You didn't think the police would have looked for her here already? When the missing person's report came in with the allegations of abuse, we did a wellness check. It's what we do, and it's a job for the police, not a couple of juvenile delinquents."

"Abuse?" Aaliyah asked. She sounded faint, shaken enough she didn't even take issue with being called a delinquent.

She shot Jared a glance, eyes wide. Aaliyah was a smart girl. He knew she was connecting the dots between Richard Travis's message to Mom—*Did he hurt you?*—and the cop's statement and coming up with violence. He was sure that despite the cop's implication, she'd realize it was his father and not him. But the fact was, he hadn't told her. She'd had to hear it elsewhere.

Would she think he was covering for his father, keeping secrets? Would she worry it would be a case of like-father-like-son?

But someone was sharing secrets, and if abuse was mentioned in the missing person report, that meant Aunt Aggie had to know, but ... what had Mom told her? And why tell Aunt Aggie, but lie to Jared when he asked? Did Mom think she was protecting him?

He'd been such an ass to her after she moved out. He wished desperately that he could take it all back.

"We'll talk about all this down at the station," the first cop said. "That yours?" he asked Aaliyah, nodding to the purse on the counter next to his mother's laptop.

She nodded wordlessly. Stunned speechless, he thought.

"ID in there?"

She nodded again. "In my wallet."

The cop grabbed for the purse, picking it up with the straps bunched in his hands and holding it out from his body like a trash bag he didn't want too close.

"Let's go." His partner gestured them toward the door with his gun. When Jared looked back, he was re-holstering it, but his hand stayed nearby. If he'd even thought of taking off, that would have stopped him. But he didn't want to run. Not in cuffs and not as a fugitive. Where would he go? He just wanted to get everything cleared up.

But they didn't go to the station right away. First, the cops sat Jared and Aaliyah down in the back of their cruiser and shut the doors. There was a cage between them and the front seats. Neither cop got into the car. One dropped Aaliyah's purse on the hood of the cruiser and reached for her wallet. The other stood outside the driver's side door on his radio. They heard him call in the address and that they had two suspects in custody for the B&E … or at least Jared hoped the code stood for B&E and not kidnapping or whatever they thought had happened to Mom. The cop read numbers off their IDs, mentioned that parents would have to be called. He also asked for a forensics unit to be sent out to Mom's place. Maybe that was a good thing? If there was any evidence to be found, maybe the police would discover it because Jared had given them probable cause to search? He had to find a bright side in all of this.

When the officer finished, he handed the IDs back to his partner, who left Aaliyah's purse on the hood while he sat half in and half out of the car, a clipboard leaned up against his open door, making notes. Names, addresses, license numbers. All that sort of thing.

He and Aaliyah were so dead. They were going to have a criminal record.

Aaliyah would never forgive him, and he couldn't blame her. Her future had been so bright … what had he done? He was never going to forgive himself.

Maybe it was better that his punishment come from the police rather than Dad.

Oh god, they were going to call Dad.

"I'm sorry," Jared said quietly to Aaliyah, shifting around so that he could sit sideways on the seat facing her.

"Yeah," she said, watching the cop making notes rather than looking at him.

"I really am," he said. "I had no idea this would happen. I didn't think."

She turned on him. "But I did. I thought about it, and I knew it was a bad idea, and I said so. But I let you go through with it. Hell, I *helped*. That's on me." Her eyes were a flashfire, but her voice hissed more like steam, almost too quiet to hear. Probably so the cop in front of them couldn't use anything she said against them.

Jared didn't know how to answer that. He was prepared for Aaliyah to hate him, but blaming herself, even partway, that was worse.

It was forever until another unit arrived to secure the scene. Officer Cuffs walked them through everything, and when he returned, there was a short, silent trip to the station, followed by finger printing and the whole nine yards. They separated him from Aaliyah almost as soon as they got to the station and his mood tanked until it took all of his energy just to follow directions. He asked about his one call, prepared to make it to Aunt Aggie, but they took that decision out of his hands. He was underage. They had to have a guardian present. Dad was already on the way.

Jared felt sick. The pounding in his head was back, and all he wanted was to time travel back to the nurse's office to rethink his life decisions. The police had re-cuffed his hands in front of him after the finger printing, but they hadn't given him back his phone or any of his stuff. All he could do was stare at his hands, or tap out his own drumbeat. Or count the crappy acoustic tiles in the ceiling. Or follow the cracks in the plaster of the wall like they were lifelines that might tell his fortune (murky, chance of incarceration).

If only the boredom was the worst part. But it was the anger at himself and the fear of what was coming next that gnawed at him.

By the time the door finally opened, he was ready to scream or confess to anything as long as it came with a deal to spare Aaliyah. In walked a woman he'd never seen before, dressed in a button-up shirt the ominous gray of a stormy New York skyline and black pants only a few shades darker than her skin. Her hair was cropped closely to her head, and had a henna sheen to it, the only spot of color beside her lips, which nearly matched her hair. She held a file, although there couldn't have been much in it. Yet.

She turned a hard look on Jared that told him how much trouble he was in. There was no sympathy there. He could try to explain, but he had the sense that she'd heard it all before.

But she wasn't nearly as intimidating as the man who entered behind her. His father.

If the detective—he was guessing she was a detective, since she wasn't dressed like a beat cop—was a brick wall, his father was a steel trap, full of spikes and ready to close on him. He looked deadly. Homicidal. The police setting seemed the only thing holding him back from tearing into Jared.

"I'm Detective Karen Anderson," she told Jared, ignoring his father for now. "I'm investigating your mother's missing person case."

Jared instinctively lifted his hands to shake, but realized that cuffed together as they were, that wasn't going to be an easy thing. Detective Anderson met his gesture anyway, and shook his one hand. She'd clearly had practice. It wasn't nearly as awkward as it could have been.

"You have nice manners," Detective Anderson said. "It seems a boy like you would know better than to break in where you're not invited."

Wow, and there it was. First shot fired.

He looked at Dad, who fought back his explosion and put a smile on his face. "Yes, he does. His mother and I raised him right. You must understand that there's been some kind of mistake. My wife isn't missing. Or, if she is, it's by choice. She—" Dad broke off and glanced at Jared, moved around the table and put a hand to his shoulder, as though it might comfort him to have it squeezed to the point of pain. "She left us. I told that to the police her crazy sister sent to question us. If Jared let himself into his mother's apartment, it was because he was worried about her."

Detective Anderson didn't even glance at Dad, so his smile was wasted. She was busy flipping through the folder in front of her, which she then laid out on the table. She slid a second folder out from underneath the first and arranged them just so. Parallel, edges perfectly aligned. When she glanced up at Jared, her gaze speared his until he felt like a fish dangling at the end of a harpoon. "Jared, the officers who brought you in read you your rights?"

"Yes."

"Good, then you understand that you have the right against self-incrimination. You don't have to answer my questions, but I hope that you'll want to clear things up. Your girlfriend is really worried."

"Aaliyah! How is she? You have to let her go. She didn't have anything to do with this. I made her bring me out here. It's all my fault."

Jared winced as his father squeezed even harder. He couldn't help himself.

Detective Anderson's gaze shot up to him then. "Sir, I'm going to have to ask you to step away from the child and take a seat. He's under sixteen, so you have the right to be here during questioning, but I don't want anything to happen here that can be misconstrued as you influencing his testimony."

Dad immediately unclenched from Jared's shoulder and raised both hands as though to show he meant no harm. He moved off to a chair at the end of the table, catty-corner to the one where Jared sat that was bolted to the floor, but he threw Jared a significant look. Jared didn't know how to read it. "Keep your mouth shut?" "Don't screw this up?" Things were already all screwed up. He didn't see how he could make them worse.

"Aaliyah is fine. Her parents are with her," Detective Anderson said finally.

"Both of them?" Jared asked. It was a stupid question. They'd both know eventually. What did it matter who was here now?

Detective Anderson just stared him down. "Let's talk about you," she said. "Tell me how this is your fault."

He stared back. Had he said that? Oh, god, he had. Was that a confession, saying it was all his fault? No wonder Dad had dug in. Maybe if he met the detective's gaze without flinching, she'd know he was being straightforward with her. If he could just explain …

"It *was* all my idea." He didn't look at Dad. He'd falter if he did, and he couldn't afford to do that if he wanted to get himself and Aaliyah out of trouble. "Dad said Mom left us, and I know she sent a text saying she had to get away for a while." If that *had* really been her. Had the local police shared the text with Detective Anderson? He gave a second's pause for her to ask about it, but she didn't, so he figured she knew. "But I couldn't believe she'd just disappear. Even when she moved out, she called every day. She broke up with Dad, but … she didn't break up with us. She wouldn't. Especially not Emily. My younger sister," he added, in case that wasn't in the detective's file.

"Why 'especially not Emily?'"

"Everyone loves Emily. And she's only fourteen. She needs her mother."

"And you don't?" She leaned back in her chair, crossed her arms over her chest, and fixed Jared with a hard stare.

"If I didn't, I wouldn't be in this mess," he answered honestly. "I just—I didn't know how seriously the police would look for Mom, and so I wanted to look for her myself."

"And what did you find?"

He blinked. "Nothing! I didn't have time. I'd only just turned on Mom's computer when the police came busting in."

"Speaking of busting in—"

"Jared, don't say any more," his father cut in. "Detective Anderson, my son only came to check on his mother. There's no crime here. Unless she's sworn out a complaint, in which case all of these questions about her disappearance are moot."

Jared's heart jumped and he watched Detective Anderson very closely. Was Dad right? Could Mom be around somewhere?

"Your son was caught breaking and entering. We don't need a complainant to charge him."

Which meant *no*. The hope died, sinking like a battleship.

"But what was broken? What harm was done?" his father asked.

Detective Anderson ignored the questions and turned back to Jared. "You tell me. We have only your word that you didn't have time to do anything. Our techs are at the apartment now. You'd do well to tell me what you did before they find it for themselves. Maybe we could even make a deal...."

"What kind of deal?" his father asked at the same time Jared moaned, "But I didn't *do* anything."

"Convince me," Detective Anderson said simply.

Jared looked at his Dad. He had no idea what to do. It sounded like the police were determined to charge him. His only hope was convincing Detective Anderson he was innocent.

Or was that what she wanted him to believe?

The police could lie. He knew that. They could say anything they wanted to get you to confess. Tell you they knew things they didn't or whatever.

"Do we need a lawyer?" his father asked.

"That's up to you."

"I loved my mother," Jared jumped in before his father could call a lawyer and he lost the chance to head everything off. Even as it came out of his mouth, he realized a guilty person would say the same thing. He rushed on. "If I didn't, why would I have left her so many messages and texts? You've got to be checking her phone records, right?"

"Messages would only prove you're smart enough to leave a false trail."

"But—" But what? He had nothing.

"If something happened, if there was an accident, you need to tell us now," Detective Anderson said, staring at him hard enough that he wanted to squirm. "Trying to hide things will only make it worse, add obstruction, tampering with evidence. Make your girlfriend an accessory after the fact. Maybe you and your mom got into it over something—maybe your girlfriend, maybe your grades—and you pushed her. She hit her head or something and you were afraid you'd get into trouble. It happens. More than you think. Just an accident."

"All right, that's it," Dad said as Jared blurted, "I didn't do anything. *I was asleep at the time.*"

There was absolute silence for the missed beat of his heart. His father and Detective Anderson both stared at him in shock.

"At what time?" she asked, very softly.

His father stood. "No more questions. This interview is over. If you're going to charge him, charge him, but we're getting a lawyer. I'm invoking for him."

Jared was shaking. He hadn't meant to say that. Did Dad—

Detective Anderson turned her sights on him. "Mr. Graham, your wife is missing. I'd think you'd want to do everything in your power to find her. I'd think you'd want the answer to these questions as badly as we do."

"Invoking," he said. "Lawyer."

He stared Detective Anderson down. Truly down, since she'd stayed seated and he now loomed.

"Fine," she said, staring back at him. Her face was stone. Her tone as chill as a mountain breeze. She slid her chair away from the table and rose as well. "I'll be back."

She left the room.

Which left Jared alone with his father.

He watched his dad, who stared daggers at the detective's back until the door closed behind her. It was a horrible eternity waiting for his father to get to him.

When Dad swiveled back his way, Jared still saw daggers in his eyes, only they'd shifted targets. "You don't say another word."

He looked around the room as Jared had earlier, only he wasn't counting ceiling tiles or cracks in the wall. He seemed to be searching for something. It occurred to Jared belatedly that, *duh*, the room probably had a camera, or a microphone at least. Of course, the police would record everything. On the cop shows, the detectives made a show of getting permission to record, but he knew that wasn't always necessary. He'd seen enough true crime stuff where people were tripped up by being left in an interrogation room alone or talking on the phone with someone while in jail. He didn't know what New York law said, but he was afraid to find out the hard way.

"I'm going to step out and make a call," Dad said. "Don't talk to anyone. Not even to yourself."

And he was gone, the door shutting behind him with a horrible finality.

"Don't say another word," he'd told Jared.

Good advice. But was he truly afraid Jared would incriminate himself or afraid he'd talk about what he might have heard Friday night? Did Dad realize what his outburst had meant? And what did that mean for him?

After what happened to Mom—what he feared had happened to Mom—was he safer in police custody?

FOURTEEN

Jared

DETECTIVE ANDERSON RETURNED twenty minutes later, just after his father had slipped back into the room, and announced that they wouldn't be pursuing charges at this time. He was going home.

Jared's breath came gushing out, and for the first time in hours, he felt he could take a full breath to replace it. Apparently, it didn't matter where he was safer. Home won over prison hands down.

"However," she said, looking hard first at Jared and then his father, "we may re-approach depending on what turns up. Neither of you are to leave the area. We'll certainly have more questions."

"Neither of us?" his father asked.

"Sir, your wife is missing. As the estranged husband, it can't come as a surprise that you're a person of interest. If you have any information or have had any contact with your wife that can help us clear things up, please don't hold back."

"I've told the police everything I know," he said.

"Well then, here we are."

"Aaliyah?" Jared asked.

"Already released."

"My phone?"

"Evidence." She pulled a slightly crinkled business card from her pants pocket and slid it across the table toward Jared. "If you think of anything you want to get off your chest ..."

His father intercepted the card, stopping it with a finger to the far end. "Thank you. We'll call if we think of anything."

Jared didn't think Detective Anderson would hold her breath waiting for that call.

His father plucked the card off the table and put it into his own pocket, then told Jared, "Let's go."

There was nothing else to do. At least Aaliyah was free. Not that her father or his would probably ever let him see her again. With luck, she was already back home.

Home. It was about to become his prison, he was pretty sure. And that would be the best-case scenario given the pent-up rage he could feel steaming off of his father.

He didn't want to get into the car with him.

He didn't have a choice.

What did he really think his father was going to do? He couldn't answer that. He wanted to think he wouldn't dare do anything. Not with the police already watching him. *The way he didn't do anything to your mother?* part of him asked. He tried to squash it like a bug.

His father stood to the side of the doorway, waiting for the detective and for Jared to precede him out. With Dad behind him, he couldn't watch for clues about what he was thinking or feeling, how he was going to react.

They had some paperwork to fill out and then he was stuck in the car with his father, slipping glances at his profile for some indication of the trouble he was in, but afraid to look at him full on and kick it off. He didn't believe in auras or force fields or any of that, of course, but there did seem to be some kind of storm cloud seething around his father, charged air ready to strike down any attempt he might make to talk himself out of things.

They were a third of the way home before his father spoke. His voice eerily calm, like he was the eye of the raging storm. "You're grounded. That goes without saying. No more dates, no more runs in the park. For now, you do all your running at track. If I hear you skip even a single practice, you're off that as well. It will be just school and home. Emily needs you anyway. She had a scare tonight, and you left her alone. I couldn't even go to her because I had to come and get you. In jail."

Jared didn't point out that he hadn't actually been in *jail*, because it had been a close thing, and anyway, it didn't matter. Splitting hairs with his father would *not* go well.

"Okay," was all he said. And then the part about Emily registered. "Is Emily okay?"

Dad spared Jared a quick, unreadable look before turning his attention back to the road. "She is. Some strange man showed up at the house. Someone from your mother's past."

Jared's blood ran cold. "A strange guy? He didn't ... do anything, right? Why didn't you tell the police about him?"

"If he'd done anything, I would have. But it was outside their jurisdiction and there was nothing to tell. He tried to talk to Emily. She ran to the Meyers'. Carla called me. End of story."

If that was all there was to it, Emily wouldn't have been spooked. But he could ask her later. He wasn't going to push his father; he was already in enough trouble.

Things were quiet for a moment before his father asked, "What did you mean 'you were asleep when it happened?'"

Jared's blood ran so cold it formed ice shards that wanted to stop up the flow all together. He'd known this was coming; he should have been thinking about how to answer. He still didn't know exactly what he'd heard. Probably nothing. Almost certainly nothing. But he couldn't bring himself to tell his father ... just in case. He had to deflect, but he was no actor. He gave it his best shot.

"I figure whatever happened to Mom had to have happened Friday night or Saturday morning, because otherwise she would have come for us. Emily, at least," he said, giving Dad the side-eye, not wanting to seem as though he was studying his father for his reaction. "I know you said she'd changed her mind, but she would have changed it back. I know it. So, whatever happened, it must have been that night after she left, when we were all sleeping."

There, that sounded likely. He might even be able to convince himself.

Dad side-eyed him as well, only not as furtively. "Jared, you're thinking emotionally. But you're almost a man now. You have to start thinking with your head. Nothing happened to your mother. She sent you a message on Saturday. Sometimes people are selfish. They let us down. Your mother … I want to tell you otherwise, but your mother has left. That's it. No big secret. No mystery. Your aunt is a drama queen. I expected better of you."

His dad was more convincing than he was. Maybe because he was right? Could this all be in Jared's head? He really didn't know what he'd heard. It could have been totally innocent, and he could be biased against his father because of the past. The law considered people innocent until proven guilty. It seemed wrong that Jared couldn't apply that to his own father, who was currently the only parent he had.

Dad sighed heavily, and Jared felt miserable. He didn't know what to believe. He didn't know what to trust—his father or his instincts. Those same instincts had pushed him to drag Aaliyah into breaking and entering and had probably cost him his girl-friend. They didn't seem so hot right now.

"We're stopping for food," Dad announced abruptly. "I'm not rewarding you for what you've done, but there's nothing at home, and we need to bring dinner back for your sister."

Jared got why his father mentioned not rewarding him when he saw they were pulling into a KFC drive-through. Kentucky

Fried Chicken was his favorite. Well, maybe second to Popeye's, but they didn't have one of those close to home.

When they got the food, his father reached around to place it on the floor behind his seat and gave Jared the drink carrier to balance on his knees. They rode the rest of the way home in silent salivation. His stomach was apparently untouched by his turmoil.

FIFTEEN

Monday Night

Emily

EMILY SAT cross-legged at the foot of Jared's bed, staring at him. "What were you *thinking?*" she asked.

She'd tried asking him at dinner, but Dad had stopped that cold, saying they were going to have a nice family dinner. Despite telling her not to, Mrs. Meyers had called Dad and told him about the guy she'd seen. She tried to defend not telling him and to pass it off as nothing, but Dad didn't want to talk about that either. He didn't want her to dwell on it, he said. If the guy was looking for Mom, he'd surely leave them alone now that he knew she wasn't here.

Instead Dad asked Emily about her English assignment and her homework. She flashed a glance at Jared, but he didn't seem inclined to talk about any of the important stuff either. He was deep in his own head. In the sulks, Mom called it, but she'd be sulking too if she'd just gotten arrested, so she couldn't really blame him. She did her best to chat cheerfully about stupid, regular stuff, pretending everything was fine.

Jared thought she was untouched by everything, that she didn't care. He didn't appreciate how hard she worked to distract them from all the bad stuff and to keep the peace. He didn't have any idea how difficult it was or that sometimes she just wanted to scream. Or worse. And if she told him, *really* told him so he'd understand, she didn't know what he'd do. She'd suddenly be the center of attention, and she didn't know what that would mean. Would he watch her like a hawk? Tell Dad? Try to get her help? What would that look like? She was terrified of being committed. Of being locked up and having something like her mental history follow her around forever. She had it together. She was handling things. Really.

But discovery would brand her.

Jared ignored the question of what he'd been thinking, busy wrapping up his game controllers to turn over to their father. At least he hadn't kicked her out. Yet.

"Jared," she said, sharply enough to get his attention. "I can't lose you too, okay? You can't get arrested. You can't ... do anything stupid."

She waited for him to blow up. For a moment, he tensed, and she was sure it was going to happen, but then his shoulders slumped and he finally looked at her.

"I know," he said.

He put down the controller he was holding and held out his arms. She didn't let shock stop her from un-pretzeling herself and jumping off the bed for a hug before he changed his mind.

Jared wasn't the huggy type, but this time he held onto her and let his head fall to hers. "I screwed up, Em," he said into her hair. "I got Aaliyah into trouble. Probably lost her. The police let us go, but they didn't say they were dropping all charges forever. Dad—"

He stopped there, but he didn't really have to go on. Dad was pissed. But he was being awfully quiet about it. No screaming.

No shouting this time. Just straight to punishment. Maybe he knew Jared felt badly enough already. Maybe he was trying to make up for Mom's absence.

"You're not going to lose Aaliyah," Emily said. "You two are ..." she scrunched her nose, but realized he couldn't see it. "You're too cute. Too into each other. She's not going to desert you."

"I don't think she'll have a choice. There's no way her parents will let her see me again."

Emily didn't know what to say to that, so she just hugged him. But he was done now. He eased up and she had to let go or risk being clingy.

He picked up the controller again, and she went back to his bed.

"That guy today was seriously weird," she said. "He scared me."

Maybe she should have told Jared while he was still hugging her so he'd keep it up. She could really use that hug right now. Instead, she wrapped her arms around herself.

"What happened?" he asked. "Dad mostly gave me the silent treatment on the way home."

She told him, and he froze, a second controller mid-wrap in his hand. "What did the guy say his name was?"

"Jake ... Cassuary. Something like that."

"He said he knew Mom from high school?"

"And that they reconnected online."

"Facebook," Jared said. "I'm pretty sure I saw a name like that come up in her messages."

"You read Mom's messages?"

"A little," he said.

"*Jared.*"

"Don't *Jared* me. Mom's missing. I want to find her."

"But those are private."

He clammed up, like there was more he wanted to say and wouldn't. Had she shut him down or was he protecting her?

Dammit, they were only fourteen months apart. She wasn't a child. With Mom gone and Dad dealing with the problem by pretending it didn't exist, they only had each other. Jared was not allowed to shut her out.

"What else did you see?" she asked.

He didn't say anything for a second. He just placed the second controller in the cardboard box with the first, and his gaming headset and ...

"Did Mom ever mention a guy named Richard?" he asked her suddenly. "Or Rick or Dick or whatever?"

Emily narrowed her eyes at him. "I don't think so. Why?"

"He was someone else she was talking to online. She met him in a cooking class."

"She did talk about some guy who was hopeless in the kitchen. I think he exploded a sauce. Maybe that was him?"

"Maybe."

"And when you say *talking*, you mean just talking, right?"

"As far as I know."

"Then why are you so concerned about him?"

"I don't know. I mean, it's not like Mom and Dad know all our friends."

"Right."

"But—"

"But what?" she asked.

"Nothing."

This was getting old. She wasn't a kid. She stared Jared down until the silence got awkward. But it also gave her time to think, especially about that thing Josh had told her. She hadn't mentioned *that* to Dad. She didn't even want to think about it herself.

Maybe Jared wasn't the only one holding back.

"Show me," she said.

"Show you what?"

"The guy's picture. The messages. Whatever you've got."

"On what? Dad took everything, remember?"

Emily held out her phone and waggled it in his direction. He grabbed it out of her hands and opened her browser. She'd uninstalled the Facebook app that came pre-loaded on her phone—who used Facebook anymore?—but he was there within seconds.

"Here," he said, holding the phone back out to her, screen first. She took it, using her thumb and forefinger to enlarge the picture. It wasn't a close-up shot, but full-body, a guy squatting beside his big, fluffy black-and-white dog that looked something like a husky, but with a big loopy tail. She thought they were called akidas or akitas or something like that. The guy was definitely silver-haired. And yes, attractive, if you were into old guys.

"That's him," she said, amazed it had been that easy to find him. Could he lead them to Mom?

"Who?" Jared asked. "The guy from today?"

He took the phone back and stared at the picture, as if memorizing the guy's face.

"No, the man Josh saw Mom out with," Emily answered.

"Little Josh?"

"Not so little anymore."

Jared eyed her like he might ask, but then he didn't. At least, not about Josh. "What did he see?"

She didn't want to tell him. It was like ratting on Mom. Jared was angry enough at her already. This would send him over the edge.

"Mom has a boyfriend?" he asked when she was done. His voice was cold. Hard. Like a frozen block of ice. But his fists were clenched. Hard. She wondered if he was digging his nails in as she had earlier.

"I don't know," she said honestly. "Maybe she just needed someone to talk to. What did the messages say?"

He chewed his lip and didn't answer.

"Jared, that silent thing makes me nuts. Talk to me."

"They didn't say much. I think he and Mom were talking

another way. Maybe text. Maybe phone. But I don't think she's with him. He sounded like he hadn't heard from her. He was worried."

Damn, damn, damn. She didn't realize how much she was hoping that this guy knew something.

Jared unclenched his hands and reached for her phone. She surrendered it, and he started typing.

"What are you doing?" she asked.

"I told him I'm Diane's son and we have to talk."

He kept staring at the phone even after he'd sent the message, maybe hoping for an immediate response. Then he started typing again.

"What did you say that guy's name was—the one who came looking for Mom? Jake Cassuary?"

"That's what it sounded like."

"Huh."

"Huh, what?"

"He said he was a friend from high school and they reconnected on Facebook?"

"I think so."

"He's not on her friend's list."

She grabbed his hand and tilted the phone so she could see for herself. As if Jared wasn't perfectly capable of reading the screen.

"That's weird."

He grabbed the phone back and scrolled around a bit more, swiping and typing. Then he stopped. "Mom blocked him."

"What?"

Again, she grabbed the phone and tilted it.

"Maybe he creeped her out as much as he did me," she said.

Jared clicked on the guy's profile. His picture was some kind of cartoon cat who looked like all his fur had been rubbed the wrong way. The background was a cartoon desert. That was all they could see. Apparently, the whole profile was marked private, and since they weren't friends …

"I don't like this guy already," he said.

"If I see him again, I'll snap a picture with my phone. Or get his plate number."

Jared looked up at her sharply. "If you see him again, you get the hell out of there. Right away. You call the police. Or run to the Meyers again."

"You don't get to tell me what to do."

"*Emily.*"

"*Jared,*" she mimicked.

He huffed in frustration, stabbed at the screen a few times, and started typing again.

✳

"*Now* what are you doing?" she asked, frustrated because it was *her phone* and it was about time she had it back.

"Texting Aaliyah. I need to make sure she's okay."

He'd moved on from Mom that easily? Yes, they'd hit a dead end, but there had to be *some* way to track these guys. If only she knew how to jailbreak their information on Facebook, if that was even the right word. She was no hacker. Neither was Jared.

She hated being helpless, but even if they could turn up current addresses or something, how would they get to their suspects? Neither she nor Jared could drive yet, and he was grounded on top of it. Dad might never let him out of the house again, and there was no way they could ask *Dad* to drive them. Maybe Aaliyah …

Something occurred to Emily just as Jared hit Send on his epic text. "Won't the police or Aaliyah's parents have taken her phone?"

"Crap, I should have thought of that." He threw Emily's phone onto the bed and followed it down, sinking onto the other end from Emily, then looking to her in an appeal for help. "So, how do I get in touch with her?"

"You'll see her tomorrow at school."

"Yeah."

He sounded so sad that Emily skootched over to give him another hug, and he let her ... until the phone rang on the bed between them and he reached for it before she could. She squawked as he grabbed it, indignant because it was *her phone*. But maybe it was Aaliyah and he had a good reason.

He glanced at the read-out, and when his face fell she knew that it wasn't his girlfriend. But still, he answered it.

"Hey," he said without any enthusiasm. "Oh, hey, Aunt Aggie. Yeah, this is her phone. Here she is."

He started to pull the phone away from his ear then yanked it right back. "Oh, sorry. Um, yeah, I don't have a phone anymore. For now. That's why I couldn't get back to you."

Emily reached for the phone in Jared's hand, but he held onto it. He was getting entirely too entitled with her phone. She could let it go or she could make it an issue. She decided to go for it, and swiped so fast he didn't have time to tighten up. She enjoyed the shocked look on his face when it was suddenly gone and launched herself up from the bed so he couldn't easily retake the phone, pressing it to her ear. "Aunt Aggie, he was *arrested*. The police have it."

She realized as she was saying it that Jared would be pissed off that she told. But, really, how could she keep something like that to herself?

"What!" her aunt said. It was probably meant to be a question, but the exclamation point came straight through the phone. At full volume.

"Well, he went by Mom's place—"

She didn't even register that Dad had flown into the room until he latched onto her hand and squeezed hard enough that she let out a gasp and dropped the phone. He caught it as it fell and put it to his ear. Emily didn't even recognize his face. It was twisted up, mouth misshapen into a snarl. Eyes narrowed and blazing, as though they could shoot tightly focused lasers. He didn't look at all like himself.

"What the hell do you think you're doing?" he snarled into the phone.

Emily was so stunned she reached for the phone like she could take it back as she had from Jared. She wanted to protect Aunt Aggie from Dad's wrath, but he stopped her with a glare and she fell back. It was like she didn't even know him.

"You started this witch hunt," Dad said into the phone. "From now on, if you want to talk to the kids, you go through me. Do you know you got Jared arrested today?"

He was blaming Aunt Aggie?

Her aunt must have said something, because Dad paused, but not for long.

"You have them half out of their minds with fear that something happened to their mother. Jared went looking for her today. He *broke in* to her apartment, and some nosy neighbor called the cops. Was that you too? Do you have the whole neighborhood on watch?"

He listened for, like, half a second.

"No, I don't want to hear it. You're getting the kids all riled up. It's bad enough that Diane left. They don't need you turning their lives upside down."

He pulled the phone away from his face and glared at it before punching the End button and throwing the phone back onto the bed.

"No more calls from Aunt Aggie," he said, catching Emily's gaze in a way that made her feel trapped. Like she couldn't look away. "She calls, you give the phone to me. She texts, you show me. You *do not* respond."

Emily just stared.

"You got it?" her father asked.

Emily had been afraid for others before, but never herself. For the first time ever, she feared giving Dad any answer but the one he wanted. She didn't know what he'd do if she argued, and she didn't want to find out.

"Got it," she said, her voice small.

She risked a glance at Jared, but he was staring at Dad. His jaw was tight. He'd break teeth if he clenched any harder. His hands were fisted. She willed him not to say anything. Not to challenge Dad. Not now.

"Good," her father said, and whirled straight around to march out of the room. He turned back almost as quickly, making her jump. "And go back to your own room. Jared needs to think about what he's done. And he's probably got homework. You do too. Neither of you are to use this as an excuse to let your grades slip, you understand me?"

Jared started to open his mouth, and Emily grabbed one clenched fist to stop him.

"We understand," she jumped in. Jared's fist was like stone under her hand, and yet she felt it compress like he was trying to squeeze out a diamond.

Her father stomped off, but he left the door open, denying them privacy to talk about what had just happened.

As soon as he left, Jared hissed. *"What the actual hell?"*

Emily was shocked. He hardly ever swore in front of her.

"What shouldn't get to us?" Jared went on. "That Mom is gone? That he's forbidden us to talk to her sister who's worried sick? That the police are investigating? Are we supposed to be hard like him and not give a damn?"

Emily started to say something, but Jared wasn't finished. "You'd better go," he said. "Before things get ugly."

She didn't know whether Jared was talking about himself or their father. He was so tightly wound....

He grabbed her phone off the bed and tossed it to her before escorting her to the door with a hand on her back. She was out in the hallway with the door shut hard before she could protest. Her head was spinning. Mom was gone; Dad was acting crazy; and Jared was starting to scare her. What if he stopped holding himself back and he and Dad came to blows? Would the police take Jared away? Dad? What then? Her whole world was a house of cards in gale force winds.

Dad *couldn't* be serious about them not talking to Aunt Aggie. He was just upset. He'd calm down. And Jared …

She didn't know what Jared would do. She couldn't even believe what he'd done already. So, Dad had taken his electronics; that wasn't the only way to reach the outside world. He had a window. Would he sneak out next? Could she stop him? Should she? Or would that bottle him up until he exploded? Or tip Dad off and get him into truly massive trouble. What if she didn't stop Jared and he got himself arrested again?

"Jared?" she said through the door, trying for just loud enough for him to hear.

"What?" he asked, his voice as tight as his fist had been.

"You won't … do anything stupid, right?"

"Like what?" he challenged.

She didn't know what to say to that. She didn't want to give him any ideas. "Anything," she said after too long a pause.

"No," he said. "I won't do anything." His voice seemed softer now. "I won't leave you alone."

She believed him. She had to.

Jared

Dad was right about one thing; Jared had a lot of thinking to do. Dad was cutting them off. He couldn't talk to the police, which was okay. He didn't *want* to talk to the police. He couldn't speak to Aunt Aggie. He couldn't communicate with *anyone*—not without his phone or computer or Xbox. Not until tomorrow at school, anyway.

It made him feel a weird, crazy kind of vulnerability. What if something happened? He considered picking up one of those pay-as-you-go phones, but without a car, he had no way to get to a store. He could catch a ride, but if Dad found out he didn't come straight home or skipped practice … there'd be hell to pay, and these days hell seemed like a literal thing.

But mostly he was worried about Emily. She'd already lost her mother—their mother. She couldn't lose her aunt too.

He had to fix this. He had to find out what had happened to Mom. Despite his father. Despite the police. He needed to know what he'd heard that night before it ate him alive. Because if there was anything he could have done …

It hurt so damn much he wanted to curl up on his bed and —*Die*, he thought. But only for a second. He'd never leave Emily alone like that. And it wouldn't solve anything. What he *really* wanted was to sleep through the pain. To wake up and find out the horror had passed. Mom was back. He would be so glad to see her, he'd forgive her for ever leaving. Emily was happy. The police were off his case. Aaliyah was speaking to him again and her parents were okay with it. Dad was … well, Dad still wouldn't be happy, except maybe that he'd been proven right and everyone could give it a rest.

He lay down on his bed. He wanted to turn his back to the door, curl up facing the wall, and shut out the world, but he couldn't bring himself to do it. He didn't know who he thought might sneak up on him, but he faced the door anyway, ready to spring out of bed in a second if Emily called out or he heard any odd noises. He was so tense he might as well have been crouched at the starting block.

With nothing to distract him, thoughts spun in his head. He relived every second of the afternoon, from dragging Aaliyah into things through the break-in and interrogation and Dad's strange outburst with Aunt Aggie. The thing that really stuck with him was what Detective Anderson had said after she'd accused him of having something to do with his mother's disappearance and he'd asked her why, if that was true, he'd left her messages and texts. *"That only proves you're smart enough to leave that trail."*

He'd told Emily that he didn't think Richard knew anything about where Mom was, because his Facebook messages sounded worried, but what if he was leaving a false trail, like Detective

Anderson had said? Or maybe the guy who'd shown up looking for Mom was returning to the scene of his crime. Maybe he'd kidnapped Mom or … worse. If Mom wasn't gone under her own steam, Dad wasn't necessarily the only suspect.

He had to take comfort in that. He didn't want to think about how angry he was lately. About how when Dad ripped the phone away from Emily *he* wanted to rip into something.

He *did not* want to think even for a second that he might be like his father. Or that Dad was worse than they knew.

He had to focus on that innocent-until-proven-guilty thing. Especially for his own father. Especially because of what Dad's guilt would do to Emily. If they lost him too, where would they go? Gram couldn't take care of them. She could barely drive, could barely hear anymore, listened to her television loudly enough to wake the dead. And after her fall a few months ago, when, luckily, she'd only bruised and not broken her tailbone, Dad was worried about her taking care of herself. He'd considered moving her in with them. But she'd refused.

Aunt Aggie and her one-bedroom apartment? She loved them, he knew that, but she preferred people in small doses. He didn't get it, because he was a people person, but she really liked to be alone.

And he was too young to take care of Emily by himself. Even if he had his license. There was no way he'd be able to afford the house and the car and electricity and whatever else his parents had to pay for.

His muscles started to cramp, and he realized he was as stiff as a board. He had to calm down. For that, he needed a plan. He needed to know he wasn't helpless, that there was something he could *do*.

Maybe that Dick guy would have some answers. He should never have pushed Emily out before checking again for a response.

His door clicked open, and Jared was immediately up, poised

like he was going to karate chop any danger. Like he'd taken martial arts instead of track.

Emily poked her head in. The rest of her followed quick like a fox. She closed the door behind her and leaned against it, as though that would keep Dad out if he'd caught her entering after he'd told her to leave.

"It's all gone," she said, tensing him up before he could even relax.

"What is?" he asked, feeling her tension but at a complete loss what was behind it.

"The messages. All of them on Mom's Facebook. We hadn't closed out my browser, so everything you entered was still there, and when I checked to see if Richard had answered, they were all gone."

She ended on a sob, as though this had been their last hope of finding Mom. Her knees started to go out from under her, and she slid to the floor before he could get to her, crying like it was the end of the world.

SIXTEEN

Jared

HE DIDN'T SEE Aaliyah at school the next day. Or the next. By Friday he was getting seriously concerned, approaching frantic. She couldn't leave him too. Even if they couldn't go out anymore, he needed to know she was all right. And that she didn't hate him.

So when he saw her in the lunchroom, his gaze somehow zeroing in on her as he entered, even though she was halfway across the room from their regular table, he stopped so short that Dugan crashed into him from behind.

"What the hell, man?" he asked, giving Jared a push to move him forward.

Jared went with it, started walking again, straight in Aaliyah's direction. He was nearly to her when he realized he hadn't apologized to Dugan ... and didn't really care. Maybe later. Right now all he could think about was Aaliyah, who either hadn't seen him or didn't care.

He was a step away when she finally glanced up, totally startled, and then looked away again to his left. At nothing.

"I'm not supposed to talk to you," she told the empty air.

"I was so worried. When I couldn't reach you and you didn't come to school—Are you okay? Is everything—" *Okay*, he was going to finish again, lamely, but she was already shaking her head.

"Mom and Dad want to homeschool me. They kept me home while they researched it. But with my accelerated schedule and my AP classes and the after-school activities to pad my college applications … They're letting me come back, but with one condition. I have to stay away from you."

Jared had thought it would be okay if he could just know Aaliyah was all right. But now that he knew … well, the relief at seeing her was a drop in the bucket compared to the pain of all the rest of it. She didn't seem to hate him. That should count for something. But this—not even meeting his eyes and not fighting for him—*this* was hell.

"Aaliyah?" he said. Nothing else, hoping to make her *look* at him even for a second, just so he could see what was behind her eyes, hoping it was more than cold indifference. When she didn't look up, he said. "Never mind. I'll leave you alone. I've caused you enough trouble."

It was the least he could do. He knew that. But it hurt like a hurdle to the chest.

He turned and walked away, headed for the food line, not because he was hungry, but out of habit. Besides, if he had food to stuff in his mouth, that might discourage Dugan or anyone else from asking questions.

He heard someone hurrying up behind him and almost didn't turn. There didn't seem to be any point, but a small hand on his shoulder had his heart leaping into his throat. Maybe it was Aaliyah. Maybe seeing him walk away …

But he turned to see her punk friend Maybell with the spiked hot-pink hair and the ripped Screaming Meemies concert shirt pinned to a tank top so it wouldn't fall off one shoulder or another and violate the stupid school rules.

"Yeah?" he said, carefully neutral. Just because he deserved any lecture she could throw at him didn't mean he was in the mood.

"It's killing her too," she said.

Jared felt a little of that compression to his chest start to ease.

"It doesn't seem that way," he answered.

"I never said this, okay? But I think she's afraid that if she looks at you, she'll cave. This is her whole future we're talking about here. Her parents want to lock her up and throw away the key. That would kill her." It was the second time she'd used that expression. Maybell was nothing if not dramatic. It didn't mean she was wrong.

"So I'm just supposed to walk away?"

She shrugged. "For now. Maybe things will calm down and her parents will ease up. Or maybe you'll find a way. But for now ..."

"Will you give her a message?"

"I'm not going to be like that nurse from Romeo and Juliet. I've seen how that ends." But she bumped his shoulder with hers as she said it, so he guessed he was supposed to smile, even if there wasn't anything funny about it.

"Just tell her I'm sorry, okay? And that I'm here if she decides ... whatever."

"Got it. You have my number?"

Jared furrowed his brows. Her number? With him and Aaliyah just barely broken up?

She snorted at him. "Oh lord, you're so not my type. I mean for Aaliyah. Look, I don't promise you anything, but if you want to send her a message to my phone, I'll make sure that she gets it. And if she decides she wants to answer, I'll let her do that. Modern day carrier pigeon, that's me."

It was the best thing he'd heard all day. All week.

"Thank you," he said, meaning it. "But why? I didn't think you liked me all that much."

She eyed him and shrugged again. All he could think was that it was a good thing the shirt with the torn-out neck had been pinned to her tank. Otherwise all that shrugging would certainly have thrown it off.

"You're okay," she said. "And I hate to see Aaliyah hurting."

"That makes two of us."

Jared rooted in his backpack for a pen and paper and took down the number Maybell gave him.

"My parents have my phone," he said, "so the read-out might say *Emily*. That's my sister."

"Note to self," she said, "don't send any nip pics."

Jared's eyebrows must have risen all the way to his hairline.

"Relax," she said, a wicked smile forming on her face. "I'm kidding."

She walked away, leaving him to stare after her.

He was startled by a sudden slap on his back, and then Dugan's voice, "Dude, you move fast. I didn't think you were her type."

Jared turned, rolling his eyes hard. "It's not like that," he said.

"Sure, sure. I didn't hear that part about nip pics."

"Oh, lord," Jared groaned.

"Do you think they're pierced?" Dugan asked, grinning from ear to ear.

"Dude, seriously?" he asked.

"What, like you're not imagining it?"

"I have a girlfriend," he answered, but it was automatic. He wasn't so sure anymore.

"Okay, so you're taken. You're not dead."

Jared just shook his head. Dugan wasn't going to get it, and he wasn't going to explain it to him.

But now he couldn't even think about food. Or grabbing it for show to take back to the table with Dugan and their other friends. Any more comments or questions like that and Jared was afraid he might throw a punch.

He walked away. He wanted to walk straight out, even though he didn't know where he'd go, but he got stopped by one of the lunch monitors. He mumbled something about being sick, and all she asked was whether he wanted a pass to the bathroom or the nurse. He *wanted* home, but that wasn't an option.

"Nurse," he said. There was too much left of lunch to wait out in the men's room. The nurse was going to get tired of seeing him, but with his mother missing, he thought she'd understand.

※

There was no track on Fridays, and Emily was hanging out with her friend Shara after school, which meant it might be hours before she got home and he could check her phone. He could hunt down where Dad had stashed his stuff, use it to get on the web, search through Mom's e-mails or past Facebook updates for clues. Maybe set up his own account to reach out to Richard Travis or try again to find a local listing for him—Emily had already gone looking.

Check news and hospitals for Jane Does, a part of his brain said, but he crushed that right down. The police would have checked the hospitals already.

His mind was like a pendulum, swinging back and forth between *something horrible has happened* and *she's fine, everything's fine, you're overreacting.* He wanted to stay on the side of the shiny and happy, but there really wasn't one. Best-case scenario meant Mom had turned her back on them, but he didn't believe it. Not after seeing her toothbrush and her laptop, not after she didn't show up for her job or call Aunt Aggie. Not with the mysteriously missing messages.

He hated that he was afraid enough of his father not to hunt his things down. He didn't know what kind of spyware Dad might have on the family's internet.

Dad had said he couldn't go running. Couldn't leave the house except for track.

He'd taken away television with the rest of Jared's electronics.

What did that leave him?

He could take a nap, but every time he laid down these days his brain tried to eat itself, gnawing on every fear like a dog with a big bone that wouldn't grind down.

Well, he had an assignment for English he was already behind on. He wasn't much of a reader to start with, and a historical novel would have been his absolute last choice, but he hadn't been given one. At least *A Tale of Two Cities* was supposed to be about the French Revolution, so surely there'd be some action and stuff. But so far he hadn't gotten past the beginning.

It was the best of times, it was the worst of times.

What the hell? It was one or the other. No way it was both. Which meant the author was being poetic. Which meant an entire book of the writer saying what sounded pretty instead of whatever the fuck he meant. Jared hadn't had a lot of patience for that crap even before his mother disappeared.

But what the hell else was he supposed to do?

Nothing.

Dad was boring him into reading.

Death by homework.

He went to his room, dug out the book, started reading, and got that nap in anyway.

*

He bolted awake when Emily got home, but was too groggy to meet her at the door. He did manage to stagger out to the kitchen, still half asleep, and ask to look at her phone. He might have greeted her first, he wasn't sure.

"Geez, Jared," she said, thrusting her phone at him, but not before looking at it herself. "Nothing new, okay?"

It wasn't okay, but there was nothing he could do about it.

"You look like heck," she said when he handed her phone back after checking just to be sure.

"Thanks," he said with a glower.

"Sorry, I didn't mean that to come out so strong. It's just ... are you sleeping?"

"Just woke up from a nap."

"I mean at night."

"Sometimes."

They stood there looking at each other. It was Friday night and he had nowhere to go. No date, not even with himself to go jogging in the park.

As if she'd read his mind, Emily asked, "Do you want to play a game? Cards, like you used to play with me when I was little."

Was she offering him a pity play date? Was he desperate enough to take it? The answer was yes, yes he was.

But he wasn't going down that easy. "What game?" he asked, as though he might actually have better things to do.

"I don't know, Garbage? Rummy, Nerts, War?"

"War," he said. Although now that she was older, she might be fast enough to give him a run at Nerts. He smiled remembering the fun they used to have, even though playing with her always started out as a chore, just something to humor and entertain her.

"You're on," she said. "You get the cards; I'll pop some corn."

"Bossy much?"

Emily stuck her tongue out at him and he laughed. Actually laughed. It shocked him so much he nearly shut it down. He had no right to laugh when Mom was ... wherever she was. But Emily needed normalcy, and so he let it die off naturally. Or maybe a little bit strangled, but she didn't seem to notice over the crinkling of the popcorn bag as she put it into the microwave.

Her phone rang as she pushed start, so she answered it and then kinked her neck so that she could hold the phone between her shoulder and her ear while she grabbed herself soda from the fridge.

She stopped mid-turn with the soda bottle in her hand. "Yeah, he's right here," she said. "We're about to play cards."

She was looking at Jared now, and he saw her eyes go wide. He heard Dad's voice coming through the phone, but couldn't make out what he was saying. What the hell was going on?

"Um, okay. You do know we're old enough to watch ourselves, right?" Pause. "Yeah. We'll be here."

She hung up and Jared immediately asked, "What?"

"Dad was checking up on you," she said. "Or asking me to, which just sucks. Oh, and he's bringing pizza and Gran tonight. He's going out."

Jared didn't say anything, but inside he was seething. Mom was missing, his kids needed him—well, Jared didn't, but any reasonable parent would assume otherwise—and Dad was *going out*? Out with the guys? Out on a date?

Dad didn't really have guys.

"Out with who?" Jared asked.

"He didn't say. Maybe it's something for work?" But Emily was chewing her lip and thinking, seeming to have forgotten all about the soda she held in her hand. Behind her, the popcorn was going mad, pinging and popping all over the place, but when the microwave went off, Emily jumped.

She nearly dropped the soda, but she made a good recovery and set it down on the counter as she dealt with the popcorn. Jared went to help, getting out a bowl and opening the steaming hot bag so that Emily wouldn't burn herself. In turn, she got out a second glass for the soda and poured him some too.

For the next half hour they played War and alternately ate and threw popcorn at each other. Like they were normal kids and this was a normal night and everything was normal. Like they were some kind of TV family.

It was nice.

Until Emily's friend Shara called even though they'd just

seen each other and she ran off to take the call in her room. They were nearly finished anyway. Jared had, like, seven cards left, and she had the whole rest of the deck. And that was that. He sat there playing solitaire for a while, but that got old pretty quickly and then he was back to staring at walls. Or taking another go at *A Tale of Two Cities.*

Or obsessing over whether or not he should ask Gran about whether she'd heard anything last Friday night. On the one hand, she was half deaf, so it didn't seem likely. And even asking her would alert Emily. Gran tended to spend the whole evening with the television on at full volume. She'd never hear Jared unless he shouted, and then … Emily.

On the other hand, could he resist asking? She was a potential witness, and right now this was the only investigating he was capable of.

But was it worth the harm asking could do when she probably didn't know anything anyway? Even if he could keep Emily from overhearing, Gran might mention the questions to Dad and then … what? What more could Dad do to him? He didn't really want the answer to that.

He tried to keep it in, but all night, all he could think was *What did you hear? What did you hear?* It repeated in his head all through the pizza Gran made them eat in the kitchen, through the game shows she seemed to find any hour of every day, which she let him and Emily watch with her even though he wasn't supposed to have TV, because it was the way they spent time together. *Finally,* Emily excused herself for the bathroom or escape, she didn't specify.

He saw his moment coming. He waited while Emily leaned across the easy chair to kiss Gran on her papery cheek. As she pulled back, Gran took both her hands with a squeeze and a smile and declared her, "Such a lovely girl." Then she let her go.

He waited until he heard a door close down the hall and then he waited still longer for a commercial. He knew better than to reach for a remote while Gran's show was still on, but to his shock, Gran beat him to it. The remote was in her lap, after all, so she didn't have as far to go. She turned the sound so far down it might as well be off.

"What's this I hear about you getting arrested?" she asked, twisting in her chair to fix him with a *look*.

He hadn't been the only one waiting for Emily to leave in order to pounce.

He pulled back in shock. "Um, not arrested, actually. Just … questioned."

"Were you handcuffed?" she asked.

Oh, hell. "Yeah."

"What? Speak up."

Was it her hearing or did she just want to hear him say it again? "Yeah," he repeated, louder.

"Did they put you in the squad car?" she asked. "Read you your rights?"

Crap. "Yeah."

"Did they drive you to the station and put you in an interview room?"

"Okay, yeah, but—"

She stopped him with a look like she was a bird of prey set to peck out his tongue if he continued. "Then you were arrested."

"Okay, so I was arrested," he said. "But they let me go."

Gran shook her head. "Jared, I love you, but you're impetuous, a hothead. I understand that you want to *do* something. But you're only getting into trouble and causing grief for your poor father. He's going through enough. Your mother is gone. If she wanted anyone to go after her, she'd have left a forwarding address."

"Did Dad ask you to talk to me?" Jared asked, suspicious.

Gran blinked her bird-of-prey eyes. "Do I need to be told what to do?"

Uh oh.

"No, I'm just saying—don't you find it weird that she's missing? That she didn't go back to her job or apartment? We were the last people to see her." *Dad* was the last person to see her. "Maybe you saw or heard something that can explain why she's gone?"

There, that seemed subtle enough. He didn't ask, "Did you hear a fight?" "Did Dad do something to Mom?" "Is she ever coming back?"

"We were right here in the same house," she said. "Your mother came, went to dinner with your father and left. I was sound asleep by that point. We all were." But those eyes, still sharp, if a little more faded than they used to be, bored right into him as if looking for some kind of flaw or giveaway on that last bit. Or maybe that was Jared's guilty conscience. Not that he had anything to feel guilty about, except pretending to be asleep when Dad came to check on him. Unless it was suspecting his father of … He could hardly bring himself to think it. Not murder, maybe, but an accident? Something he covered up out of fear. Whatever it was, Jared had to know.

"Right," Jared said. "Of course. Just, like you say, I want to do something. I feel like Mom would have left some clue.…"

"If she did, the police will find it." She looked past him suddenly, said, "Oh!" and pressed the volume button on the remote until Jared's eardrums were about to shatter.

Her show was back. They were done here.

Jared excused himself a second later. Like Emily, he leaned in to give Gran a parting kiss on the cheek. She did not squeeze his hand or tell him he was a lovely boy. Instead, she craned around him to see the next clue. He tried not to take it personally.

SEVENTEEN

Saturday

Emily

EMILY WAS STRUGGLING to focus on homework at the breakfast bar when the call came in. She'd have preferred the kitchen table, but Dad had tax stuff and his laptop spread out all the way across it and he was NOT in a good mood. He never was when doing paperwork, but Jared made it worse that morning by asking with a sneer how his night had gone and who he'd been with. Emily seriously thought Dad was going to lose it. His fists clenched until she was afraid he was going to use them.

He looked at Jared like his gaze could stab right through him. "You little snot, I'm your father. You will *not* question me."

Jared faced off with him, his own fists clenched. "Mom's *gone*. I think you owe us more than that."

Dad's eyes blazed. Emily willed Jared to shut up.

"I don't owe you a thing," Dad said. "If anything, you owe me for supporting you all these years, for coming to get you at the police station and not beating your ass for what you did."

Emily gasped, at the curse and the threat.

"I'll tell you what," he went on, "the next time the police take you in, they can keep you. How would that be?"

Jared's eyes burned just as bright. "You make good on that threat, and I'll tell them—"

He stopped himself, fear suddenly chasing the anger off his face.

"Tell them what?" his father asked. His voice was low and deadly calm.

Jared didn't answer that. He turned on his heel, went to his room, and closed the door too hard but just short of slamming. He hadn't come out since. That was hours ago.

But the call—

When the phone rang, Dad snapped, "I'll get it," even though Emily was closer.

She didn't argue. She hadn't dared say a word to him since his fight with Jared. She could practically feel him fuming, as if he was a furnace turned up too high and she was in the blast radius.

He grabbed their landline off the wall, and she stayed right where she was, the better to hear. She didn't even shift in her seat. She barely breathed to keep from making any noise and being ordered away.

But she still couldn't hear anything but his side of the conversation.

"Yes."

Pause.

"You did? Where?"

"Uh huh. Do you need me to come down there?"

"Oh, I see. Thank you, officer."

Dad hung up, and stayed for a moment staring at the phone. When he turned, Emily was watching him. She thought she'd heard Jared come out of his room as well, but she couldn't pull her gaze away from Dad to look.

Emily wanted to ask about the call, but after Dad's reaction to Jared's questioning ...

"They found your mother's car," he said, looking Emily in the eyes. "At the Poughkeepsie train station."

"And?" Jared asked from the hallway. No confrontation in his voice now. Just stress and worry.

"That's it. Just the car. Makes sense that if she was at the train station she probably took a train."

Emily let out a breath, for a second so relieved she felt almost boneless, like she could melt off the stool. "That's good, right? Now that they know, they can trace where she bought a ticket to, track her down."

She was watching Jared now though, and his face didn't light up like hers. Why wasn't he relieved? Didn't he want to find Mom as badly as she did?

When he didn't say anything, she looked back to Dad. There was no happiness there either, and she started to get a bad feeling in the pit of her stomach.

"Em," Dad said, very gently, like he was about to tell her something horrible. "If they find out where she went, they're not going to hunt her down. They'll know she left on her own, and that's her choice. They won't bring her back."

He approached to hug her, and she slid off the stool and backed away instead. He wasn't going to hug her and make it all right. Nothing was all right.

"But if they could just talk to her or make her talk to us ..." she said.

"Em, they're not going to do that. I think you have to accept that she's gone."

"No!" she yelled, startling even herself. "No, I will not accept that. Mom's gone and you don't even care!"

Now she was the one who ran to her room. And slammed the door. And locked it. She even considered putting her desk chair under the knob, since the door only had one of those simple screwdriver locks, but she didn't really think Dad would come after her. She threw herself down on her bed and grabbed the meerkat stuffed animal they'd gotten at the zoo last year when they all went as a family, and she hugged it to her like it was Mom.

It didn't hug back.

But a darker pressure started to build. She needed to do something about this pain. She was the only one who could.

*

Jared stayed behind in the hallway, staring at his father.

"What?" Dad challenged, bristling all over.

"I don't know," he said honestly. "I just … want this to be over." *I want everything to go back to the way it was.* But that wasn't going to happen.

"They want us to come in later," Dad said. "I think they want me to walk them through whatever they find in the car."

"You said 'us.' They want *us* to come in?"

"Me. But I'm not leaving you home alone."

"Dad, I'm almost sixteen."

"And not mature enough to keep from making stupid decisions like breaking into your mother's place."

Jared growled his frustration. "What would you have done if it was Gran missing?"

"Not that. Speaking of Gran, I'd better go wake her. She had a bad night with her leg spasms, but she'll want to know what's going on. Maybe she won't mind staying a bit longer to keep watch on things."

Things. Meaning me. Jared steamed. He didn't say another word. Any of the ones crowding his mouth and mind would get him into more trouble.

He moved silently and glaringly out of the hallway to let his Dad pass and considered his next move. He thought about going to Emily, but there was nothing he could say to comfort her. He had no computer access, so he couldn't try to find his mother's credit card companies and passwords and statements, look up train tickets … Anyway, the police would be doing all that the legal way, using subpoenas or whatever. They'd be looking at video from the train station and surroundings. He wondered if they'd share what they found with the family.

In the absence of anything useful, all he could think was that Aaliyah would want to know. Maybe it was self-serving. Maybe he just wanted an excuse to see her, but it was all he could think to do. If he stayed in his room or in this house any longer, he'd go insane. He'd never risk sneaking out if Dad was home, but once he went out and Gran was settled with her shows …

She'd make the perfect alibi.

The wait nearly killed him. Dad got Gran up. Offered to scramble her some eggs, though she refused, saying he needed to get going and Jared could take care of her. Dad tried to talk to Emily, but she wouldn't open her door and he wouldn't yell through it. Then, finally, Dad was gone, and Jared was left to make his grandmother scrambled eggs and toast, remembering when she used to chase them all out of the kitchen, insisting that she had it. She'd make them eggs-in-the-nest—well-buttered bread with the centers cut out, toasted in the frying pan with eggs cracked in the centers. Occasionally, she'd take potshots at Mom for her "fancy food," like the eggs Benedict or crème brulée French toast that she'd try out on them. Jared never really understood it. Even Mom's oopses were pretty awesome. He figured Gran was just jealous that someone else was cooking for her "little boy." She'd been older when she had Dad and had never gotten over calling him that. Still, it was weird and unfair, and if he was Mom, he'd have said something, but she never did. At least not where he could hear.

Anyway, Gran thanked him and patted his hand and asked after Emily. He couldn't just leave her, though the compulsion to get out, to go see Aaliyah, was overwhelming. Instead he sat and talked to Gran about how upset Emily was and how much homework he had and how he'd probably be back in his room all day doing it.

"Playing video games, more like," she said with a teasing glint in her eye.

"Not possible. Dad has all my controllers."

"Ah," she said, shoveling egg onto her toast and not noticing as half of it dropped off again on the way to her mouth. "Well, maybe later you can take a break and take your sister and me out for ice cream or something. Won't that be nice? Anyway, I have to take a swing by the pharmacy."

She took the bite of half-egged bread.

"Gran, I don't have my license."

She waggled the bread at him, "Excuses. You can drive with another adult in the car, yes? I've been an adult for more than three-quarters of my life now. I think I qualify."

Jared smiled because he was supposed to, but anxiety churned in his stomach. Now he'd have to get back before she wanted him with no idea when that would be. It would be risky, but he was already grounded and disconnected from everyone and everything. He didn't see what else Dad could take from him.

He couldn't lose his nerve.

"All right, Gran. We'll go later. I need to get some work done first, and I don't think Emily is in any mood to go out."

"Let me just take care of these dishes, and—"

"Not a chance. I've got these. You've got your shows?"

"Such a sweet boy," she said. Ah, there it was. "Would you grab me my cane? Your father hustled me out so fast, I forgot it in my room."

Jared went for the cane and came back to find his grandmother trying to stand even without it. She could probably have made it, but he rushed to her side anyway. He handed her the cane and took her other arm in his, escorting her to the living room and settling her into her favorite spot. He even made sure she had a blanket for her feet, and a cup of water and the remote within easy reach before he retreated to his room, chased by the volume blast from the TV.

He closed his door and locked it and immediately went out the window, thankful his father hadn't yet thought to nail it shut, and that their house was a one-story ranch-style, so he didn't have to drop from an upper floor. He slid the window closed behind him—not as easy from this side—and quickly looked around. He couldn't see the street from around the side of the house, not from behind the blind his father had built to hide the garbage cans, which meant no one could see him either. Perfect.

But he had to come out from behind the blind sometime. He felt pretty stupid peeking around it, realizing as he did that it was way more suspicious than just walking across his own yard. Luckily, there was no one to see. As soon as he hit the sidewalk, he started a fast walk, like he was out for one of his runs, even though he wasn't really dressed for it. Far sooner than he would have normally, he started to run. People were used to seeing him race through the neighborhood, and if they couldn't catch him, they couldn't stop him for a chat. His mother's disappearance was big news. Everyone seemed to want to give their gossip the personal touch with direct contact.

Even running, it took him almost half an hour to get to Aaliyah's neighborhood. It would be even longer on the way back, since he'd be tired and less motivated. He didn't have a lot of time to waste. As soon as he got to Aaliyah's block, he cut through a back yard, hoping it wouldn't be like at Mom's complex and that no one would call the police. He couldn't afford for Mr. or Ms. Persad to catch him. He fervently hoped neither was out gardening or mowing or grilling ... well, it was a little early still for that.

He managed to get to Aaliyah's window around the side of the house without being seen. Thankfully, her yard wasn't fenced off, though the same couldn't be said for her neighbor's place with the backyard boundary made up of really aggressive rose bushes. He'd found a slight space between two of them, but squeezing through had left his forearms bleeding where his shirt was pushed up. He'd never understood the appeal of the vampire flowers.

Now that he was here, her window in sight, his nerves kicked into overdrive. What if Aaliyah didn't want to see him? What if he was caught and got her into even more trouble? What if her parents called the cops? Technically, he supposed, he was trespassing, since he certainly hadn't been invited.

No guts, no glory.

He stepped up to the window after making sure that the coast was clear and rapped on it with his knuckles.

At first, nothing. Then, "Did you hear something?"

Crap, someone was inside with Aaliyah. She couldn't have moved on so quickly, could she?

His heart squeezed. He was torn between staying and going, but his body made the decision for him. He was frozen. He couldn't move if he wanted to. He'd come to see Aaliyah. Now he also had to know who she was with. Did that make him a creepy stalker boy?

"I'll check," said a second voice, and Jared let out his breath in a gush. A girl's voice. Maybell.

Sure enough, Aaliyah's curtain was yanked aside, and Maybell's pale face and hot pink hair appeared in the window. She drew back, startled to see someone right on the other side of the window. Then she looked back over her shoulder. Jared couldn't hear what she said next, since it was in a hush, but it wasn't exactly a mystery.

There was a pause that seemed an eternity, and then Aaliyah appeared, pushing Maybell out of the way and raising the window.

Jared's heart actually leapt.

"Aaliyah," he said. "I—"

His words dried up at the angry look she was giving him. "Jared," she hissed, cutting him off. "You can't be here. If my parents find you ..." She didn't say what would happen, but he had an imagination.

Maybell nudged her so that they could both see out the window. "Congratulations, stud," she said with a smirk, "I'm no longer the bad influence."

Aaliyah gave Maybell a quelling look, but it had no effect on her.

"I'm sorry. I just hadn't heard anything and ... They found my mother's car. I thought you'd want to know."

Immediately, Aaliyah's look changed to one of heartbreak. "They found her?" she gasped.

Ouch.

"No, not her. Just the car. At the Poughkeepsie train station."

She leaned out a little farther. "So that's good, right. It means she's okay?"

"Maybe. Dad's at the station now. They have questions for him."

"Ah, that explains what you're doing here."

"What I'm doing here—Aaliyah, I had to see you. I know you don't want to talk to me, but ... I have to know you don't hate me. And you have to know that I'm sorry."

"Maybell told me."

His heart sank. He'd told himself that the reason he hadn't heard from her was that Maybell hadn't given her his message. "But you didn't write."

Were those tears in her eyes? "I didn't know what to say. I thought a clean break would be best."

"So, this is it then?" Damn, his voice broke. With Maybell as a witness. He snuck her a quick glance, but she wasn't sneering for once.

"What else can it be? My parents are never going to let me see you again."

"I thought ... I don't know. Maybe they'll get over it?"

Aaliyah and Maybell shared a look that Jared felt like a shot to the heart. He was on the outside in more ways than one.

"I don't think so," she said quietly.

"Maybe you'll defy them?"

"Jared, I have to go. You have to get out of here before you're caught. It would be bad for everybody."

He looked at Maybell. "But she can stay?"

"Dude, I didn't almost get her arrested." She held up her hands, "Look, ma, no handcuffs."

Aaliyah hit her friend, knocking her hands down. "I really am sorry," she said to Jared, looking him straight in the eyes for what he was afraid might be the last time. "I don't hate you," she said more quietly.

Then she closed the window and let the curtains fall in front of it, shutting him out.

Despite his worry about time, Jared didn't run or jog home. He couldn't. It was all he could do to keep one foot moving in front of the other. He watched them as he went, only glancing up from time to time to look for obstacles or street signs.

His heart was broken. It no longer mattered if Dad caught him or if Gran ratted him out or … anything.

Nothing mattered.

But as he turned onto his street and his heart dropped like a stone, he realized he was lying to himself. That police car in their driveway *again*. That mattered.

EIGHTEEN

Saturday

Jared

OHCRAP, ohcrap, ohcrap! Had Gran discovered him gone? Had she called the police to report it, thinking he was a runaway? Had the police changed their minds and come to arrest him?

Or ... had they found Mom? Not her car this time, but *her*.

That thought had Jared running for the door despite all the other possibilities. As he hit the yard, he thought about going for his window instead. Maybe he could get back in before anyone noticed he was gone—if that wasn't what they were there for. But he realized immediately he was too late. One patrol officer stood beside her car, straightening from putting something into it or grabbing something out, and she spotted him, instantly going on alert.

"You the son?" she asked.

His deer-in-the-headlights look must have given him away. He could run. He was good at that. Unless she was really in shape, he could probably outpace her. But how would that look?

And if they were here for him, would that be resisting arrest? Probably. Anyway, he had to know. If they were there about Mom ...

He nodded, gave up on the idea of running, and started toward her at a walk. "What's going on?" he asked.

"We're serving a warrant on the house. It might be best if you stay here, out of the way."

"If my family's inside, there's where I need to be." Would Dad still be at the police station answering questions? Probably. That would leave Gran and Emily alone. Not that they couldn't handle themselves, but ... he should be there. And they'd definitely have discovered him missing when he didn't come out of his room when the police showed up. Maybe they'd even searched his room already.

That thought got him moving. Not that he had anything to hide, but the *violation* of it.

The cop stayed behind rather than escort him, which he didn't understand until he looked around and saw the neighbors gathered like vultures over a carcass, waiting to pick at the remains of their dignity.

He hurried toward the house, knocking on the door when he hit it ... just in case. Of what, he wasn't sure. Maybe someone on the other side who might take exception to him entering. There was no immediate answer, so he used his key, thinking the knock was probably warning enough that he was coming. The blast of sound from Gran's shows didn't hit him the second the door opened, but the sight of her and Emily huddled in the foyer did. Emily had her arms wrapped around Gran, who had one arm wrapped around her in return and the other white-knuckling her cane. Their gazes shot to him as he came through the door, and Emily flung herself at him, nearly overbalancing Gran at the loss of support.

"Jared, where have you been?"

He didn't answer right away, taking it all in. A head had poked through the door from the garage when he entered, noted his arrival with a glare, and disappeared again. It was one of the cops who'd arrested him in Poughkeepsie. So, not the local police then. Was that normal? Maybe finding Mom's car in Poughkeepsie settled the case firmly in their jurisdiction? But didn't finding the car at the train station mean Mom had taken off? Why were they here? At the house. In *the garage.*

From which he'd heard that horrible noise the night Mom disappeared.

"We've been worried sick," Gran said, refocusing his attention.

Crap. He hadn't meant to worry anyone. He hadn't meant to get caught. And *what was going on in that garage?*

"I had to get out. Dad has me trapped here with nothing to do all day," he said, too distracted by what was happening to worry about a cover story.

"What?" Gran asked at full volume. "Don't mumble."

Oh hell.

Jared repeated himself. Louder. Loudly enough, probably, for the cops to hear.

"I thought you had homework," Gran said.

"I … do." He answered. He hadn't lied to her about that, just misrepresented when he was going to do it.

"Where did you go?" Emily demanded. "You didn't go back to Mom's place, did you?"

As if there'd been time. He glared at her for making him air his dirty laundry in front of Gran, who'd no doubt report everything to his father.

"I went to see Aaliyah, okay? She won't talk to me, but I had to see her. Tell her I was sorry."

Even with rheumy eyes, Gran could pull off the same predator's glare Dad had. Like she was a raptor and he was prey who'd just moved and given away his location. "Well, now you've seen her. I hope you made it count, because if you think you were grounded before …"

"Don't tell Dad!" Emily pleaded, turning back to her.

Gran looked down her nose at Emily. "I'm certainly going to tell him. I won't lie to my son."

"No one's asking you to lie. Just ... leave it out. Jared's already in enough trouble. Dad will kill Jared if he finds out."

It was a figure of speech, but it sent chills up and down Jared's back. They didn't stay there, but spread to his heart, freezing it until it could barely beat.

"Obviously, he's *not* in enough trouble. Not enough to keep him from getting into more."

Emily's big eyes pleaded for all they were worth. He didn't know how Gran could resist. He never could. Even Dad usually gave in.

"Well then," Emily said, "think of it as *Dad* has enough to worry about."

It was weird, his sister fighting his battle for him, but these were the kind of battles she fought best—battles of persuasion.

Gran chewed her lip and didn't respond. Maybe Emily was getting to her.

"Did the police say what they're looking for?" Jared asked.

"I didn't ask," Gran said. "The warrant is on the counter."

How could you not ask? Jared thought.

Wasn't she the last bit curious? Or terrified?

He crossed over to the counter, hoping no one would stop him. The cop outside had said he wasn't supposed to touch anything, but he was sure that didn't apply to the warrant. He grabbed it and started skimming, looking for the important information, then had to make himself go back and read more carefully. The first time he was too frantic, too panicked. All he could see were words. He couldn't make any of them out individually.

He gasped when he found it. *Blood, other bodily tissue or effluents and any objects containing traces of blood or other tissue.*

He looked up at Gran and Emily, huddled together again now that he'd removed himself. He didn't know how to ask and not freak out Emily, so he read the whole thing again, more slowly still. Trying to take in every word. He knew the police needed evidence to get a warrant. He was hoping it would be spelled out so that he'd know what they had.

He needed to know whether something had happened in that garage, whether he'd heard what he most feared. He needed to know whether to come forward. He wasn't trying to protect Dad. Not if he'd hurt Mom. But he couldn't accuse him of anything—or lead to an accusation—unless he was sure. For Emily's sake at the least.

"Did they say anything?" he asked Gran. "About why?"

"No, they just gave me the warrant and went about their business."

And Gran had dropped it on the counter like a hot potato.

He did the same and headed toward the garage.

"They want us out of the way," Emily protested.

"I won't get in anyone's way."

He got to the entrance to the garage, which they'd left open, but the officer stopped him before he could get within a couple of feet of it. Jared realized he'd been watching the entrance and keeping an eye on any comings and goings in the house at the same time. Nothing Gran or Emily or he said would have been private. Not that they'd said anything incriminating, but they *could have*.

"I'm sorry, son," he said. "You can't come in here."

"I'm not your son," Jared snapped back. But he didn't move. The smell of bleach stopped him. And if he could smell it …

From where he stood, he could see someone dressed in a black vest with CSI displayed in bright yellow reflective lettering spraying something on the floor of the garage. In CSI and shows like that it was always Luminol, something that made blood and other fluids fluoresce under black light. The tech wasn't alone. There was another doing the same to Dad's barely-used workbench and tools. Someone stood beside him. Not a tech. Slim charcoal gray pants, a dove gray button-up shirt tucked into them, the black of her gun and holster stark against the lighter fabric. Her hennaed, close-cropped hair gave her away even before she turned around—Detective Anderson.

Her gaze met his with no stops along the way. Her mouth was set in a grim line. What had they found?

"Stay right there," Detective Anderson said, hand out as though she could hold him back from a distance. "Lopez, the lights."

The officer who'd been standing by the door making sure no one interfered with the search hit the garage lights as the CSI exchanged his Luminol for a black light. Jared held his breath, feelings rushing him like traffic coming the wrong way up a one-way street. Fear was first. That they'd find something. Or that they wouldn't, but only because of the bleach he smelled. At least he was seeing it all first hand, so he'd *know* whether or not they found anything. They wouldn't be able to put him off in order to protect him or their investigation. No one could play games with him over what he could see for himself.

His breath caught, as almost immediately the black light raised an eerie glow from the concrete—ghost-bright, streaky blue arcs, as though someone had tried to scrub something away, but only managed to smear it across the floor.

He watched the other crime scene tech circle around the glow, snapping pictures. Then the black light moved on, across the garage. But there were no other glows.

Jared hissed as the overhead lights were flipped back on, suddenly too bright, and he blinked his eyes to adjust, then stared at the spot where he'd seen the glow, as though it might still be there and tell him something. Then he looked up to see what Detective Anderson was making of it. She was looking right at him.

"But," Jared started. Again, he had no idea how he meant to continue. He really should keep his mouth shut, but the impulse to *know* was too great. "But … I smell bleach. Doesn't that—"

She exchanged a look with the crime scene tech still holding the black light, as though they got that a lot.

"Walk me through the last time you saw your mother," she said, spearing him with her gaze.

He froze, like he was a deer and she was the headlights. "I, uh, thought you weren't allowed to question me without my dad or a lawyer."

"Choudhry, did you hear a question?" she asked the officer with the black light.

He shook his head. "No, ma'am, I did not."

"No question," Detective Anderson confirmed, watching Jared. "I just thought you might want to help."

"Let me ask you a question first," he said, hoping she'd go for it. "Why are you here? I thought you found Mom's car. Why aren't you asking at ticket counters, reviewing camera footage, all that?"

Anderson's gaze seemed to soften, almost to pity. Jared steeled himself and his breath caught. He wasn't going to like what came next. He wasn't sure he could take it. He almost told her "never mind," but he couldn't bring himself to do it. He had to know.

"Didn't anyone tell you?" she asked.

Jared shook his head.

Detective Anderson sighed, and took a second to decide on words before saying them. "We found her car," she said gently. "But there was blood. Someone tried to wipe it away, but they didn't catch everything. We did."

Jared swallowed hard at the lump, maybe his heart, which seemed to be caught in his throat. It didn't help.

"Blood?" he asked, sounding strangled.

Detective Anderson approached, put a hand to his arm, stared him in the face. "Jared, we're checking every angle, but we think there might have been foul play."

His legs started to go out from under him, but he caught himself on the wall, which was a good thing, because suddenly Gran snapped out his name from behind him, a helluva lot closer than the front foyer, "Jared? Jared, what's going on? What's happening?"

Crap, Emily would be right behind her. She couldn't hear this; she'd be devastated. He had to protect her as long as he could.

Maybe the blood wasn't Mom's. Maybe it was old. Maybe the bleach in the garage was Dad trying to get rid of the stain from an oil leak. Maybe—

But he knew it was time to speak, to tell Detective Anderson what he might have heard and let her deal with it. The police were already investigating. They'd already served a warrant. He couldn't make it worse, and he wouldn't have to carry the should-he/shouldn't-he burden around any longer. It was eating him up. If she'd just tell him it was nothing or too vague to be of any use, he could breathe easy, knowing he'd done what he could. But not right now. Not with Gran and Emily listening in.

We'll talk later, he mouthed to the detective. Then he turned to Gran and ushered her away. "Nothing," he said. "I think they're just finishing up. Maybe we should get Emily out of here for a while. I'll drive."

Emily

Emily did *not* want to be gotten out of there. All she wanted to do was throw herself at the police and insist that they were looking in the wrong place and they needed to be out there *finding her mother*. She was in tears again, and it made her feel small. Like a kid. Someone the police wouldn't take seriously.

It ticked her off. She was angry and destroyed all at the same time.

There was blood, the detective had said. Jared probably thought she hadn't heard. She was sure Gran hadn't. But now it was stuck in her head, bouncing around with those other two terrible words—foul play.

They thought something had happened to Mom.

Something bad.

"Come on, Emily," Gran said. "Let's go to the Alps Sweet Shop. My treat. I think we all need something nice. Chocolate makes everything better. It's like defense against the dark arts."

Gran quoting Harry Potter? It couldn't be. Her world was all kinds of upside down.

"I want to stay here," Emily said. Only it was more of a sob. "I want to wait for Mom. Or Dad," she added, when she realized that was only going to get her Gransplained to, and if Gran said something bad about Mom right now, Emily would lose it. It was bad enough the police were prowling the house, implying that Dad ...

"Emily," Gran said—her voice strained, like she was working not to be sharp, but it didn't come naturally. Emily was starting to hate the sound of her own name. Everyone seemed to use it as a rebuke. "We're going." She announced. End of story. Like Emily had no say at all. She was so tired of it. So sick of everything.

Make me.

But she only said it in her head. She didn't know if she would have said it to Gran in any case, but the police were there. With a lifetime of being the good girl and keeping the peace, she couldn't suddenly rebel the way she desperately wanted to. She didn't dare send the message that the Grahams were a family of troublemakers. Not after Jared's arrest and Dad's questioning. Not with her mother running off ... because anything else had to be a mistake.

"Give me a minute."

She didn't wait for an answer that might not be what she wanted, but retreated to the bathroom to wash her face and ... she wanted to do more. She wanted to release the scream building inside. The pressure of pain that wanted to collapse her. She needed to divert the pain. Focus it.

But Jake followed her to the bathroom. "Everything okay?" he asked.

She glared. Stupid question.

She ran the water, splashed it over her face. Let it run as she lathered her hands. She knew he hated the waste. She did too, but for now it was her only way of rebelling. She scrubbed like she could wash everything away, reality along with the tears. She slammed off the faucet and rubbed the towel over her face until it was raw.

"No," she said finally, emerging from the towel. "It fucking isn't."

Jared reared back as if she'd struck him, and she felt a weird release, like either her curse or his shock had vented the bubble of pressure/pain building inside her. Enough that she might live through leaving the house. If they weren't gone too long. If nothing else happened while they were out. If it did ... She didn't know how much more she could take.

Jared moved instantly aside when she went to brush past, like he knew she was all sharp edges right now and might cut him.

She blinked at the sunlight as they stepped onto the front porch. It seemed wrong. There was nothing sunshiny about their day. But the giant orb in the sky hadn't gotten the memo.

"Sir, I'm going to have to ask you to stay back," someone said.

That was when Emily realized that they weren't alone, but had stepped out of their house into what looked like a neighborhood fire drill or something. People stood gathered in twos and threes, some with their dogs or kids, staring at their house or pretending not to stare but talking to each other and shooting glances. It was a female cop who'd been talking, and it was to Mr. Meyers, who stopped in his tracks.

"I'm not trying to get inside," he said instantly. "We just want to make sure the kids are okay. See if they need anything."

He gestured behind himself to demonstrate the "we" he referred too, and Emily looked beyond him to see Ms. Carla and Andrew hanging on to each other. Well, she was hanging on to him and he was tolerating it. In her experience, teenaged boys didn't generally allow that sort of thing from their mothers. At least, not in public and not for long. Not that anyone was focused on them.

Emily swept the crowd with her gaze, noting who else had come out. Seeing Samantha from way down the block with her mother and their Yorkie. And then she froze. It was him—that creepy guy who'd come looking for Mom.

"We're fine," Jared started to tell Mr. Meyers. "Gran—" but Emily reached over blindly and yanked at her brother's sleeve, stopping the rest of his words.

"It's him," she said. "That guy Jake."

She pointed. She didn't have any other choice, because she'd been the only one to get a look at him before, but he saw her pointing and instantly started edging down the block.

"Wait!" Jared shouted. "You!"

Jared

The guy bolted, and on instinct Jared bolted after him, leaping the stairs like they were a hurdle and racing across the driveway for the street. The cop tried to stop him, but he saw her lunge coming a mile away and swerved without slowing, evading her reach. She was yelling something, but the blood was rushing in his ears, and anyway, he didn't want to hear it. All he wanted was to lay hands on this guy, shake answers out of him, and put the fear of God or Jared into him. He needed to learn not to go around scaring little girls. Jared's hand clenched and unclenched in anticipation of grabbing their quarry.

He could feel other feet pounding the pavement behind him, and knew with the instinct of a runner how far he was ahead of the cop. She was never going to catch up with him.

The neighbors got the hell out of the way as stalker-guy Jake raced down the block. He had a head start, and he was long-legged, so he had a helluva stride, but Jared was faster, and was gaining on him until Jake took a sudden dodge between two houses. Jared zagged as well, but suddenly there was no sign of Jake. Either he'd zagged again or broken into one of the homes … No, there hadn't been time for that. Jared kept running and burst out from between the houses. He looked left and right. No one. The cop was hot on his heels and he made a sudden decision. Jake had dodged left before. Maybe it was his default. He ran two blocks in that direction before giving it up. There was no sign of the guy. None. Maybe he'd done track in his day. Hell, maybe he still ran marathons. Old wasn't dead.

Jared wanted to slam his fists into something in frustration.

Behind him, the cop's steps slowed as well, and he could hear her talking into her radio, letting dispatch or whoever know they'd lost the suspect. Then she grabbed Jared by the arm, and not gently. "What the hell were you thinking, kid?" she asked. "You could have been hurt."

"Running?" he asked.

"Catching," she said, in a way that implied he knew very well what she'd meant. "Who were you chasing?"

She steered him back toward home, and he told her on the way, all about Emily's first encounter with the guy and how he'd creeped her out. He didn't mention their Facebook research. There wasn't anything to tell.

"*And?*" she said pointedly.

"And what?"

"That's what I'm asking. You don't run down some guy because he showed up at your house."

"You do if your mother's missing and you think he might have answers."

"*Do* you think that?"

"Maybe." He shook his arm out of her grip. "It was worth a shot. Now we'll never know."

She blew out a breath through her nose so hard he expected a snot wad to come shooting out. "If he's been watching your house, he's a potential witness. You've given us a name.

Provided it's not false, we shouldn't have any trouble finding him. And just in case, you and your sister can provide a description. But if he comes around again, *you call us*. You do *not* go running off on your own."

Jared's hand shot up to his forehead, and he saluted her. "Ma'am, yes, ma'am."

She didn't appear amused. "I'm not kidding. You need to take this seriously."

"Trust me, I'm taking everything very seriously."

Detective Anderson met them at the driveway and gave him a look sterner than any of the officer's words, but it was still nothing to Gran's look. She was still standing on the porch, and he realized he'd left her high and dry without anyone to help her down the stairs. Well, Emily, but if Gran lost her balance, he wasn't one hundred percent sure Emily could catch her. Gran looked like she was going to box his ears. She'd done it once when he was a kid and had run into traffic after a ball. His ears had rung for a week.

They all went inside, where he and Emily gave their descriptions to the police, and less than five minutes after she called it in, Detective Anderson had the guy's license photo to show them and they confirmed the identification.

"I want to remind you that he hasn't done anything wrong," she said. "I don't want you overreacting if you see him. I don't want you to do anything but call us if you're concerned."

"If he hasn't done anything, why did he run?" Emily asked. It seemed a reasonable question to Jared.

"If someone hollered and started running after me, I might do the same thing."

He didn't like that answer.

"Wait," Emily said suddenly. "If you're here with us, who's interviewing Dad?"

Apparently, Emily had all the good questions today.

"Don't you worry about that."

"Will he be home soon?" she asked.

"I can't say."

"But this Jake fellow," Gran said, "you're going to find and interview him too? He seems awfully suspicious to me. Much more so than my son."

Detective Anderson looked her full in the face. "We'll find him."

She made no other promises.

"Then I think we're done here," Gran said. "You have work to do, and I need a lie-down after all this excitement. Emily, help me to my room?"

Jake was surprised it wasn't him; she usually insisted on him or his father escorting her. Probably she meant it as a rebuke because he'd left her on the porch while he tore off after that guy, but it actually worked in his favor. He needed to talk to Detective Anderson alone.

"I'll walk you out," he said.

Gran gave him a sharp look, but couldn't really say a word. He'd already been dismissed from her side.

NINETEEN

Emily

THE HOUSE WAS DEADLY QUIET. She'd heard Jared come in after seeing the police out, but he'd gone straight to his room and wouldn't talk to her when she asked what had taken him so long. He was shutting her out. Hiding away in his room, though she didn't know what Dad had left him to do there. Gran was napping. Dad was still at the police station.

Detective Anderson had mentioned blood and foul play. Those three words ate away at her soul. *Blood, foul play.* They chased each other around like a puppy chasing its tail, snarling and snapping, only none of it in good fun.

She thought of that Emily Dickinson poem they'd read in school that always stayed with her, parts of it, anyway.

> The Soul has Bandaged moments—
> When too appalled to stir—
> She feels some ghastly Fright come up
> And stop to look at her—

That was how she felt, as if her soul was having a bandaged

moment, and her blood was leaking through, hemorrhaging. She wished she could get to the other part of the poem, the one that always gave her hope …

> The soul has moments of escape—
> When bursting all the doors—
> She dances like a Bomb, abroad,
> And swings upon the Hours,

She didn't know entirely what it meant, but she liked the sound of dancing like a bomb, being explosively present. Swinging upon the Hours sounded like she owned time and was outside even physical laws. Like she was truly free.

But then reality returned, in poetry and in life:

> The Soul's retaken moments—
> When, Felon led along,
> With shackles on the plumed feet,
> And staples, in the song,
> The Horror welcomes her, again.…

It could have been written for her.

Mom was gone and they'd found blood. If that wasn't horror, the word had no meaning. The pain of it was shackling her to the bitter earth.

The police were questioning Dad. He was a suspect. There was no way around it. He wasn't just "walking them through things." Not for hours on end.

But he couldn't have hurt Mom, could he? Not like … that.

She thought of the night Mom had left the first time, when Dad had grabbed a fistful of her hair and yanked, and her mother had cried out in a way that went straight through her heart. When Jared had run with her to the Meyers' house and the police had come, though she didn't know who had called them. The only call Ms. Carla had made was to their place, trying to calm things down, get someone talking. But no one answered. Andrew didn't show any interest in her or Jared—he never had —but the fight was different. He raced out, either to see for himself or to try and stop it, as though Emily and Jared hadn't already tried. Mr. Meyers ran after his son. Either could have made the call. Or Mom could have gotten free and made it herself.

She and Jared knew about the police because the cruisers sped past the Meyers' windows, which they'd been peering out as though they could see anything from them. Emily had been desperate to get back—she'd never wanted to leave in the first place—but Ms. Carla practically held them hostage until Andrew and Mr. Meyers returned and said the police had things in hand. And that Mom refused to press charges. Neither one looked comfortable with that. Andrew's face was a thunder-cloud, and his fists were clenched, like she'd seen with their father, with Jared when he got angry. Mr. Meyers' face was more closed off, like he'd put a lid over his feelings, locking them away. He hardly met Jared's gaze and bypassed Emily's alto-gether, but she could see the tension around his eyes and the clench of his jaw.

She didn't know why she always thought of Ms. Carla as Ms. Carla and Mr. Meyers by his last name, but she noticed that Jared did it too. Maybe it was their way of keeping their distance when he seemed to want to draw them closer.

She had to be thinking of the Meyers as a way to avoid thinking about Dad, because they certainly couldn't have anything to do with Mom's disappearance. It wouldn't make any sense. She could see someone having a private "talk" with Dad about keeping his hands to himself, but no one could have anything against Mom.

Except maybe that Jake guy, if Mom had snubbed him. *Or Dad,* said the internal voice she was trying to ignore.

The pain flared, and she reached for her bedside table and the envelope she had stashed there, folded over and over on itself to protect and hide the razor inside. Her razor. A straight edge taken from a box of spares for one of Dad's cutting tools in the garage. He'd never missed it.

She unfolded the envelope. She thought about going to the bathroom, getting a clean towel, in case ... But the need was too urgent. She might see someone on the way who could stop her.

She held the razor in one hand and ran her fingers over the blade. Not hard enough to cut. Not yet. Just enough to make sure the edge was still sharp. Still smooth. She had no idea how many times it could cut before she'd need to replace it. Skin was probably easier on the blade than what it was intended for, but she swabbed it with alcohol each time after use. She didn't know what that would do to the metal, but she had to make sure she didn't get infected. She wasn't *crazy*. Or at least, she didn't think so. She just ...

A sob broke out of her, and she raised the blade to her arm, just under her last cut to her left shoulder. She didn't know why she chose there. Some people, she knew, cut their thighs or other areas easier to hide. She'd never be able to wear tank tops, and she'd have to wear a t-shirt over her bathing suit probably forever, but that was all fine. She didn't want to be exposed. Not in any way.

The blade dug into her skin. No, words mattered. *She* dug the blade into her skin, and the sharp sting made her gasp. She'd gone in a little hard. Too hard, but she needed that first shock. All of her was focused on the pain, on the slow progress of the blade into her skin. She wanted to make this last. To count. The pain would last, but not this sharply. Not immediate and real and the full focus of her world. It would die down and all she'd be left with was a scar, like the older one she could feel straining as she pulled taut the skin around it for her cut.

Then her attention was grabbed by a sound from the front of the house. The door opening. Everyone was already inside. Except her father.

Dad was home.

The razor slipped in her grip, and she cried out as the blade dug deeper than she meant it to before she unclenched her hand and let it drop, making a bloody mark on her sheets.

Oh hell.

Holy hell.

She was bleeding, and pretty badly. She had to get this cleaned up before Dad came to check on her. Or called a family meeting. Or whatever he might do. There was no telling.

Emily slapped her hand over her shoulder and ran for her hamper. She was pretty sure there was a used towel there. She'd get blood all over it, but she could do the laundry before anyone else got to it. She could hide this. She yanked out clothes one-handed, dropped them to the floor. The blood was now dripping down her arm, escaping her hand which made a crap Band-Aid.

Ah ha, the towel!

She wrapped it around her arm, trying to make a tourniquet, but it was a bath towel, and too thick for that. She had gauze and other stuff she'd smuggled into her bedroom for things like this, but it wouldn't do her any good until she got the bleeding to stop. She didn't think it was as bad as last time, at least, but the blood kept her from getting a good look.

There was a knock at her door.

Oh, holy hell.

She'd locked it, hadn't she? She was sure she'd locked it.

"Em, Dad wants to talk to us," Jared said through the door. At least it was Jared.

"I can't right now," she answered, hoping he wouldn't hear any of the stress in her voice. She was staring at the door now, so she saw when the knob started to turn. She leapt for the door, just in case, and almost got hit in the face when it opened inward. She hadn't locked it. How had she not checked? Panic clawed at her heart.

She jumped back out of the way and slapped a hand over her towel, as if that might hide things. She knew she looked guilty as hell. Hopefully, Jared would be too wrapped up with his own stuff to notice.

"What did you do?" he asked.

So much for that.

"Nothing," she said. "Monster zit popped. It's kind of gross." The lie had worked on Ms. Carla. Of course, that was with a bandage and not a towel going bloody as they spoke.

Jared looked down the hallway. "There in a minute," he called out. Then he fixed Emily with a no-nonsense look. "Let me see it."

He *couldn't* know. Though he certainly would if she showed him.

Emily backed away. "No. My business. Nothing for you to see."

He reached out, lightning fast, and grabbed her. She just managed to bite down on her shocked outcry. She could *not* let Dad hear and come running. She didn't know what he'd do, but he'd be angry. That wasn't even a question.

Before she could protest, Jared had the towel unwrapped and was staring at her arm. Emily looked as well. The blood had stopped except for a tiny wetness at the far end of the wound, but her arm was still smeared with it, and the towel was trashed.

He looked from the cut—from the half dozen or so smaller cuts and one larger on her arm—and up into her eyes. "Emily, what have you done?"

She pulled her arm out of his hold, but not too roughly, afraid to start the bleeding off again. "Nothing. I told you it was none of your business. Let me get cleaned up and I'll be right out."

"Not my business?" he asked, his voice rising. Emily shushed him hurriedly. "Not my business?" he asked more quietly. "Like what Mom was going through was none of our business? Maybe if we'd pushed it ... made her press charges ..."

It was so close to what Emily had been thinking herself that a new sob broke out of her. "Go. Just go," she said, before she could ugly cry all over him.

"Please," he said, gently, shocking her into listening, "let me help?"

Her heart broke. She stared at her brother, horror and hope and pain all warring. Could she trust him?

"You won't tell Dad?"

She held her breath waiting for the answer.

"I don't know what to do, Em. You need help."

She jumped at him, grabbing both his arms and squeezing, radiating the panic she felt, letting him see the terror in her eyes. "You *can't* tell Dad. You can't. Or Gran. If you want to help me, the best thing you can do is keep this to yourself."

"But Em—"

"No, I mean it. If they find out. If they ... have me committed or checked into a hospital or something for my own good the first thing they'll do is take away my phone. It's my only link to Mom. She could try to contact us again. You don't know!"

"But—"

"And something like this could follow me. I don't know what that would do to my chances for college or ... I just don't *know*. You can't tell anyone."

"Can we talk about this later? I told Dad a minute, and he doesn't have any patience. He'll be in here any second checking up on things."

"I'm not going anywhere until you promise me."

"Fine," he said, glancing toward the hall like he could see through the door. "For now. But if it happens again ... Let me get a wet towel from the bathroom to help you clean up."

She had to pry her mouth open to tell him she already had bandages and alcohol handy. He looked like she'd punched him in the face, like hurting herself had hurt him. He was gone before she could apologize and back before Dad could come looking for them. He held a towel and a tube of triple antibiotic cream. "I didn't know if you had this," he said.

She shook her head, too overcome to thank him. Jared made her sit on the bed, where his face twisted again at the sight of the bloody razor. Then he took her arm and so gently she barely felt it, swiped the wet towel over her shoulder, carefully avoiding the cut, and taking several passes to remove the blood. Then he asked her where her alcohol and everything was. She pointed to her drawer below the one where she kept her razor, and he got everything out, including the cotton balls to go with the alcohol. She bit her lips to keep from gasping at the pain as the alcohol burned away the germs and kept her lips clamped as he spread the ointment. Then he gently wrapped her shoulder in the gauze she had and secured it with the medical tape. Emily rolled down the sleeve she'd bunched up when she started, and they both eyed the spot.

"Throw on a sweatshirt or something," Jared ordered. "Just to be sure. I'll take care of this stuff."

He used the pharmacy bag in which she'd kept her supplies to bunch up the bloody towel, using the end to grab the bloody razor off the bed when she moved.

"Don't—" she started to protest.

"Do not even tell me to leave it. That's not happening. This is coming with me. And later, we're going to talk."

He folded the bloody razor into the towel and added the used cotton ball to the bag, jammed everything down until it fit and then tied the bag off and left the room with it.

Emily was left staring after him. She had to hope he didn't encounter Dad in the hall and that, if so, he was a better liar than she was. She didn't hear anything, so she figured she was okay. But she'd better get out there.

Dad was waiting for them in the kitchen.

"Where's Gran?" Dad asked as Jared entered, hot on her heels.

She moved aside so she wouldn't get incinerated by the glare he was aiming her brother's way.

"Still sleeping," Jared answered. "I didn't think you meant me to wake her."

"Then what took you so long?"

"I did," Emily said, afraid to volunteer anything else and get caught in a lie.

His gaze as it fell on her was slightly less blistering. He took a breath, his chest flaring out and then flattening, his emotions—or at least the outward expression of them—doing the same. It was eerie to watch.

"I'm sorry, kids. This must be hard on you. What I have to tell you isn't going to be any easier. Why don't we sit down?"

Neither one of them protested. Dad sat on one side of the table. They both sat on the other. It felt symbolic.

Dad didn't start immediately, and Jared said. "The police already told us about the blood."

Dad blew out another breath, this one slow and controlled. "They did, huh? I'm sorry about that. I hope they didn't scare you. From what they said, it wasn't much. A papercut or a nosebleed or anything could have caused it. It wasn't enough to … to mean anything."

"Then why did they ask you to come in?" Emily asked before Jared could. For some reason, Dad found Jared's every question a challenge. It was better coming from her. "Why did they search the house?"

"Protocol," her father answered without hesitation. "They've got to do their jobs. Your mother's been missing for a week now by their count. They've got to do due diligence."

She already knew the answer to her next question, but she had to ask it. To see if Dad would be honest with them. If they could believe him on this, maybe they could put faith in other things. It felt flimsy. Everything felt flimsy right now, like her life's story was written on tissue paper and anything would tear it to shreds.

"Are you a suspect?" she asked.

He met her gaze. Firmly. No wavering. "Yes. The police seem to think so."

"Do they have any … evidence?" It wasn't what she wanted to ask, which was, "Did you do it? Did you hurt Mom?" But she couldn't bring herself to voice it. She didn't think he'd say yes, whatever the truth, and she wasn't confident she could tell if he lied to her. The question would only set Dad off and probably not illuminate anything.

Or she was being a coward and couldn't face the answer.

The evidence question was already skirting the line.

"No," he said, his voice hard now. "No evidence."

He rose from the table, a little roughly, and Emily tried not to jump back. "I'll let Gran sleep. This has been stressful for her, I'm sure. Come get me when she wakes up. I want to talk to her too."

He walked to the cabinet in the kitchen where they kept all their meds and shook out two pills from the big bottle of migraine tablets Mom always kept on hand. Then he took them dry and left without a word, headed for his own room, maybe to lie down.

Emily looked to Jared, who was staring after Dad.

"What do you think?" she asked.

"I don't know," he answered.

He didn't ask what she was talking about.

"If you go back to your room, I want you to keep the door open," he said.

Emily gasped. "No way. You're not my ..." *father* wouldn't come out. "You're not the boss of me. I'm not giving up my privacy."

He stared at her. "Emily, I caught you *cutting*. And based on the scars, not for the first time. If I see your door closed, I'm going to come in. If it's locked, I'm going to open it. Or call Dad." He reached out to grab her hand, and she yanked it out of reach. "Em, you have to understand. I can't let anything happen to you. If I keep quiet and something happens ... I can't take that."

His voice broke.

Her big, bad brother's voice broke.

She felt like crap. But she couldn't give in.

"You going to follow me to the bathroom too? What about school? Jared, you can't watch me all the time."

He dropped his head to the hand that had tried to grab hers, banging it on that rather than the table. His whole posture was defeated, as though he'd deflated onto the table. She couldn't think of what to say to puff him back up.

She put a hand to his shoulder, and he raised his head slowly. His eyes were red and moist but no tears had fallen.

"You're right," he said. "I can't. So, you have to promise me, Em. You made me promise that I wouldn't leave you or do anything stupid. You have to promise me the same."

She stared into her brother's face, her mouth dry, panic rising up like lava from a volcano, burning away all moisture. "I don't know if I can," she whispered, and it hurt. "With everything going on … I need an outlet."

"Not this one, Em. Promise me. Next time you feel something like this coming on, reach out to me. We'll get through it together. You can't keep hurting yourself."

She knew it was true. And yet it wasn't. She could very well keep on. She would have if he hadn't caught her. What did she do now that he had?

"I'll try," she said. It was all she had. She couldn't lie to him, but she couldn't make a promise she didn't know if she could keep.

"You have to do more than try."

The bossiness of it, telling her what she had to do, set her into full rebellion. "If I told you to stop seeing Aaliyah, could you do it?"

"That's different," he said.

"How?"

"It's not hurting me."

"Isn't it? Maybe there's no blood, but don't try to tell me it doesn't hurt."

"It's not the same," he said mulishly.

Maybe it wasn't, but the focus was no longer on her, and

while her mouth was still as dry as a lava tunnel, at least she could breathe.

*

Jared waited until everyone was asleep that night. At least, until he could be pretty certain everyone was asleep. Gran had gone home. Emily had gone to bed hours ago. He knew for sure, because he'd already gone in once to check on her. Just to make sure …

Dad had gone to his room too, but Jared couldn't be absolutely sure he was asleep. He didn't snore every night. Or at least not all night every night. Not that Jared made it a habit to listen outside of his door, but those nights when the high of a track meet that went well or something else kept him up, sometimes he heard it, and sometimes he didn't. When Dad was sick, he snored like a cartoon bear. Sleep was easy to determine then.

Tonight he had to take it on faith. Dad was usually asleep by eleven, but things had been anything but usual lately, so he gave it until midnight. It wasn't hard to stay up—not with worry about Emily and Mom and what he'd told the police about the night she disappeared swirling around in his brain. Probably he could have taken one of those pills Mom sometimes took to sleep and still not have been hit by the Sandman.

Still, he wasn't going so far on faith as to sneak out the front door. It tended to seal too well, so that opening it sounded like opening an airlock. If Dad wasn't deeply enough asleep, he'd be caught. Emily's fear was like a disease, spreading to him. He didn't know what Dad would do if he discovered that Emily was cutting or that Jared was sneaking out. He didn't want to find out.

His window had worked well enough when he'd ducked out to see Aaliyah. It ought to work again. Jared set the bag of Emily's bloody supplies near the window and struggled to raise it slowly and silently. It mostly worked, maybe because it had been so recently used. No one would hear a thing, unless they were specifically listening for it … and maybe not even then.

He put one leg out, grabbed the bag, balanced the rest of himself, and slid out over the windowsill, lowering himself to the ground. The window was harder to close from this side, but he slid it mostly back down, leaving enough space to wedge his fingers under when he wanted to come back. Then he considered, which he really ought to have done before leaving the house. He didn't dare put it into their garbage can in the blind by the side of the house. Tomorrow was garbage day, and Dad might have something to contribute to the can before it went to the curb. Sometimes he even took it out himself rather than delegate to Jared. He *might* not be curious about a pharmacy bag sitting there, but if he spotted the blood … And he wasn't the only one who might. What if the police came back around? What if they searched the garbage? What would they make of the bloody bandages? The razor? There would be questions, and he'd promised Emily.

He'd keep silent for now, but he felt queasy about it. He wished he knew he was doing the right thing. Emily needed help. Keeping quiet wasn't going to get it for her.

He'd take care of that after all this was over, he promised himself. No matter what Emily said, no matter whether he felt he was betraying her. Once Mom was found and everything was okay again, he'd speak up. Though maybe he'd start with a school counselor or someone. Not Dad, who'd probably berate Emily and make everything worse. He wouldn't understand. Hell, Jared didn't understand. How could she hurt herself like that? But at the same time, maybe he did understand. He sometimes wanted to punch something, and not something soft. While pain wouldn't be the purpose, it would surely be a side effect.

So, he couldn't hide Emily's evidence in their own garbage can. He could bury it somewhere, like the park, but there were two arguments against that. For one, he hadn't planned ahead and brought anything to help with the digging. For another, dogs like Stanley might scent the bag and get curious enough to unbury it. The safer bet would be a neighbor's can, preferably one already filled so he could bury the bag deep.

He started with the Palchikovs next door, feeling like he had a big target on his back. Just his luck the moon was three-quarters full tonight and shining on the neighborhood as though to searchlight him. But as he got close, a light came on over their side door. Probably on a motion sensor. He shied away, looking for an easier target.

The Meyers were the next house down. Approaching their can didn't set off any lights or alarms. And, best yet, it was so full the hinged lid of the plastic can hadn't closed all the way. There was even a hole torn in the side of the top bag where it looked like a crow or something had gotten at it. He could smell the bag as he got closer. Rotting chicken. Damn, anything would have to be desperate to want a piece of that. Maybe not the crows then. Turkey vultures?

Didn't matter.

Jared took a deep breath and held it as he approached the can. He lifted the lid and carefully eased it back so it wouldn't drop against the can and make a noise. Then he lifted the top bag, set his in its place and put the original back on top of it. He reset the lid, glanced around guiltily to make sure he hadn't been seen, and started to back away. He had a thought as he did, worried that the vultures or whatever would be drawn to the blood. He was about to reapproach, bury it deeper, when he heard a sound at the Meyers' side door, the one closest to the can. It was—oh hell, it was opening!

Jared spun on a dime and took off running down the street, racing past his house just in case he hadn't been fast enough and he was spotted. All anyone would see was his back. They'd never see where he circled around the block and came at his house by cutting through backyards from the other side.

All he could think was *shit, shit, shit.* Had he been seen? Was that why someone had opened the back door? Or was it a horrible coincidence, someone coming out to add something to the garbage at just the wrong moment?

His pounding heart said it didn't matter. As long as they hadn't seen him. As long as no one got curious enough to look and see what he'd tossed out.

He didn't like leaving it to chance. Wishing and hoping.

He didn't see what else he could do.

TWENTY

Emily

OMG, Em, I heard about the police being at your house. U OK? Call me.

That was how it started. A message from Shara she didn't have the energy to answer. Not after everything—the police, the blood, Jared catching her …

She'd turned the notifications off, put the phone on the charger, and forgotten about it. Or tried to. She'd checked once more before going to bed, just in case Mom had called. Or texted. Or anything. Because the blood in her car couldn't mean what everyone seemed to think. It couldn't.

No message from Mom, but increasingly worried messages from Shara. And even a couple from Josh. And Marissa from art class. And then it seemed like anyone she'd ever texted with had gotten in on the act, letting her know word had spread about the police and her mother's car. But that fast? And how? Had it made the news? Had one of the looky-loo neighbors spread the word? Maybe Andrew Meyers. Or Samantha, or one of the kids from their bus stop. She hadn't been paying attention to who was around, not after spotting creepy-Jake in the crowd.

She didn't know what to say. She started and deleted about a million texts to Shara and then settled on. *Not okay. Not ready to talk. But thank you for caring.*

Josh was even harder. *Okay as I can be,* she lied. *Thx for checking in.* It was more and less than she wanted to say.

She debated on Marissa, on asking her to spread the word that they were fine and just wanted privacy, but no one was going to honor that. Kids would talk. She supposed it was better to know what they were saying.

In the end, she just turned off the notifications again and went to bed.

But it was morning now, and habit awoke before common sense. The first thing she did was reach for her phone. It had gone crazy. She scrolled through her messages, looking for anything from her mother. Knowing it wouldn't be there, but unable to stop hoping.

Nothing. But she paused at a message from Aunt Aggie. *I know your Dad won't let you talk to me, and I don't want to get you into any trouble, but I'm really worried about you and Jared. I hear you kids today use Snapchat for messages you don't want anyone to see. I've just set up an account as AofGG (Anne of Green Gables, in case you're wondering). You can reach out to me any time.*

If you need to get out of that house, just say the word. I'll be there in an instant, despite your father.

Please delete after reading.

Emily deleted right away, feeling paranoid about it. Had she been quick enough? Did Dad have some way to read her texts? Had she left it there too long?

One way to find out. If he'd seen the texts, he'd find some way of blocking her access to Aunt Aggie, maybe blacklisting her number or changing the password to their router so Emily couldn't get on the Internet, although she could always use mobile data ... unless he shut that down too. She had no idea what he was capable of. But she felt ridiculously paranoid when she tried logging onto Snapchat on her phone, and it worked just fine. She logged into the account she barely used, since she and her friends mostly texted, found AofGG and sent her a friend request. It was accepted nearly instantaneously, and a chat window opened up.

Are you okay? Aunt Aggie asked. She must have been waiting by the phone.

Emily's eyes got misty, just like that.

No, she said honestly. *You know they found Mom's car? They found blood?*

I know about the car. Didn't know about the blood. A lot of blood or …? I hate to ask.

Not a lot, I don't think. But enough to worry them. They searched our house. They've questioned Dad.

She felt a little funny writing it. Disloyal, but … this was her aunt, and she needed to talk to someone.

Do you feel safe with him? Aunt Aggie asked.

Emily stared at the words. She almost shut the chat down right then. It was a crazy question. No wonder their father didn't want her talking to her aunt, if she was going to stir things up like that. Emily's stomach felt like a pit of acid. And not quiescent acid, either, waiting for something to fall in and be devoured, but the kind that sloshed its banks and ate through everything around it.

What do you mean by that? Why wouldn't I feel safe? she asked.

Emily, I know about the fights. The abuse. Your mother kept pictures.

Emily stared for a second before closing out of Snapchat. The conversation would disappear within seconds. Like it had never happened.

If her aunt had copies of those pictures … if she'd shown them to the police, then it was no wonder they were focused on her father. Emily was angry. And the worst was, she was mad at herself for being angry, because if Aunt Aggie was right, if there were pictures, that meant what she and Jared had seen was only the tip of the iceberg. Dad's abuse hadn't been limited to one or two fights—not that even that much was okay. Mom had been in pain and she hadn't seen the extent because it was too painful to know. Or because Mom had been protecting them.

Something exploded behind her eye, and she thought at first it was one of those migraines that sometimes came on like an icepick to the eye or a blinding blow to the temple. And it *was*, but brought on by the grenade blast of the truth she'd been keeping from herself. About when and why the cutting had started. To punish herself. Because she deserved it. Because deep down she *knew*. She knew and hadn't saved her mother. No wonder she'd left.

She must have cried out, because Jared burst through her door a second later, hair sticking straight up, lines all over his face like he'd bolted straight out of bed and still had the imprint from the creases on his pillow. He stopped when he saw Emily half propped up on her bed. No blood. No emergency that he could see.

"Em? What's wrong? Everything okay?"

His voice was still thick from sleep, as if his tongue hadn't woken with the rest of him.

"Migraine," she said. He'd run in to rescue her, the least she could do was let him. "I just need medicine and to lie down."

One of her eyes, the one the pain had exploded behind, seemed to be twitching, and tiny prisms were starting to form at the edges of her vision. This was going to be a bad one.

"Be right back." Jared left more slowly than he'd come, and Emily considered sinking down on the bed, but she'd have to be upright to swallow the tablets, so she stayed, watching the door.

She'd have to tell Jared. If there were pictures, they might be the reason someone besides them had been nosing around Mom's social media. Someone might have been on a search and destroy mission. If so, any evidence had probably been erased already, like Mom's Facebook messages. And no one would have any reason to do that but the person who'd hurt her. Dad.

Sickness stirred in her stomach, and that acid that wanted to eat everything was suddenly clawing its way up her esophagus. She ran for the bathroom, flattening Jared against the wall as he returned with the meds. She got to the toilet just in time to empty her stomach into it. Nothing but acid. It burned out her throat as it poured out, until she was coughing from the rawness, bringing up more bile. Her stomach continued to clench and heave, long after it was empty, leaving her doubled over and miserable. Tears leaked from her eyes, snot dribbled from her nose. Her throat was a raw wound.

She hadn't managed to close the door behind her, and Jared came in now, helping her perch on the edge of the tub, flushing the toilet, handing her toilet paper so she could wipe her nose. He'd set the pills and the water he'd brought down on the counter, but Emily reached for the water, unable to speak what she wanted. Jared saw her outstretched hand and figured it out. He handed her the water. Then, once she'd taken a sip to soothe her throat, he handed her the pills.

They scraped going down, and she took another sip of the water trying to ease their way. But only a small sip. Her stomach was already rebelling again, unsure whether it would keep its new contents.

"Let's get you back to bed," Jared said.

She could only nod. She risked one more small sip of the water before handing it back to him. He tried to take her arm, to help her back to her room, but he felt six million degrees hot, and she cried out in actual pain at the touch. It was a side effect of the migraine, she knew that. It made all stimuli feel like too much. Light was a supernova, sound was a brain-blast, touch was either scalding or freezing or pins and needles. Yeah, this was going to be a bad one.

Jared drew back and watched her progress carefully, close enough that he could help if she needed him, but not enough to touch.

When Emily laid down, he asked if she wanted him to cover her up, but even that seemed like too much. She shook her head, gingerly so the movement wouldn't hurt and asked to be left alone.

Jared withdrew and she prayed for sleep. Or death. Any kind of release from the pain.

＊

She woke some time later to voices outside her door. Her head still felt heavy and pressured, as though it had been filled up with sand. And slow, like thoughts had to filter through it and some got trapped along the way. She couldn't make out any actual words at first, as though the sand stopped up her ears as well, but eventually she caught, "… wake her?"

"'M awake," she said, semi-coherently.

The voices outside stopped.

"Emily?" her father asked. Almost gently.

That had her worried.

"Who did you expect?" she asked. Her throat protested.

The door opened and her father's face appeared. "You feeling any better?"

"Some." Maybe sitting up would let some of the heaviness drain away. Maybe.

She started to rise to sitting, slowly, testing her head. The change of position made her dizzy. She stopped halfway up, let her stomach settle. By that time Dad was fully into her room with Jared looking in from the doorway.

He settled on the edge of her bed, and reached to brush her sweat-dampened hair back from her forehead. She flinched away, afraid his touch would hurt like Jared's. *Not* because she was afraid of him. Not because she truly believed …

"Sorry," she said, the word grating her throat. "Everything hurts right now."

He took back his hand, trying not to look hurt.

"I understand," he lied. "We were discussing whether or not to wake you. I wanted to let you sleep, but Jared thought …

Well, we didn't want you to hear things first on your phone, on your own. We thought it might be best coming from us."

She was suddenly all over chills.

"Hear what?" she asked, before her imagination could run wild. Maybe it wasn't what she thought. Maybe—

"A body has been found," Dad said, as gently as he could. "No one is saying it's your mother, but … The news got wind of it, and they're speculating. I've got a call in to Detective Anderson, but she hasn't responded. Probably busy at the crime scene. Or maybe the local PD is handling that. I put a call in there as well."

"I'm getting up," she said, starting to swing her legs around and hoping her father would move so it wouldn't get awkward. He did.

"Are you sure you're up to it?"

"I have to see."

And she didn't want everyone crowding into her room, trying to watch on her small screen. She wanted them out as soon as possible. The bloody stain from the dropped razor was still on the sheets, and Dad could *not* see that. She should have changed the sheets and cleaned her room right away. She didn't know what other evidence there might be. Jared had taken care of things, but had he gotten it all? She was too fuzzy-headed to be sure or cover her tracks now.

"I'll be out in a minute."

He looked at her doubtfully, but left the room, closing the door behind him, giving her privacy. A sob broke loose from her, broken off by the pain of it.

Deep in her heart, she knew it was her mother. Their town was quiet. It wasn't that they never had killings, but usually it was in the heat of the moment or drug related, and the perpetrator was caught then and there. No mystery. What were the chances one woman was missing and it was another woman's body who turned up? And how could she hope it was someone else's mother or daughter or sister who lay dead? Yet she did. She prayed it wasn't *her* mother. But she knew ... She knew.

Her stomach clenched again, like someone squeezed it in a fist, sending the bile shooting upward. Emily ran for the bathroom for the second time that day. She only made it to the sink this time, and spewed everywhere, even into the hair that fell in front of her face. She was a mess. Sweaty, vomity, teary, snotty.

She wanted to collapse onto the cool bathroom tile, but she couldn't. If it *was* Mom, the police would come calling again. She had to pull herself together. Right now she couldn't even stand herself. She needed to get cleaned up before she could go out there, as urgently as she felt the need to see what was going on.

She started the shower, and while she waited for it to get warm, she scrubbed her teeth hard and fast. Then her tongue. Then her whole mouth. Everything she could reach. She had to get the taste of acid out of her mouth. She rinsed and spit, and then stepped under the shower and gargled the water pouring down on her before doing the fastest lather, rinse, and repeat in the history of her world.

Her stomach miraculously stayed calm, and the water hardly hurt hitting her temperature-sensitive body. The towel felt like sandpaper as she dried off, but she felt a little better for being clean. She put on her softest sleeping pants and an oversized T-shirt her Mom had given her with a baby goats in pajamas pattern and padded out into the living room, where the horror on her father's and brother's faces stopped her in her tracks. She thought she wanted to know, but did she really? As long as she didn't see, the police hadn't called, there was a chance. Still a chance. Even though ...

She didn't know what got her moving again. It was no conscious thought, but suddenly she was there in the living room. Her brother and father had taken either side of the couch, leaving her the middle, but she didn't want to touch anyone right then, so she took the recliner. She didn't recline, but sat there on the edge of her seat, watching the TV screen. It showed a park. And crime scene tape. And uniformed officers with their backs to the camera, standing between the reporter and any actual view of what was going on.

It didn't stop the reporter—male with a navy-blue windbreaker, hair blowing in the breeze that also swayed the one tree visible in the shot—from painting a word picture of what was going on.

"—keep you apprised of this developing story. For those just tuning in, a body was discovered by a couple out walking their dog on this blustery Sunday morning. More accurately, the body was found *by* the dog, a golden retriever named Molly, who got curious about some underbrush and wouldn't come when called."

Get to the point! She screamed internally. No one wants to hear about the dog! Except maybe their viewers. Certainly not the family the body might belong to.

"When they went to check on what was holding her up, they discovered a woman's shoeless foot, which quickly led to the discovery of the rest of the body, which had apparently been dragged into the underbrush."

Emily made a pained noise, but no one looked away from the television.

"The police aren't speculating at this point about the identity of the body or how long it has been there, but a source close to the investigation—"

The reporter stopped as a voice off camera told the reporter he was going to have to move back, that they were expanding the perimeter, and the camera panned over to show a tall Latino man with a mane of hair and a beard and mustache that had gone too long untrimmed, like he'd been working for days straight. He had a badge hung around his neck, a gun at his waist and a jacket that didn't do anything to hide it.

Emily let out a breath she hadn't realized she'd been holding. Not Detective Anderson. Maybe that meant this case wasn't connected to their mother's disappearance. Hope was a razor around her heart, allowing it to expand, but cutting each time with the edge of probability.

When Dad's phone rang, he jumped. Literally jumped. They all looked at each other, and Dad, remote in hand, paused the television to answer it.

"Hello."

Pause.

"Thank you for calling. I saw the news—"

The police then. It had to be. Probably he wouldn't have even answered for anyone else. Not right then.

"I'm sorry, could you repeat that?" He looked sharply at Jared and then Emily, who tried desperately to read what was happening on her father's face. She wished he'd put the call on speakerphone.

"Jared and Emily?"

Jared and Emily, what? she wanted to scream.

"Okay, yes, we'll be there as soon as we can. Emily isn't feeling so well, so give us a little time. Did she ..." he stopped, closed his eyes, breathed through whatever he was going through. "Never mind. Not now. I'll find out soon enough."

He hung up the phone, and Jared pounced. "Did she what?"

Dad looked at them, his face drained of color, a horrible sadness falling like night over his features. "I don't even know how to say this but to say it. I never thought—" he ran his hand roughly over his face, maybe as a stall. "Kids, that body they found, they think it might be your mother's."

Emily didn't even gasp this time. She was too numb. She thought she'd known, but suspecting and confirming were two different things. The worst had happened. She thought she should cry or collapse or something, but all she could do was sit there in stunned silence.

"They want me to come down to the morgue to identify her body," Dad continued. "So until then, we don't really *know*." Yes, they did. The police wouldn't make a mistake like that. They wouldn't traumatize the family if they weren't pretty certain.

"And they want you two down at the station. They have some questions. There'll be an advocate there for you. I don't like to let you go alone. I'm—*we're*—all we've got now. Just the three of us."

He got up off the couch to sit on the coffee table, which swayed under his weight, but allowed him to reach for both Jared and Emily's hands. Emily glanced at her brother, who looked ... *guilty?* About what? Not wanting to take Dad's hand? She led the way, taking Dad's hand tentatively. What she really wanted was a hug, but she wanted it from Mom. Someone to comfort her and tell her it was all okay or, better yet, not even happening. But that was the one thing she could never have.

"We've all got to help the police now in any way we can. We have to find out what happened to your mother."

But did he mean that really and truly?

TWENTY-ONE

Jared

THEY TOOK JARED FIRST. He'd thought they'd talk to him and Emily together. Or at least at the same time, so Emily wouldn't be left alone in their waiting area, but for whatever reason, his name was the only one called. Maybe she'd be next and wouldn't have long to wait.

He squeezed her hand before he followed the officer who'd called him into an interrogation room. He didn't have far to go. He and Emily had been sitting on a bench in the station, watching people at their desks or officers hurrying from one place to another with news sure to make or shatter someone else's day. The room they took him to was different than the interrogation room he'd been in before—Detective Anderson's ... or her department's, anyway. It was an industrial sort of gray instead of putty or dun or whatever they would have called the blah beige-brown slathered on the other station walls. And it had a popcorn ceiling painted white rather than acoustic tiles, but it was still boxy and without windows. This one didn't even have a two-way mirror, proving that cop shows didn't always get it right. Although, he supposed that if they filmed the interrogation, as they probably always did to cover their butts or collect evidence, no one had to be on the other side of a mirror. They could watch real-time on a screen somewhere or view the recording at their leisure.

There were a man and woman already in the room. The man he recognized from the news they'd been watching when the call came in—the detective with the wild hair, tamed now that the wind wasn't having its way. His badge was no longer hanging from a cord around his neck, and his gun had been tucked away somewhere, but otherwise, he looked just the same. He met Jared with a hand outstretched and introduced himself as Detective Diaz.

The detective started to introduce the woman already seated at the table, but she rose and cut him off to introduce herself.

"Hello, Jared. I'm Mrs. Kapoor from Child Protective Services. The police have requested that I be present in case you or your sister need my help."

That explained why the police were calling them one at a time, if CPS had sent only one advocate for them to share. Mrs. Kapoor was trim and tiny, wearing flats, Jared noticed, as if she didn't need extra height to give her presence. She had on a power-red skirt, a dove-gray jacket—a way better gray than the walls—and a patterned shirt that tied them both together. She looked competent, but Jared's anxiety didn't ease. His mother was dead. He was being questioned. This wasn't going to be anything but painful, with or without Mrs. Kapoor.

Still, he was polite. He took her hand and thanked her for being there. Then he looked to the detective. "What happened? Can you tell me how my mother died? Whether she suffered?"

"Please, sit," the detective said, indicating the chairs at the table. There were four chairs and three of them, but he knew where he would sit. The detective had chosen one side of the table and Mrs. Kapoor the other. The symbolism was clear. He sat beside his advocate.

"Okay, I'm sitting. Please ..."

"We don't know for certain yet that the woman we found is your mother. No identification was found on her."

"Then her purse was taken? It could have been a robbery?"

"We're not speculating at this point."

"But you must have some theory. How was she killed?"

"Jared," the detective said gently, "I didn't ask you in so you could question me. Once we have more information, we'll share it. For now, I have some questions I need to ask you."

Detective Diaz reached down beside his chair, and, for the first time, Jared noticed a bag there, a big paper shopping bag with no logo. But from it he pulled ...

Jared's mouth went dry and he started to sweat all at the same time, making it clear where the moisture had gone.

The detective held the pharmacy bag Jared had disposed of the other night. It had a hole torn into the side like the crows or whatever had gotten to it as they had the other exposed garbage, but that didn't make any sense. The bag shouldn't have been exposed. He'd been careful to cover it. Yet at least half the contents were gone ... unless the detective was waiting to pull them out of the bag as well, waiting to catch Jared in a lie. The only thing he could see still there was the bloody towel.

Diaz set the bag down on the table in front of Jared and let him look at it for a second. "Want to tell me about this?"

"What is it?" Jared asked. He had to try twice. The first time he didn't have enough moisture for more than a rasp.

Diaz stared, his eyes practically boring into Jared. He'd bet Diaz was killer at staring contests. He didn't even blink. "It's a bag. With a towel drenched in blood. That you disposed of in your neighbor's garbage."

Oh, holy hell. He *knew*. How?

"Um—"

Mrs. Kapoor put a hand to his arm. "Jared, you don't have to answer any of their questions, you know that, right? And if you wish, you can ask for a lawyer to be present."

"I'm sure Jared wants to help with our investigation. Right, Jared? You'd like to help us clear things up?"

Jared's gaze jerked away from Mrs. Kapoor toward the cop. "Clear *what* up? What do you think this is?"

"I'm waiting for you to tell me."

Crap, crap, crap. How did he tell the truth without making trouble for Emily? Without making things look bad for himself? What else did the detective have in that bag?

"Emily cut herself accidentally," he said, gambling that it was nothing, hoping he didn't sound as guilty as he felt. "And it bled kind of a lot. She didn't want to upset Dad, who's going through enough, so I helped her clean it up. And then I threw it in the neighbor's can so Dad wouldn't find it."

Diaz was still staring. It was disconcerting. No doubt it was meant to be.

"Your sister cut herself?"

"Yes." Keep it short. Don't volunteer information. Wasn't that what the lawyers always said in the cop shows?

"Accidentally?"

"Yes."

"So you were disposing of this for your sister?"

Crap, what was he implying?

"She didn't ask me to. I just did it."

"And she'll corroborate all of this?"

"Yes, talk to her."

"We will. What made you feel the need to conceal this from your father?"

"Why are you making a big deal of it? This isn't—Wait, you don't think that's Mom's blood, do you? Test it! You'll see."

His heart was pounding now. The police couldn't actually think this was evidence! Yet the detective acted like this was about far more than a bloody bag. He acted as though he thought *Jared* had done something to Mom.

"Why are you getting so defensive?"

"Detective," Mrs. Kapoor jumped in, "what are you driving at?"

He didn't look away from Jared. "I'm trying to get the big picture. A young man disposes of a bloody towel the night before a woman's body is found in the park. It seems suspicious at the very least."

"Talk to Emily, she's right outside." Only, he wished he could talk to Emily first, so she'd know what story he told. She had to know he hadn't given away her secret, that he'd protected her. Or else, *she* might give it away. If the detective thought she was a danger to herself or others ... cops were mandatory reporters, weren't they? Child Protective Services were most definitely. The last thing Emily needed right now was to be locked up in some hospital, away from her family.

"In a minute. You never answered my question—why would you keep this from your father?"

"I told you, he's got enough going on."

"But he never believed your mother had come to harm. He told us she'd left by choice. To tell the truth, he never seemed that concerned."

Jared had known that Detective Anderson wasn't the only one on the case and that she had to be in touch with someone in their local PD. He guessed Detective Diaz was that contact. He wondered which detective Dad had talked to during his earlier questioning. And how he'd done.

Jared had no idea how he was doing. Or what to say next. Did he tell Detective Diaz that Dad had had to deal with him getting almost arrested at Mom's place? Did he know about that already?

"Just because he didn't seem concerned doesn't mean he wasn't. If nothing else, he had to worry about me and Emily. We were upset."

"But he wasn't," Detective Diaz said again.

Jared sat back in his chair and crossed his arms. He wasn't going to get baited.

When Jared didn't answer what he figured wasn't a question to begin with, Detective Diaz moved on. "You said you heard something the night your mother disappeared—a crash and a muffled cry, maybe coming from the garage?"

Oh hell, was this about him or about Dad? Who did they suspect? Was the plan to keep him off balance—make him feel targeted so he'd point the finger at others? What the hell was he supposed to do?

And what had happened to Mom?

*

Emily sat on that bench in the middle of the station and did her best not to think. The bench was hard and bolted to the floor. As wrung out as she was from the migraine and the vomiting, as much as she wanted to sleep and wake to find this was all a bad dream, there was no way on God's green hellhole that was going to happen.

For a while she stared off in the direction Jared had gone, as if she might suddenly gain the ability to see and hear beyond closed doors.

But her imagination kept drawing her to the morgue with her father. And the image of a woman's body, hidden under a sheet but for the feet sticking out at the bottom—sickly gray-blue, mottled, very clearly dead flesh. She'd seen enough television that the vision came unbidden, as much as she tried to push it away. The sight of the medical examiner, whose image remained fuzzy, pulling back the sheet. Her father looking ...

That was where the vision fell apart. She couldn't imagine the look on his face. She couldn't—*wouldn't*—imagine the rest of her mother's body on that slab. It would be too early for the autopsy, so she wouldn't have that horrible Y-incision. Surely she'd have been cleaned up, though. There wouldn't be blood or dirt and leaves caking the body. Would her face show the horror of her death? Would peace have stolen over her at the end?

There were tears pouring down her face, and one of the officers passing by noticed, stopped.

"Are you okay?" he asked. "Are you with someone? Should I get them for you?"

Emily shook her head, and started wiping the tears away with her fingers. "They took my brother in for questioning. I guess I'm next. My father's at the morgue."

The officer's face immediately changed, from slightly detached sympathy to real feeling. "You're with the woman they brought in this morning?" he said, but it wasn't really a question. More a confirmation to himself, so she didn't answer. That's what she was here to find out, anyway. Maybe the police had made a mistake. Maybe she wasn't "with the woman they brought in."

"Let me get you some tissues," he added. "Do you need someone to sit with you? I'm sure they wouldn't have left you on your own if they planned to be long."

"Tissues would be good," she said. The new tears were stopping up her nose and kicking up the pressure in her head. "But I don't need anyone."

"I'll be right back."

She didn't watch him walk away, looking back instead toward the interview rooms, hoping Jared would emerge and they could go home. Only they wouldn't be going home. It would be her turn next.

What she saw instead was a tall man with silver hair parting ways with a woman in a white button-up shirt with a badge clipped to her belt. A detective or plain-clothed cop. One she didn't recognize. But she recognized the man, at least from his picture.

The officer who'd stopped to talk to her returned with the tissues. She took them and thanked him quickly, hoping he'd leave the same way. She didn't want him to be there when Richard Travis walked by.

Luckily, the officer didn't linger, and Emily rose from the

bench as Richard Travis approached, headed toward the door, hurrying to intercept him.

"Richard Travis?" she asked, standing right in his way.

He stopped dead in his tracks, staring down at her. "Do I— Emily?" he asked, stunning her. "Are you Diane's daughter?"

Her mother's name from his lips hurt, but it was just one more droplet in the pool of pain. "Yes," she answered, barely a whisper of sound. She cleared her throat and said, "Can we talk?"

She indicated the bench she'd been sitting on, and Richard looked quickly toward the exit, as though bidding good-bye to his chance to escape the cop shop. But then he nodded and led the way, sitting far enough toward the center that she could regain her seat at the end without being too close. As if he'd seen her there.

He waited for her to begin with whatever she had to say. It was hard to think through the headache, but this was maybe her only chance to question him, and she couldn't let it go. She studied him for a second. Nice face. Tanned, like he was an outdoorsy type person, or at least worked outside. Gray eyes, that silver hair, a full head of it. Plain black long-sleeved T-shirt with a logo over the pocket that said *Lush Landscaping*, the words curved around the silhouette of a blooming tree. So she was right about him working outdoors. Or he was just a big fan of landscaping.

"You wanted to talk?" he prompted.

"You knew my mother," she stated unnecessarily.

He nodded.

"How well?" That was abrupt. She hadn't even thought of the question before it was out of her mouth. Apparently, her subconscious was guiding this interview.

There was something in his eyes. More than sadness. Loss. She felt answering tears starting up again and grabbed angrily for one of the tissues the cop had brought, dabbing her eyes and offering the box to Richard Travis, who shook his head to refuse. Of course not. Real men don't cry.

"We're friends," he said. "Nothing more. Not that I didn't— don't—really like your mother." *He'd used the past tense and then corrected himself. Did that mean he knew she was dead or that he'd already accepted that it was likely?* "But she was married, and not in any head-space to move on."

"What does that mean?" she asked. Because it sounded like he'd have been perfectly willing to have an affair with her if she'd been into it.

"It means ... look, I don't know if I should be talking to you about this." He looked around to see whether anyone was paying them any attention. "I should go."

Emily snapped out her hand to grab his arm. "Don't," she pleaded. "I need to know. I have to make sense of all of this. Please. Nothing you can say is any worse than what's going on in my head." He had no idea.

Richard gave her a sad smile and patted her hand. "Okay," he said. "You can ask your questions. I don't know that I'll answer them all, but I'll do my best."

"What did you mean before?"

He sighed. "I meant that your mother and father did not have the best relationship. Even if she'd been clear of the marriage, I'm not sure she'd have been ready to move on to another relationship."

"You're being careful," Emily accused. "You're choosing your words, which I get. I mean, to you I must seem like a kid, right? Well, I'm no kid. And even if I was, these last few weeks ... Well, there's nothing like the sheer horror of losing your mother to grow you right up. So whatever you've got, I can take it."

He studied her the way she'd studied him when he first sat down. She straightened her spine and stared back at him.

"Okay," he said again, this time like he meant it. "No sugar coating. Your father was awful to your mother. You have to know that. And she had to get out. She was torn up about leaving you kids, but she wasn't planning on that being long term. She just had to get out and get established before she could do anything, so she could show a court that she was a good bet for custody, so that he couldn't use you to manipulate her or suck her back in."

Her head was going to explode, and not just from the pressure.

"Dad said she left us. And she did, for two weeks. I guess while she got *set up*, but that's a long time to stay away from us, so when he said she left for good ..."

Richard worked his jaw, as though chewing on it. His face said it didn't taste right at all. "She'd never have done that."

Stupid tears. She wiped them away, the tissue abrasive, her eyes stinging.

"I didn't think so," she said. "I never did." But she realized as she said it that she was lying. She had believed it, at least a bit. And on some level she hadn't even acknowledged, she'd been angry at her mom for leaving them for so long. Jared had been a lot more honest with himself about that.

Richard leaned toward her then, just a little, and it made her lean in as well. "I don't understand why your dad did everything he could to hold on," he said. "He had someone else. Your mother knew it. I don't know why he wouldn't let her go."

Emily reeled back. "Someone else?"

"Crap, I'm sorry. I shouldn't have said that. Forget I mentioned it."

"Who?" she asked. No way could she forget it or let it go.

He looked pained, but he answered. It was too late to take the words back, and he knew it.

"She never said. But she once found a hair band in their bed that wasn't hers. Or yours. And there was other evidence."

Emily's eyes widened. She thought of that red scrunchy she'd found in the kitchen, the one that didn't belong to her mother, that she'd borrowed anyway. Was that the one? She shuddered at the thought of having worn the hair band belonging to the other woman. And her father having left it right there on the counter. Could he have intended Mom to see it that Friday night? That wouldn't make any kind of sense. Not if he wanted to reconcile, like he'd said.

"Why were you talking to the police?" she asked.

He shifted on the bench like he was uncomfortable, either at the hard wood or the questioning. "I imagine they're talking to everyone who knew your Mom."

"That's not an answer."

"Yes," he said. "It is. I'm sorry, but I really do have to go. I have to pick up my little girl from the sitter's."

"You have a little girl?" she asked.

Now his eyes softened. His whole face lit up. "I do. Her name is Jessica. She's five years old."

He rose from the bench, but almost as an afterthought, he stopped and dug his wallet out of his jeans pocket. Emily had no idea what he was doing at first, and then he pulled out a business card for his landscaping company with the same logo as on his shirt. It had his name, a phone number, and a website.

"Here," he said, handing it over. "This is my number. If you or your brother need anything … well, I don't know what I can do, but I'll try to help however I can. I really cared for your mother."

Again, the past tense. It was like a stab to her heart, although it was her brain that throbbed with it.

She whispered her thanks, and he was gone. It was only after he vanished that she wondered what had happened to him and Jessica's mother. Were they divorced? Had she died? And if so, how?

She was looking down at the card when a shadow fell across it. She looked up into the face of the same cop Richard Travis had been shaking hands with, the woman in the white button up shirt with the belt badge. Her dark hair was back in a tight, low ponytail, which seemed to be the default hairstyle of all the women cops she'd seen, despite what television would have her think about always-flowing hair. Her eyes, a surprising shade of brown that was almost amber, looked understanding rather than hard, although undoubtedly that could change depending on the situation.

"Emily Graham?" she asked. When Emily nodded, she said, "I'm Detective Elizabeth Wong. Your brother is talking to Detective Diaz, but they should be done any moment. Would you like to come with me?"

If she said no?

But she didn't. She nodded again, starting to feel like a bobblehead, and followed Detective Wong down the hallway, almost surely to the interview room she'd been in with Richard Travis.

She left the door open and leaned against the wall, motioning Emily to a seat. "Your advocate should be here in just a second and we can start then. I saw you talking with Richard Travis?"

It wasn't phrased as a question, but she heard the rise at the end, clearly indicating that it was.

She shrugged. "That all right?"

"Of course. I didn't know you knew each other."

"We didn't." Why did it feel like the interrogation had already begun? "I recognized him from his Facebook picture."

"Ah, you're on Facebook? I thought the kids had all abandoned that for other things."

Was there a trap here somewhere? She didn't have anything to hide, but still, Detective Wong was making her nervous.

"No, I'm not, but Jared and I checked Mom's page after she left us. We were looking for clues about where she'd gone."

"Did you find any?" she asked.

"No, we'd have told the police right away. Or Dad."

"Did you read her messages?"

There was the trap.

"No." That had mostly been Jared, and she wasn't ratting him out.

"Delete any of them?"

Emily stared? "Why would we do that?"

The detective smiled, as though to put her at ease. Emily didn't trust it. "You love your mother, don't you?"

Present tense. Emily's heart leapt. The seesaw of hope and despair was going to kill her.

"Of course."

"So you'd want to protect her, say if there was evidence of an affair and you thought your father might find out?"

Her head was definitely going to explode. Despite the meds, her vision was starting to tunnel again. Richard had said there was no affair. Was he lying? Was Detective Wong just fishing? Or was there someone else?

"I didn't think you could question me without my advocate."

"We're just making conversation."

The door pushed open, and in walked another woman, significantly shorter and more colorful than the detective. Her skirt, anyway, which was warning flag red.

"I want to go home," Emily said to the new woman immediately, standing up to leave. "If no one is going to tell me what happened to my mother, then all I want to do is go home and lie down. I have a blinding headache, and it feels as though it's going to explode at any moment."

"Do you need medical attention?" the new woman asked.

"I need my mother."

The new lady, her advocate, she presumed, looked infinitely sad. "I'm so sorry. I don't know whether the detective has told you yet. Probably she was waiting for me. We've just received word that your father made a positive ID. The woman found in the park this morning was your mother."

TWENTY-TWO

Jared

HE'D NEVER REALLY THOUGHT Aunt Aggie looked that much like Mom. Not until the shock of her appearance at the police station. She was dirty blonde where Mom was a strawberry blonde, had blue eyes instead of their Mom's green. She also tended to wear her scrubs even when not working, though then she paired them with jeans instead of drawstring pants. Today, though, she wore a colorful cardigan over a t-shirt without any pattern. No frolicking dogs or kittens chasing yarn or cows jumping over the moon. And she'd done up her face, like she thought you had to get dressed up for the police. Or maybe it was to cover up red, puffy eyes, because looking closely, her eyes *were* red. And suddenly she reminded him of Mom, so powerfully it was like a mule-kick to the gut.

Emily ran to her as soon as she opened the door—the police had finally left them alone after they'd dropped the bombshell about Mom. Dad was going to be several more hours, and they had to call someone for them. Emily had insisted on Aunt Aggie, and whether their father relented or was never consulted, Jared didn't know, but he was glad to see her.

Aunt Aggie hugged Emily back for all she was worth, then shifted her to one side and held out an arm for Jared. He joined them, hugging both carefully, afraid if he gave in to his emotions, he'd hug too hard. He buried his face in Emily's shoulder.

It was Emily who shrugged out of things way too soon, and he realized he'd probably hit her bad shoulder. The one she'd cut.

"Can we go home?" Emily asked.

"Absolutely. I think I may have to sign something or … Just give me a minute, and I'll be right back. I promise."

She left, and Jared turned to Emily to finish the conversation they'd been having when Aunt Aggie came in.

"So Mom found a hair band in their bed? It seems a stretch from that to an affair."

"Really? Can you think of another explanation for how it got there?" she challenged. "Apparently, there was other evidence. I don't know what it was."

"What color was the scrunchy you found?"

"Red."

"Mom doesn't wear red." Not usually. As a strawberry blonde with a complexion that tended toward the rosy, it emphasized the red in her skin and make her look, she said, like an Oompa Loompa.

"Exactly."

He chewed his lip, because something had occurred to him.

"But it's Carla's signature color."

They stared at each other, and he watched the realization hit Emily.

"And *someone* in that household ratted us out, told the police I'd dumped that bag in their trash and turned it over to them. But if they saw me, why leave the bag in the can long enough for it to get pecked apart before they removed it?"

"Maybe they didn't know what it was you'd done until the

birds dragged the bag out and spread the contents all over. And once they saw blood, they probably freaked."

"Maybe." It made sense. He didn't know if he'd have done the same in their place—reported it to the police rather than asked someone about it directly—but he might have if someone in the Meyers family had gone missing. It didn't lessen the feeling of betrayal, especially knowing Ms. Carla might have been betraying them and their mother all along.

The door opened again, and this time Mrs. Wong returned with their aunt to make doubly sure they were okay and that they wanted to leave with her. When they confirmed it, they were released. Emily led the way out, as if she couldn't wait to get out of the station. He seconded it.

"Stupid question," Aunt Aggie said as they walked to her car, "are you kids okay? Do you need anything? Want me to stop anywhere? Are you hungry?"

Jared didn't point out that those were multiple questions. Emily got into the back seat of their aunt's old hatchback, leaving him the shotgun seat. He answered for them both as he got into the front.

"I don't know if okay is the word I'd use, but we're holding it together." At least he hoped he was answering for them both. "I think we just want to get home. I'm not sure either of us can eat right now, but if we get hungry, maybe we can order in?"

He looked back at Emily, but she had her eyes closed and was resting her head against the car window, and didn't notice.

"I understand."

They lapsed into silence as she worried about backing out and then getting out of the station parking lot and onto the road, then she asked. "Did the police tell you anything at all about how she died?"

"No. Has the news said anymore?"

"Not that I've heard."

Silence again.

He heard movement in the back seat and glanced back again

to see that Emily had unbuckled her belt and was now laying across the backseat as best she could, curled up on her side, one hand under her cheek and the other shielding her eyes.

She barely woke when they got home, and only long enough to shuffle to her room and collapse onto her bed. Jared checked on her about five minutes later, just to be sure ... She was snoring faintly, sleeping in the position she'd fallen in, it looked like. He envied her the oblivion.

Which meant that he was left with Aunt Aggie. Better than being alone right now. Or with Dad, though he felt the pressure to entertain her somehow. Or to play host.

He offered her something to drink and was getting them both sodas when she asked, "How's Aaliyah?"

Right, they hadn't spoken in a while.

"Next subject," he said.

He was glad he had his back to her so he couldn't see the sympathy or whatever would be on her face. Anyway ... Mom. She was all that mattered right now.

He didn't actually wait for Aunt Aggie to come up with a new question. He turned with the sodas in his hand and caught his aunt's gaze before asking, "Did Mom know who Dad was having an affair with?"

Her eyes widened. "How do you know about the affair?"

"Doesn't matter." He wasn't going to tell her Emily was talking with strange men in police stations. "We do."

She took her soda and sat down at the kitchen table—the same table where they'd been sitting when Dad told them Mom had left them. The pain hit him again, like a blade to the heart. He wanted to collapse to the ground with it, but he couldn't. The search for the truth had kept him going this far. He had to see it through, wherever it would lead. For Mom.

"She said it was a neighbor. Someone close. That's all I know." It solidified what he already suspected, but it was another blow just the same. The Meyers' home had been their safe place when their parents had fought. Now he knew it was all a lie. But how could Carla want to be with his father when she saw what he did to their mother? Did she blame the victim, think that Mom must provoke him? Did she think he loved her too much for her to ever be in Mom's shoes? Did she believe she could change him?

Was Jared any better, needing to believe his father wasn't guilty so they could keep their dysfunctional family together? Not necessarily for himself, but for Emily, who still believed in their father, as far as he knew, and who seemed the safest from Dad's wrath. So far. But what if she went through a rebellious period or started reminding him of Mom? Who knew what might set his father off next. He had to know the truth. And he had to do something about it, whatever it was.

"What do you think happened to her?" he asked, the words coming quietly, as though his vocal cords could hardly stand to let them lose into the world.

Aunt Aggie took a sip of her soda. Stalling. Then she said, "I don't know. I don't want to speculate. But, I *do* want you and Emily to know you can come live with me. I'll get a bigger place. You'd have to change schools, but—"

Jared was shaking his head. Panic had started welling up at the thought, and he didn't do panic. He couldn't. He was afraid if he started right now he might not stop. It was all too much. "I can't think about that right now," he said quickly.

"Of course. I just wanted you to know the offer is there, so you wouldn't worry."

In case his father was arrested. That's what she meant. *In case his father had murdered their mother.*

"Listen, I really appreciate you picking us up at the station and … everything. But it's been a really horrible day. I need to check on Emily and then I just want to go and lie down. I hate to leave you alone out here.…"

He spotted the tears his aunt wasn't allowing to fall. He was so stupid. He'd only been thinking about his own pain, but Aunt Aggie had lost her sister. They'd been together their entire lives, and alone since Pops had died of pancreatic cancer four years ago, almost a year to the date after G-ma had gone. He and Emily were all she had left.

He got up from his seat and went around to hers, hugging her from behind. She held onto his arms where they wrapped around her, and he felt the tears start to fall.

"I'm so sorry," she said, releasing him to try to stem the tears with her hands. "I told myself I had to keep it together for you, and you're the one comforting me."

He hugged her a little harder, then released her to pull up the next chair over and sit beside her rather than loom behind. He put an arm around her, resting his head on her shoulder. Her tears were making others prickle behind his eyes, but he wasn't going to give in to them.

She sniffled and let things go that way for another minute, then she gave him a watery smile and rose to find tissues. "I'm okay," she said, even though she wasn't. None of them were. "You go check on Emily. Lay down. I'll be fine. I'm going to turn on the news, in case they release anything before the police see fit to tell us. I'll let you know if I hear anything."

He stared after her. "Are you sure?"

"Positive."

He took her at her word. He had a burning need to check on Emily again, not only to see that she was still okay, though that was his main concern, but because he needed her phone. Aaliyah had to know what was going on. Not because it would bring her back, but because she'd known and liked his mother. Mom had liked her too. He didn't want her to hear it on the news.

Emily was still sleeping in the same position. He took a second to watch her, knowing she wouldn't wake. That would take an act of god. She looked so peaceful in sleep. He wished it would last when she was awake.

He found her backpack where she'd thrown it onto her dresser and dug through it for her phone. He knew her numerical password, and keyed it in. He thought he'd have trouble figuring out what to say to Aaliyah, especially since Maybell would be the one relaying the message, but he didn't.

I'd call with this news if I could, or better yet, tell you in person, but since I can't … I didn't want you to hear this on the news instead of from me. They found Mom's body this morning. I guess the car at the train station was meant to throw us off. I wish … so many things. But anyway, I wanted you to know.

He wished he could hold her, he wanted to say. But he couldn't, so what was the use. It wouldn't change anything. It wouldn't make things all better, but if he still had Aaliyah, something positive in his life, maybe he wouldn't feel so lost and hopeless right now.

TWENTY-THREE

Jared

DAD SENT them to school on Monday—afraid, he said, that otherwise they'd have nothing to do all day but dwell on their sadness. They needed distractions. They needed their friends.

It didn't go well.

Jared nearly got into a fight when Andrew Meyers veered from his usual path to tell him how sorry he was to hear about their mother. Jared wanted to punch him. He didn't even know why. Maybe he just wanted to punch *something*. Maybe it was because Andrew didn't look sorry, but then why even make the effort. Was he looking for Jared's reaction? Did he know about his mother and Jared's father? Was he sorry Jared's mom was gone because it freed up the field? What would happen now? Would Carla leave Mr. Meyers and Andrew like their mother had left them? No, not like that. Mom had always planned to come back until someone made sure that wasn't possible. That's what Richard Travis had told Emily, and Jared had to believe that.

He clenched his fists hard, but didn't use them. Andrew walked away unscathed.

But it was a near thing, and getting nearer with every stare, every whisper, every expression of sympathy. He wanted to shout at everyone to stop. Just stop. But the worst was, he almost hoped they didn't, because he wanted to lash out. One stupid comment or someone staring too long, and he would throw down. He had so much pent up anger—at his father, at himself, at all the assholes who couldn't understand how someone else was feeling and leave him the hell alone.

He had to go. If he stayed, he was going to hit something. Some*one*. And he couldn't. He'd be no better than Dad. The thought killed him. He had to get counseling. Or something. Because pushing the feelings down only made them build up until he risked an explosion. Maybe Aaliyah was right to leave him. Maybe he wasn't safe to be around. The thought sent him to the office, where he saw Emily sitting on one of the four chairs in the waiting area while a teacher talked to the woman at the desk.

Emily didn't even look up at him, but slumped in on herself. And that was when he realized they were two sides of the same coin. When things went bad, Jared wanted to lash out. At Mom. At Dad. At anyone in his way. Emily turned inward, beat herself up. Self-destructed. She kept the peace for everyone but herself. Dad had messed them up but good.

"What are you doing here?" he asked.

She finally glanced up, and he could see that she was done in. Her face was red and blotchy from crying, her face bone white. She didn't even have it in her to respond.

Jared turned to the counter and interrupted the teacher, though he did at least say "excuse me." She went silent at the disruption. "We need to go home," he said. "Emily and I. We shouldn't have come. It's too soon." Dad was their guardian. He was the only one the school could call. Jared had no idea how he'd react. He didn't really care. He'd leave with Emily right now if he had to, even if it meant they were marked as skips and had to walk all the long way home. "Can you call our father?"

The teacher put a hand to his shoulder. "I'm so sorry to hear about your mother," she said.

If he heard it one more time he was going to explode.

"I'm Ms. Castillo, your sister's Language Arts teacher. I brought Emily in because I'm concerned about her. I thought maybe she could see a counselor. Maybe you want to see one too?"

He'd just been thinking he needed to see someone. But not now. Not here. Not anything that might get into his school record and mess up his chances for college and escape. But would it help Emily?

"Jared," Emily said, finally rousing herself. "I want to go home."

"You don't want to see a counselor?"

She shook her head. "I want to go home and sleep."

"Can I talk to you?" Ms. Castillo said to Jared. "In private. Just for a minute?"

He looked at Emily, whose eyes pleaded with him to get her out of there, and said. "Give me a second."

Ms. Castillo took him off to the far corner of the office, in plain sight, but hopefully out of earshot of Emily and the office assistant.

"I'm worried about your sister," she said. "She's showing signs of depression."

He was confused. "We've just lost our mother. She's grieving. Isn't that natural?"

"I mean even before that. She's been distracted. Some of her poetry has been very dark, and today she can't stop crying. I don't want to criticize your father, but I don't know what he was thinking sending you back to school so soon. The school district has a special counselor we share among schools. We're lucky enough that she's here Monday and Thursday afternoons. I was hoping to get Emily in to see her."

"I don't think one meeting is going to help her. She wants to get home, and, honestly, so do I. We need each other right now more than anything. I'll talk counseling over with her and my father, I promise."

She didn't look satisfied with that. Not at all. "Please do. Your sister is so bright and talented, but she's tormented."

I know, better than you think. But he didn't say it. He didn't think Emily would want to talk with a counselor. Therapy couldn't help if you weren't honest, right? And Emily couldn't afford to be honest. Not with her secret. Yet there had to be a way. People got help.

Emily

The rest of the week was a blur. Emily slept a lot, aware once or twice of Jared checking on her as she was on the edge of sleep— just falling or just waking up. She was going to scream if he didn't stop watching her like a hawk. Or if he asked one more time whether she was okay.

Dad was out so much, talking to the police, checking in at his office, making arrangements for Mom's funeral pending the eventual release of her body that he finally had to let Jared and Emily stay by themselves. He didn't make them go to school. Not until Thursday when he and his lawyer were going down to the police station. It sounded like he expected to be there all day. Thursday he wanted them at school—at the very least, to make up any tests and missed assignments and get a schedule of upcoming work so they wouldn't fall behind, since he didn't know what was to come.

That sounded ominous.

It felt like the police were closing in on Dad, and Emily didn't know what to think. If he did it, she wanted him in jail, but if he didn't … She still couldn't imagine it. As bad as it ever got, she couldn't imagine him killing Mom. Killing anyone. But weren't the families always surprised? How many stories were there about spouses or kids sticking by their husband or wife or father or whoever? No one wanted to believe. She knew she didn't.

Jared had finally told her about what he heard the night Mom disappeared. He hadn't wanted to worry her, but knew it might come up in the questioning or, worse, the trial if it came to that. He wanted her to hear it from him. She'd noticed Dad treating Jared differently. Ice-coldly. She wondered whether it already had come up. Really, Dad was hardly saying anything to either one of them. He was distracted and distant. As much as Emily wanted her mother back, she wasn't sure she felt the same way about her father. The only thing she knew was that if her father hadn't hurt their mother to begin with, she'd never have left. She'd have been home and safe and *alive*. Maybe Dad wasn't the only one who'd gone distant.

But despite all of that, she still couldn't believe her father had killed her mother. While part of her feared the worst, the rest of her couldn't accept that he was that kind of monster.

But the police didn't seem to be looking for an alternate explanation, which meant it was up to her. She couldn't sit around waiting for Jared's surveillance to drive her nuts or for her father to be arrested. She had to do something.

Maybe provide him with an alibi. If Ms. Carla *was* her father's mistress, it was possible what Jared had heard was him sneaking out to meet her after Mom was gone. Maybe he'd just crashed into something in the garage. She didn't know how that explained the blood they'd found, but that could be old. There was no telling when it had fallen there.

Maybe Dad was protecting Ms. Carla by not confessing to the affair. Or protecting her marriage, anyway. But if it meant saving her father ... people had to face the consequences for their choices.

The question was how to get at the truth. She could maybe find out for certain about the affair by returning the hair band to Ms. Carla and seeing how she reacted. If she accepted it, Emily could tell her that she *knew*, ask her about that night. And if she didn't admit the band was hers? Same thing, she guessed. Tell her about how her mother had found the scrunchy and where.

Tell her what Aunt Aggie had said about it being a neighbor and hope she cracked. The question was how to go about it. And when.

She couldn't tell Jared. He might try to talk her out of it. Or go with her, but she was certain that if Ms. Carla was going to say anything, it wouldn't be with Jared around. Not that there was anything wrong with him except that a) he was a guy, and b) he didn't do subtle. He wouldn't cajole or question; he'd demand. It wouldn't go well.

She couldn't go when Dad was home, because he'd want to account for her whereabouts, and she didn't know what he'd think about her going to the Meyers. She dreaded it herself, especially after they'd given that bag Jared had dumped to the police. What would they make of that? Did they think he was getting rid of evidence for their father? Guilty himself? There was no way they could suspect the truth.

One way to find out. She just had to pick her time.

Jared

Thursday afternoon, Jared stayed for track. While the coach claimed he understood about Jared's mother, he was going to get cut if he missed another practice. It was bound to happen, but not today. He couldn't lose that too. Not right now.

It was like he carried a force field around him. Most of the team had come up to him before he'd left on Monday to tell him they were sorry about his mom. But no one knew what to say next.

They couldn't ask *Hey, how's it going,* afraid they might get a sad-sack story about his loss rather than the juicy details of the investigation they really wanted. And they couldn't come right out and ask about those. Too ghoulish.

Except for Dugan. He didn't have a filter to speak of. "Dude, how's it going? They arrest anyone yet?" He punched Jared in the shoulder as he asked, like he was being playful.

Yeah, right.

Jared glared.

"What?"

"Never mind," Jared said, turning away, continuing with his stretches.

"No, really, what?"

One of the other guys came over, put Dugan in a "playful" headlock and dragged him away, muttering something to him Jared couldn't hear, hopefully that he was a heartless son of a bitch and should leave Jared alone.

He was thankful for that at least.

Jamal, one of the guys who hadn't yet expressed sympathies approached him, and he knew what was coming. He pretended to be so absorbed he didn't notice him there, but it didn't work. Jamal waited him out, determined. Finally Jared looked over. "You too?" he asked.

Jamal shifted from one foot to the other and back, clearly uncomfortable. "I was sorry to hear about your Mom. I remember her buying ice cream for the team after our win against Pinewood. She was a nice lady."

Jared gave a nod, afraid to try his voice.

"If there's a service. If it's open, the team and I will be there."

"You've already talked about it?"

"Yeah, a little."

He wondered what else they'd said.

"Thanks."

Jamal nodded and turned away.

When the coach called them to start, he tried to outrun his thoughts. If he'd known what was going on at home, he'd have raced in an entirely different direction.

TWENTY-FOUR

Emily

SHE WAS GOING to do it. This afternoon while Jared and her father were out and there was no one to stop her. She'd told Shara her plan after Language Arts, and when she couldn't argue Emily out of it, she sighed and made Emily promise to at least keep in touch and let her know how things went. "I get it. You have to know," Shara had said. And that was it exactly. She *had* to know.

Heading out now, she typed to Shara, keeping her promise. *Wish me luck.*

She didn't really believe in luck, but she did believe in thinking good thoughts. If you put out negativity into the world, that was what you got back. If you were hit with it yourself— and it didn't get much worse than your mother murdered and your father suspected—you absorbed it. Radiated it like something radioactive, poisoning people around you. She didn't want to do that. She hoped Shara's positive vibes could counter her negative.

Ms. Carla worked from home, though Emily had no clear idea what she did. Something to do with customer service or support or something, but from a home office instead of a call center. So, she'd be home. But what about Andrew? As a senior he was on half-days and usually worked the afternoons, but she had no clue about his work schedule, and she wanted to catch Ms. Carla alone. If she saw Andrew's car out front, she'd have to abort the plan and try again later.

She never got the chance. The doorbell rang, and when she went to answer it, she was shocked to see Ms. Carla standing there, a disposable lasagna pan covered in foil in her hands.

Her heart started to beat harder. It was go time. Already.

She opened the door, and Ms. Carla offered up the pan. "I made baked ziti for you all. With meat sauce. I thought you might need a good home-cooked meal."

Trying to take over for their mother already? Pain flared like a fire that had been stoked, but she beat it back. She had to be pleasant. Invite her in. Win her confidence.

"Thank you so much," she said, taking the tray. It was heavy, and she needed two hands. She cocked her hip to hold open the door. "Do you want to come in? I have something for you too," she said quickly, before Ms. Carla could form a "no."

"Oh, okay, thank you," she answered, surprised.

She held the door to let Emily continue on and entered behind her. Emily stowed the baked ziti in the fridge and turned back. "Can I get you anything to drink? Soda? Water? I'm afraid that's all we have."

"No, thank you. We were all so sorry to hear about your Mom. It must be awful for you. Please know that you can come to us for anything."

Yeah, and you'll go to the police with it, Emily thought but didn't say.

"Have the police told you anything at all?" Ms. Carla asked. "Do they have any idea who could have … hurt your mother?"

Her gaze was avid, her hands clenched in front of her. She wasn't asking out of idle curiosity. Worried about her lover?

"My Dad would know more," Emily said, studying her with the same intensity. "They've spent a lot of time talking to him."

"So, he's a suspect?"

"I guess the spouse is always the prime suspect."

"But there are others?"

"I don't know. Maybe. Have they talked to you?"

Carla clutched at pearls she wasn't wearing. They weren't her style. "What would they want with me?"

This was Emily's moment of truth. Did she slam Carla with what she suspected or take a more circuitous approach? Apparently, her mouth decided for her, unable to wait. Or maybe it was her heart that couldn't take any more uncertainty.

"Maybe to talk about your relationship with my father."

Carla took a step back, her face changing. Emily saw guilt flash across it before she got it under control.

"I don't know what you mean." But Emily knew she was lying.

Emily went to her backpack on the counter and unzipped the front pocket where the scrunchy was stashed. She turned and tossed the hairband at Carla. "Here, my mother found this."

Carla let the words strike and the hairband fall to the floor, failing to catch it. For a second there was just shock, and then she said, "But—she *told* you?"

It hurt, that confirmation. Like a knife to the gut. That Dad had betrayed Mom like that, that he'd lied and snuck around. That he had a motive to get Mom out of the way. Maybe more than one if Mom had life insurance or he didn't want to pay alimony or share custody. It was crazy, but people had killed before over stuff like that.

"I found out on my own," Emily said.

"Maybe that's for the best," Ms. Carla said, her voice changing now, from the friendly, motherly neighbor to something harder-edged. Emily didn't understand it. Shouldn't she still be trying to ingratiate herself with her boyfriend's family, especially now that they knew?

Emily did her best to keep eye contact, though looking at the woman who'd come between her parents was a sickening thing. "Were you with him that night after Mom left? Can you give him an alibi?"

"I can do better than that," Ms. Carla said, taking a step forward. Emily didn't know what it was—something in her eyes or her body language—that made her take a step back, away from the woman she'd known for years, but suddenly it was like someone else was standing there. A complete stranger. She wanted space between them. A lot of space.

She took another step away....

TWENTY-FIVE

Jared

"EMILY!" Jared called as soon as he was through the door.

The house was eerily quiet. He panicked instantly, cursing himself. He should never have stayed for track and let Emily go home alone. Not knowing how fragile she was.

He threw down his backpack, calling her name again and again, louder each time and frantic by the third.

There was no answer.

He grabbed the wall to help with the turn as he slid into the hallway. Her door was open. That had to be a good sign, right? Unless being alone she didn't feel the need for privacy.

He dashed to her door and froze in the doorway at the sight of the blood. So much blood.

Jared raced to Emily's side and saw instantly that the blood had come from her wrists, which were cut, a bloody razor blade still in one hand. He felt for a pulse, terrified he wouldn't find one. The second it took him to find her heartbeat was the longest of his life.

Her eyelids fluttered at his touch, but that was all. She didn't move. She didn't wake.

He looked around for her phone but didn't find it. Thoughts rushed him, but he pushed them aside, focusing on what to do next. Run for the phone or wrap her wrists and *then* call 911? He didn't want to delay the ambulance getting to Emily, but he didn't know how much blood she had left to lose.

He grabbed open her drawer, the one where he knew she kept Band-Aids and things and found a roll of gauze, which he quickly wrapped around and around her closest wrist, pulling it as tightly as it could to put pressure on the wound and stop the bleeding, then tearing it off with his teeth. When he got to the second, he noticed something he hadn't before—a note just beyond her outstretched hand, easily missed because it was soaked red with blood.

Oh, Emily. His heart was pounding and ready to burst. His fault. All his fault.

He quickly wrapped the other wrist and then couldn't help himself. He reached for the typewritten note.

I'm so sorry. I know I hurt everybody with what I did. Hurting Mom … I can't live with it anymore. I hope you can forgive me.

No! Jared couldn't believe his eyes. A suicide note and a confession? It wasn't even possible. Emily would never have hurt their mother. It didn't make any sense. And how was anyone supposed to believe she'd gotten Mom's body to that park? Even if she could drive, how on Earth would someone her size have lifted and dragged Mom's body into the underbrush?

She couldn't.

Which meant someone had staged this scene. Jared had left Emily alone with a killer on the loose.

He ran for the phone and called 911, telling the dispatcher to hurry, that his sister was bleeding. Her wrists cut, giving their address.

"She cut her own wrists?" the dispatcher asked.

"She sure as hell didn't. Someone cut them for her."

"Did you witness this? Do you know who hurt her?"

"No, dammit, just get here. Hurry!"

He hung up, even though she told him to stay on the line. He had to think. What did he do now? The note was ridiculous, but what if the police believed it? His first instinct was to grab it before they got here and shove it down the garbage disposal, but it was evidence. Surely the police would see how ridiculous it was. If so, it would only prove that someone had done this to Emily, staged things to frame her. Maybe the note would even have the killer's prints and would break the case wide open. But with Emily's history of cutting, which they'd see written on her skin, he couldn't be sure. He didn't know how the police would react.

Dad. He had to call Dad. Not to make sure of where he was—at the police station and so unable to have done this—but so that he could rush home. With Emily out of it and Jared not her parent or guardian, he didn't know if the paramedics would even be able to treat her. But surely they couldn't just let her bleed....

He dialed Dad and it went straight to voicemail, which meant he probably had his phone turned off. Jared had no idea of his lawyer's number. Or even his name.

He tried the detective who'd given him his card yesterday, Detective Diaz. He picked up on the third ring, answering with his rank and name.

"Is my Dad there?" Jared asked in a rush. "Emily's hurt really bad. He's got to come home. I've called 911. The ambulance should be on the way, but Emily needs him."

"Slow down," the detective said. "Hurt how? What happened?"

"I don't know," he answered, self-loathing burning like bile up his throat. "I wasn't home. I went to track. It was selfish, I know, but I never thought ... Someone cut her wrists."

"Someone?"

"It wasn't her," he insisted. Did he mention the note? There was still time to get rid of it. "She'd never do that."

"I'll tell your father. I'll be there as well." That didn't make him feel any better. Detective Diaz had been perfectly willing to treat Jared as a suspect. He didn't think he'd be any less willing with Emily.

The detective disconnected, and Jared rushed back to Emily.

She was so pale. "Emily," he said, "stay with me."

He reached for her hand, but was afraid to touch it. He didn't want to move anything and quicken her bleeding. Instead, he reached for her face and gently cupped her cheek. Then, as much as it hurt him, he pulled back his hand to slap the cheek gently, trying to wake her. Weren't you supposed to keep someone alert? Make sure they didn't slip off?

"Wake up, Emily. Tell me who did this to you."

Her eyelids fluttered, but didn't lift. Her lips parted, but no sound came out. Jared's heart was beating hard enough for the both of them.

He heard sirens in the distance. Seconds left to figure out what to do with that note. Keep or destroy? The police would assume Emily had hurt herself no matter what, but the note made her into a killer.

The indecision froze him until it was too late. The sirens were right outside their door now, and he raced to let in the paramedics and guide them to Emily. A police car was right behind them, and they waited a second for the officer to come through first, probably to make sure there was no danger, since Jared had insisted someone else had hurt Emily. Jared chafed at the delay, but it didn't last long. The officer's clearance of the house was only cursory before he waved in the paramedics. Jared was pushed aside as they rushed in with a stretcher and left it in the hallway as they worked on Emily because it was too big to make the turn into her room.

The police officer, after giving Emily a once-over, bent at the waist to get a better look at the note without touching it. Jared realized he should have done the same. His prints were on the note. He hoped they weren't the only ones.

"Did you do the gauze?" one of the paramedics asked, looking over his shoulder at Jared.

"Yes."

"Good job. Next time—and hopefully there won't be a next time—put pressure on the wounds yourself for four-to-five minutes."

Damn, he'd done wrong.

"Is she going to be okay?" Jared asked.

"She's lost a lot of blood. We're going to do our best. You got this?" he said to his partner. "I'll get the paperwork started."

His partner nodded, talking softly to Emily. He couldn't see what else was going on because she was between him and his sister.

The first paramedic rose and passed Jared on his way out the door to the tablet he'd left on the gurney. "Can you answer some questions for me? I'll need a parent or guardian, but you can get us started on the paperwork."

"Dad's on the way."

"Good. Let's start with that—patient's name and guardian's name."

Jared gave him all the information he could. When he asked whether Jared knew where her insurance card was, he went for her backpack. He kept his in his wallet. He hoped Emily did the same. He found her phone first, and shoved it into his pocket as he continued digging for the wallet. He came up with it, and the paramedic was entering the information onto his tablet when another siren came wailing, and shortly thereafter, Dad, his lawyer and Detective Diaz came pouring in, making the house suddenly seem small.

Dad rushed right for Emily's room, but the officer inside stopped him at the door. "I'm afraid this is a crime scene," he said.

"A what?" he asked, stunned.

"You can ride with her to the hospital," the paramedic inside said. "Would you let my partner know we're ready to move her?"

Dad walked woodenly back to us, like he'd almost forgotten how to walk even though he'd been doing it all his life.

"Your partner's ready for you," he said to the paramedic, who was already moving down the hallway, no doubt having heard like Jared had. Their house was anything but soundproof.

Dad looked at Jared, "What the hell happened?"

Jared sank down into a seat at the kitchen table. He understood forgetting how to walk, because it seemed his own legs had forgotten how to hold him up. "I stayed for track. I was going to get kicked off the team if I missed another practice, and I never thought ... Someone made it look like Emily hurt herself. And there's a horrible note, but she didn't write it. I know she didn't."

"How?"

"For one thing, it's a print-out. Why would you type your suicide note, unless you were sending it electronically? You wouldn't. Emily wouldn't."

"You left her alone?" his father said, his voice dangerously even. The calm before the storm.

"And I hate myself for it, okay? I'll never forgive myself. You want to trash me too?"

Dad looked like he wanted exactly that. And probably would have gone for it if Detective Diaz hadn't been right there watching. But with his wife murdered and his daughter an attempted suicide—or so it appeared, even if Jared said differently—he didn't dare do anything but the caring father routine. Jared feared what would come later.

His father turned away rather than say anything at all, only to turn back a second later. "I can't ride in the ambulance and leave Jared home alone," he said to the detective taking it all in. "I'll have to drop him off at my mother's and meet Emily at the hospital."

"I can get him there," the detective said. "You should be with your daughter."

Jared had been about to protest as well. Emily needed Dad. He sure as hell didn't, but it was better that it came from the detective. If he'd said anything, Dad would have been dead set against it automatically.

Dad chewed on that. He didn't appear to like it one bit, but he forced out a grudging, "Thanks. I'll call Mom now."

He stepped out their door to have the conversation on their stoop. No one followed him, but Jared had to wonder whether the sirens had brought the neighbors out again to watch their family drama.

He remembered Emily's phone when he had to move it in order to sit in the detective's car—up front, at least, rather than in the back like a suspect. He had to force himself not to scroll through it right there, not to draw attention to it. The detective might confiscate it as evidence. If he found anything, he'd turn it over, but ... he had to look for himself. The detective would never tell him what he discovered. If someone had hurt Emily—no, not *if*; someone *had* hurt Emily—then he had to know. But if he had any doubt, even knowing Emily, knowing she would never have done it, he couldn't trust the police to see through to the truth. Luckily, Emily's phone case was blue, her favorite color, rather than pink or polka dotted or whatever. The detective only glanced over as he shifted the phone to another pocket.

"New phone?" he asked.

"Yes," Jared lied.

He left it at that.

*

Gran put him to work the second he walked through the door, maybe thinking to distract him. Maybe because she needed help Dad had been too busy lately to give her.

He took out the trash, cleaned up enough that he filled a

second bag to go out, and grabbed a third. He dumped them all and wheeled the can to the curb, since tomorrow was pick-up day. Then he scrubbed counters, washed dishes ... He was midway through the dishes when his hands started to shake. He hadn't realized he was in shock, but something must have worn off, because suddenly he wasn't distracted and numb, but full-on shaking, the glass in his hand threatening to crack from the force of the bottle brush banging against it.

He had to put it down before it shattered in his hand. He stood there, wrist-deep in suds, mind suddenly full of *oh crap, oh crap, oh Emily, you've got to be okay.* He knew she was. That same instinct that had told him something had gone horribly wrong for Mom told him that Emily was going to make it, but what kind of pain was she in? And what were they doing to her at the hospital? Was she free to move or had they strapped her down, thinking she was a danger to herself or others? Had she woken up? Had the police been right there—taking pictures, making accusations?

What was Dad saying? Was he supporting Jared's statement that Emily couldn't have hurt herself or Mom? Or did he see a way to get himself off the hook, maybe thinking they'd go lightly on Emily because of her age and what he could claim as mental disturbance?

Jared needed to be there. He had to protect Emily.

Gran called out from the living room, which was just off of the kitchen beyond a weird sort of half wall below with cabinetry above and below like stalagmite and stalactites, leaving only a narrow space between them as a pass-through for food. "You done in there?" she asked. "I don't hear the water running."

He glared, though she couldn't see him. Emily had almost died and she was worried about whether he was slacking.

"I need air," he said abruptly. He didn't care what she thought of that. Suddenly, he couldn't breathe.

He walked right out the front door, then around the side of

the house where there were no windows and pressed his back to it. The closest neighbor's yard started only a few feet away, on the other side of a palisade fence. It was the most privacy he was going to get. He gulped in air and tried to still his shaking hands enough so that he could read the screen of Emily's phone when he unlocked it with her code.

He called Dad before anything, looking for an update, but the phone went straight to voicemail again, and Jared left a message begging him to call with news. Maybe he could get Gran to drive him over to see Emily, but he didn't even know if they were allowing her visitors. Or if she was awake. He didn't think Gran would go for it without the okay from his father, which wasn't going to happen if he wouldn't pick up his phone.

It was only after he hung up that he realized Dad would know the call came from Emily's cell phone and that Jared had it. Hopefully, he'd be too distracted by Emily to think anything of it.

Jared sank to the ground until his butt hit it, back still up against the wall. He pressed the icon to bring up Emily's messages. There were half a dozen unread, but only two he was concerned with. The top one was from her best friend Shara, and said, "Be careful. Text me after."

That got his full attention. He opened the dialogue to see what had come before that.

Heading out now, Emily had written. *Wish me luck.*

Heading out where? She'd been found at home. And going to do what? Why had she talked to Shara about it and not him?

He hit the phone icon to dial Shara. He had to know.

"Tell me everything!" she answered. "What did she say? Did she admit it? How did it go?"

Jared's hands started to shake again. Shara sounded so breathless with anticipation. She was going to be devastated with his news.

"Shara, I'm sorry, this is Jared," he said. "Emily's at the hospital. I need to know—what was she going to do?"

"At the hospital? What happened? Oh my god, is she hurt?"

Crap. He was going to have to tell her. "She … The police think she hurt herself, but I told them she didn't. That someone must have hurt her. That's why I need to know—do what? Why did she need luck?"

Shara was silent for a moment, maybe trying to decide whether she was betraying a confidence. "She was going to talk to the lady your father was having the affair with. She thought she could provide an alibi or something."

How on Earth had that turned into … this? Had it gone badly? Had Carla told her something she couldn't face? But no, there was that weird letter. Even if Emily could have hurt herself, she'd never have hurt Mom. She was being framed.

"Would you tell that to the police if they ask?"

"Of course, but … Jared, what's going on?" She sounded scared. He knew the feeling.

"I don't know yet. But I'm going to find out."

"Are you sure that's safe? If something happened to Emily …"

"That's *why* I have to find out."

He hung up and immediately scrolled to the next message. From Aaliyah's own number. She must have her phone back. It was a sign of how worried he was about Emily that he'd called Shara before checking it.

Jared, I hope you got my message through Maybell earlier this week about how devastated I was to hear about your mother. But that's not enough. I'm sorry I let my parents come between us. I was so mad at you at first.

But now I understand and I hate that I haven't been there for you. I hope you can forgive me. I know I probably screwed everything up, but I wanted you to know I'm here now if you need me. I can't even imagine what you're going through.

A laugh-sob burst out of him. *Now?* He'd desperately hoped Aaliyah would come around, but *now*, when all he could think of was Emily and saving her? Everything was so messed up.

He wasn't ready to answer yet. He didn't know what to say. Not after all this time. He'd done wrong, but so had she. She'd abandoned him when he needed her. He understood it, but it didn't make it any easier. Maybe at some point they could move past it, but he was living in a nightmare he couldn't wake up from. His options were to bring Aaliyah into that nightmare or keep her out. With what was happening to the women in his life, the kindest thing he could do was let her go.

He put the phone back in his pocket and made himself get up. Go back inside. He'd done everything he could for now. Except maybe turn the phone over. Would Shara's information convince the police that Emily had a motive to hurt herself or move them on to another suspect?

That struck him. He'd been thinking *someone* had hurt her, in an abstract kind of way because he just couldn't imagine it being anyone he knew. But what if Ms. Carla hadn't liked Emily's questions? What if she'd decided to frame Emily to protect Dad? Or herself? Was it possible that Carla Meyers had killed his mother to get rid of her rival? But then, what about what he'd heard the night of his mother's disappearance?

Nothing about any of this seemed right. If the killer was going to hide the body in a public park where it would be found, why leave her car at the train station as though she'd left town? It was as though there were two people, one who wanted Mom's body to be found and one who wanted to cover up the murder. Mom's body … he still couldn't even process that. He knew she was dead, had known deep down even before they pulled her body out of those bushes, but he couldn't accept it. Maybe if he'd seen her at the morgue. But he was glad he hadn't. He didn't want that image haunting him for the rest of his life. It would be bad enough at the funeral after they cleaned her up and tried to make it look like she was just sleeping.

Would she look as pale and lifeless as Emily had when he found her with her wrists slashed? That visual would stay with him forever.

The phone rang before he got inside, and he paused at the corner of the house to answer it. *Dad*.

"What are you doing with Emily's phone?" Dad hissed, before he could even say "hello."

"What the hell?" burst out of him before he could be smart about things. "Emily's in the hospital, Mom is dead and *this* is what you want to talk about? I'm worried sick. How is Emily?"

Dad took a breath. Jared could hear it on the other end of the line. He could almost hear him counting down to calm. "Still unconscious," Dad said finally. "They've got her bandaged up and gave her a transfusion, but with the blood loss and meds for the pain, she's still out of it."

"What are the police saying?"

"Well for one, they're wondering what happened to her phone. They didn't find it when they found her. Or in her backpack, which they've taken for evidence."

"I came across it when I went into her backpack for her insurance card and I stuck it in my pocket and forgot about it." Until he was in the car with Detective Diaz, who'd asked him about it and would now catch him in a lie. Would he wonder what else Jared had lied about? How much trouble was he in?

"I'll give it up as soon as someone comes for it. What's going to happen with Emily? Can I see her?"

"No one can right now. They've got her under observation, and once she's awake … She's going to need counseling. They've got her under at least a seventy-two hour-hold."

"What? She didn't *do* this!"

"Jared, they found signs of cutting. Did you know about that?"

Jared had already been caught in one lie. If the police tested the blood on the bag he'd dropped in the Meyers' garbage, they'd know it was Emily's. He'd told them as much. They'd put two and two together.

"I only just found out," he said.

"And you didn't tell me." Every word fell like a gavel.

"I was trying to protect her."

"Well, how did you do? Your sister is in the hospital fighting for her life."

If his father had plunged a knife into his chest it couldn't have hurt any worse. He fell back a step as though he'd done that very thing. Only the wall was holding him up. The shock, the pain, lasted only a second until his anger overwhelmed it. He bucked himself off the wall and stood at the corner of Gran's house ready to square off with his father on the other end of the phone.

"Yeah, because this is all my fault. The cutting couldn't have started with you and Mom fighting or you throwing Mom around. Emily being in the hospital doesn't have anything at all to do with you not knowing what's going on with your own daughter."

Dad growled. "You little shit."

"I want to live with Aunt Aggie," Jared said, throwing the last of his caution to the wind. "Me and Emily both, when she's out of the hospital. It's not safe for us with you."

There was silence.

And then, "Emily can decide for herself when she wakes up."

He didn't say anything about Jared, and despite the fact that he'd made the decision, it hurt, like Dad had twisted the knife he'd plunged into Jared's chest and his heart was being cut to shreds.

Jared hung up. He hurt so much he could barely breathe. He hadn't been thinking. If he went to live with Aunt Aggie, nearly an hour away, how was he going to get to the hospital to visit Emily when she woke up? Because no way was anyone keeping him away. How was he going to see Aaliyah again or get revenge for Mom and Emily? He was still months away from being able to get his drivers' license, and then he'd need access to a car.

But he couldn't live with Dad any longer. Even if Dad wasn't the one to hurt Emily, and he couldn't have been since he'd been at the station at the time, he'd still set everything in motion with what he'd done. He was still an abuser, and Jared couldn't live in fear that Dad would turn on him and Emily. He'd failed to protect Emily once. It wasn't going to happen again. He'd give up track. He'd give up everything to stay home for her. If only she was okay. He didn't really know what he believed in, but he sent up a prayer, promising anything in return for Emily's recovery.

Despite what he'd said to Dad, his next call wasn't to Aunt Aggie. He wanted to live with her, but he couldn't leave town yet. He had unfinished business. And he wasn't giving up Emily's phone just yet. Right now it was his lifeline. The police could come for it, but they'd have to find him first. He went into the settings and turned off the phone's GPS. Then he made a call and went back into the house only long enough to let Gran know he was leaving. He wasn't going to worry her the way he'd worried about Mom, even if it killed his head start.

TWENTY-SIX

Emily

EMILY FLOATED up to the surface. Everything was floaty. Dreamy. There was pain there somewhere, but it was a distant thing. Far far away in a galaxy long ago ... or something like that.

But there was a thing. Something she had to remember. Something she had to tell Jared. Or somebody. It was Jared, right? Her brother? Thoughts were like clouds that skidded away as she tried to touch them. Only clouds didn't skid.

They ... something.

She floated, head filled with nothing but a vision of clouds floating like she was. Not skidding ... drifting, that was it.

Sometime later she surfaced again. There was something urgent. Something she had to tell Jared. If only she could remember.

She tried to lift her hand to her head, as though it would help her remember, but she couldn't move it. Not one or the other. Her hands were so heavy. Or were they bound? Either way, they wouldn't move. She couldn't reach out for the thought, bring it closer.

Jared was in danger. If only she could remember.

The thought skidded away like a cloud.

Only, clouds don't skid, she told herself as she went under again.

❋

He left to meet Aaliyah. Despite the earlier resolution to keep her away for her own protection, he needed an ally. He'd just have to be strategic about it, keep her safe. More than that, if he was honest. He couldn't bear to leave town without seeing her.

He told her to meet him a few blocks away. He didn't want to stay too near Gran's place and chance that she'd send someone to bring him back or call Dad to send someone, maybe even the police. He couldn't risk them coming for him or for Emily's phone. Not yet.

That meant he had to loiter at the corner where he said he'd meet Aaliyah, afraid the whole time that someone would call the cops like they had at his mother's place. He was beyond relieved when Aaliyah drove up. He got in as quickly as he could. She drove off the same way. Not burning rubber, but certainly not sticking around.

"Where do you want to go?" she asked, risking a look away from the road to take him in.

"Somewhere we can talk." Between his mother's death and Emily's near-death, he thought his heart was too broken to beat even for Aaliyah. Their relationship was way to the back of his mind. Or should be. But the very sight of her made his pulse rate jump. Just because he *shouldn't* want her didn't mean he didn't.

Maybe this was a mistake.

"Coffee shop?" she asked.

"Aren't you afraid someone will see us? Report back to your parents?"

Her mouth twisted. "I don't care about that anymore. I spent a lot of time hating myself for giving up on you, especially after I heard about your mother. I didn't know if you'd even want to hear from me, but I had to try. I told my parents my future didn't mean all that much if I went into it as someone I couldn't respect, who'd desert her friends in their hour of need."

He looked at her, but it hurt too much. He had to look away

again, because hope was rising, and all hope had been to him lately was a lying bitch.

"They understood that?" he asked, gazing out the window.

"Not exactly. Dad gave me a speech about there being different rules for you and me—girls and boys, black and white. About how I was never going to get the benefit of the doubt, so I couldn't give people any cause for doubt in the first place. About having to get into the system to change it. Basically, anything he thought would change my mind."

"And your mom?"

"She gave me back my phone. I think she understood that you can't let other people, even your parents, define who you are. If all you ever do is what's expected, what you're told, you never change the world. You never expand anyone's mind."

Like the police seeing Emily as a cutter and stopping there. Only Aaliyah was saying so much more and he felt like he was only getting the tip of the iceberg.

"I'm glad you texted," he said.

"Me too. I'm so sorry to hear about your mother. What's happening with Emily?"

He told her. Everything. They'd reached the parking lot at the coffee shop now but didn't get out. Aaliyah just pulled into a spot, turned off the car, and swiveled in her seat to give Jared her full attention. It was so good to have her back in his corner. He'd always had friends, but they were hang-around friends, the kind you had fun with, did specific things with like go to the movies or the mall or indoor skydiving. Not the kind you really *talked* to. Not until Aaliyah. When he lost her, he lost more than his heart.

And now he'd be moving away. He told her that too. He didn't know what this conversation meant in terms of them, but he couldn't keep that from her. Especially if he was going to ask for her help. She had to know everything.

When he finished, she said, "Wow," and left it there for a minute, absorbing everything. Then, "Do you really want coffee?"

"No."

"Then what do you want to do?"

"Really? I want to find out the truth. I need to confront Carla and clear Emily's name."

Aaliyah pulled back in shock. "She's already hurt your sister," she said. "What makes you think it's safe for you? Because there'll be two of us? Even if she doesn't do anything crazy, why would she confess?"

"I don't know," he said, scraping his fingers through his hair and raking his scalp, as though the sensation might stimulate his brain. "I have Emily's phone. Maybe I can bluff her out, make her think there's something incriminating on here. Maybe she'll come after me for it."

"Jared!"

"That's where you come in. I don't want you inside with me. I'm never going to put you in danger again—of getting arrested or anything else. I'll have Emily's phone on speaker, so you'll be able to hear everything. Plus, I've looked it up, and there's an App that lets you record phone calls, in case we get anything useful for evidence. The law says it's okay if you have the consent of one of the parties. Well, I'm consenting. You'll be on the other end of the line, so you'll be consenting too. No matter how you look at it, we should be covered. Anything else the phone picks up while on speaker is just happenstance, right?"

Aaliyah's eyes were wide, frightened. "It's a good plan, except for one thing—the part where you head into danger."

"My mother ..." his voice gave out on him for a second. He swallowed down the pain before he choked on it and started again. "My mother's been killed. My sister nearly so. I can't sit on the sidelines. I have to do this for them."

"Your mother wouldn't want you to put yourself in danger."

"Like you said, at some point, you have to make your own decisions. Well, I've decided."

She leaned in and took both of his hands in hers. "You really are an amazing person. I can't believe you wondered why I'd pick you. I can't imagine picking anyone else."

He stared at her, shocked to silence. She didn't know about his anger, how he sometimes wanted to lash out at his father or the world. He'd have to tell her that too. Everything. Let her decide, if he survived this. He wasn't going to let the anger rule him, but he wondered whether that was just something he told himself. Maybe it all started with denial. Maybe what he had to do was face it. Work on it every single day. Like Emily would have to face her issues. Maybe they could work on them together.

He leaned forward and kissed Aaliyah. He suddenly couldn't help himself. She met him halfway. But it felt strange to be kissing her right then with everything else going on, and he didn't let it last.

Aaliyah looked sad as he drew back, and he said, "It's not you. It's the timing."

"Sure," she said. "Let's get this done. What's the App?"

He told her, and she downloaded it as they sat there in the parking lot. Then they were off toward the Meyers' house, hopefully to find his mother's killer.

TWENTY-SEVEN

AALIYAH PARKED across the street from the Meyers' house. "You sure you want to do this?" she asked.

"I'm sure. Are *you* still okay with the plan?"

"My part's easy," she answered.

"Okay then." Jared took out Emily's phone. "I'm calling you now."

Aaliyah's phone rang, and she played with the buttons before answering it. "Got it."

Then she set the phone down in her cupholder, grabbed him by the face, and kissed him one more time. "For good luck," she said, "and in case—"

"Nothing is going to happen to me," he said.

"It better not."

He tried to give her a reassuring smile before getting out of the car, but he knew it wasn't a very good one.

As soon as he was out, he minimized the call window and blacked out the screen, hoping it would take more than a wrong move to accidentally end the call. Then he headed toward the Meyers' front door and rang the bell.

For a minute, he didn't think anyone would answer. He

shifted from foot to foot, rang again, and finally heard footsteps headed his way.

His heart pounded, then seemed to stumble when Andrew peered through the window at him rather than Ms. Carla. Well, crap, he hadn't planned on company. Or maybe Andrew was alone and he'd have to come back later.

The door opened, and Andrew stared down at him, brows lowered, like he was confused to see him there.

"Jared?" he said. "What's going on? I saw there was an ambulance at your house earlier. I figured everyone would be at the hospital."

So he'd been home then? What about Ms. Carla? Should he abort the plan? Come tonight he'd be at Aunt Aggie's, almost an hour away. Getting back here would be tough. He had to at least try. Now, before the police arrested Emily or anything else could happen.

"Is your mother home?" he asked.

"Mom? Why do you want her?"

"I just do. Can I come in?"

Andrew stepped aside, and Jared took that as an invitation. He moved past him into a house laid out much like their own, except the wall between their kitchen and living area hadn't been blown out, so the place had a more closed-off feel to it. And something in the kitchen smelled amazing. All tomato-garlicky.

"You cooking?" Jared asked, surprised.

"Not me. Mom's got ziti in the oven. She just ran out to the bakery to grab garlic bread to go with it."

"So she won't be long?" Jared asked.

"Shouldn't be. What's this about?" He didn't offer Jared a drink or a seat. In fact, he stayed between Jared and the kitchen as if guarding the way. Maybe that was okay, because it meant he wasn't between Jared and the door. Which was an odd thought, but something about the intensity of Andrew's stare was starting to make Jared nervous.

And he realized something else. "You never asked who the ambulance was for," he said. "Or what happened."

Andrew's brows lowered like storm clouds. "I didn't want to be nosy." Nothing about his tone was convincing.

"It was Emily," Jared said, studying Andrew's reaction.

Something was seriously wrong here. A normal person—a *concerned* person—would have asked if she was okay. Andrew just waited for more.

"The police think she cut herself," he continued, though he really didn't know what the police thought.

"Is she going to be okay?" Andrew asked. Finally, a normal question, but the way he asked it didn't put Jared at ease. He'd never shown a speck of concern for Jared or Emily, but suddenly seemed very invested in the answer.

"We don't know."

Andrew relaxed at that, and it was the weirdest reaction. Jared wished he could talk to Aaliyah and get her take on things as she heard them on the other end of the phone.

"So then why are you here rather than at the hospital?"

"They won't let me in to see Emily yet, and ..." Did he tell Andrew? Something was definitely going on here. He couldn't leave until he figured out what it was. Maybe Andrew hadn't asked about Emily because he already knew. Maybe his mother had told him. Yet she was making ziti and running errands like it was all nothing.

Screw it, he'd come this far. He was all in. "I think your mother may have been the last person to see Emily. I need to know if she has any idea what happened."

"I don't think so," Andrew said, his tone spooky as hell.

"What don't you think?" Jared ventured, mind going again to the door right behind him. "That your mother was with my sister or that she can help me?"

"Both. You're not dragging us into your troubles." He stepped forward, one arm outstretched as though to grab Jared's shoulder and show him to the door.

Jared stood his ground, despite all the hairs on his body now standing on end and his fight or flight response screaming for retreat.

"I'm not leaving here without—"

He never even saw the fist flying for his face. The next thing he knew, he was on the ground, looking up blearily at Andrew looming over him with his fist clenched and his face twisted with rage.

"You may be right. Maybe you're not leaving here at all," he snarled. He glared down at Jared with such hatred his heart started to pound. Murderous hatred. "Dammit, your family can't do anything right. Your bitch mother wouldn't file assault charges to get your damned father out of our lives. Your dad can't even get arrested in this town, no matter what evidence the police have on him, and your sister—"

Jared lay stunned for a second before rearing up. All the rage, all the pain and fear and frustration he'd been feeling concentrated in his fists. *He* could be angry at his mother for leaving. *He* could hate what Emily did to herself, but *Andrew*? Andrew had no right.

Jared flew at him, fists flying. Andrew blocked the one headed for his face. A big, obvious swing. But he missed the second, aimed straight at his solar plexus. Andrew's breath burst out of him, and he doubled over in pain. Jared brought up a knee, ready to connect with his nose, but never got there. Andrew grabbed him around the middle, sent him crashing again to the floor, coming down hard on his tailbone and stunned into immobility long enough for Andrew to get another blow in. Jared flinched to the side just in time to catch it on his cheekbone rather than his already damaged nose. Already his vision was clouding as everything swelled, closing off his sight. He had to end this quickly.

He rolled, hard, but Andrew pushed back, scrambling to disengage before he could get rolled under. He got to one knee, but Jared kicked hard and heard something pop. Andrew bellowed in pain and fell back to the floor, clutching for his leg. Jared got on top of him, sitting on his chest, glaring down. His fists were still clenched. He wanted to send them flying for Andrew's face. Or to lift and slam his head into the floor. Or a million other things. He wanted Andrew to hurt.

There was a sound, someone calling his name in terror, and he realized it was coming from his phone. From Aaliyah on the other end of it. She couldn't know what was going on, but she was there listening. Recording. He could beat Andrew to a bloody pulp, but it wouldn't get him the answers he needed. And it wouldn't bring his mother back.

"What *about* my sister?" he asked, glaring down at Andrew.

He stopped fighting long enough to glare back, fire in his eyes saying the fight wasn't over. "Your sister is weak," he spat. "Like your mother. Like *my* bitch mother—cheating, lying, trying to shield your lousy father. As if her loyalty was to him. Not to me or my Dad. Oh, she said she was covering for me, but we all know that's a lie. If she cared about me or my father, she'd never have been slutting around."

Jared's blood went cold. "Covering for what?"

He had to swallow down the blood coating his throat from the broken nose in order to ask. Between that and the swelling, he hoped he could still be understood for the recording.

Andrew brought his head up suddenly, right into Jared's face, hitting his damaged nose and sending the pain supernova. His vision blacked out, the world twisted, and the next thing he knew, he was pinned under Andrew, his vision clearing just enough to meet the gaze of a madman. There was no sanity left behind Andrew's eyes. Just empty gaping holes that only violence would fill.

"Don't play any dumber than you have to," Andrew said, his face far too close, his weight making it hard for Jared's chest to expand. His head was already swimming. "You don't care what I think of your sister. Ask me what you're really here for. You want to know about your mother's murder."

"My mother?" he gasped, struggling for enough air. "But why would you—"

"Because!" Andrew shouted, his spittle flying in Jared's face. "Because your father hit her that night. Bounced her head off of something the way my fist bounced off your face. And not for the first time. Remember when you came running to our house? Your mother wouldn't press charges then either. She could have stopped everything that night. Your father. My mother's affair. But she didn't."

"I don't get—"

Andrew lifted his head, slammed it into the floor as Jared had wanted to do to him. His vision blacked again, and terror spiked like lightning through his brain. He'd walked right up to his mother's killer. Put himself in Andrew's hands. And now he was possibly going to die the same way.

But the worst was the realization of how close he'd come to *being* Andrew. He shared the same angers. The same impulse control issues. He didn't want to believe he could be one bad decision away from murder. Maybe it would be best if he let Andrew take him out. If he could leave some of his DNA behind, something that would get Andrew caught, the world would be a better place.

Andrew didn't know or care about the crisis raging through Jared. Malice gleamed in his eyes as he stared him down. "I saw her that night, sitting in her car, bleeding," he said, reveling in the pain he was causing Jared, devouring it. "I offered to call the police. To sit with her. But she refused. She was bleeding and he was to blame *and she wouldn't do a damn thing about it.*"

"So you blamed the victim?" He struggled to get the words out.

Andrew leaned more of his weight onto Jared's stomach, forcing out the very last of his air. "So I gave her something to complain about until she was never going to complain again. If she wouldn't accuse your father, I'd make sure the police found her body. And enough evidence to arrest him."

There was another sound from Jared's pocket. Aaliyah telling him help was on the way. He could only hope it wouldn't come too late. But it drew Andrew's attention, and he shifted, just enough for Jared to suck in air. It hurt like hell.

Andrew grabbed roughly for Jared's pocket, digging for the phone.

"If you wanted Mom found, why leave her car at the train station?" Jared asked, hoping to distract him.

It was no use. Andrew came up with the phone. He resettled his weight on top of Jared and raised it to his ear, the look on his face absolutely chilling.

"The girlfriend, I presume?" he said. "Or are you the bitch sister?"

Jared willed Aaliyah to stay silent. He didn't want Andrew going after her next. Especially if he didn't live through this. If he wasn't there to throw himself between them.

No, not even an option. He had to take Andrew down. He couldn't let him hurt anyone else.

"You don't have to tell me," he said. "I have the number now. I have one little thing to take care of here, and then *you're next.*"

He smashed a finger to the phone, disconnecting the call, and when that wasn't enough for him, he smashed the phone itself onto the ceramic tile of their floor, right beside Jared's head. Once. Twice. When it cracked, the sound shot right through him.

And then he was alone with a murderer. Truly alone.

Slowly, Andrew smiled down at him, his lips stretching like they might peel back from his face. It was a death's head grin. Maybe it was his failing vision or even his concussion, but it seemed like Andrew had become something less than human.

"You want to know the truth before you die?" he asked. "You can take it to your grave. My mother saw me come in that night, all bloody. I enjoyed telling her what I'd done. For us. And still she covered for him. Finding the car, driving it to the train station, cleaning up the evidence."

"Did my father know?"

"Screw your father! He started all this. One way or another it was all his fault. I don't know what my bitch mother told him or what he knew, but *he* did this to my family and yours."

He'd had enough talking. Andrew grabbed Jared by the hair, ready to slam his head into the floor again. Like he'd done with the phone. Once. Twice. Until he cracked.

TWENTY-EIGHT

JARED LOOKED FOR HIS MOMENT. He could *not* leave Andrew free to terrorize Emily and Aaliyah. He'd failed to protect his mother; he was damn sure not going to fail them.

The sound of sirens suddenly split the night.

Andrew's hold on Jared's hair loosened in shock over the sirens, and Jared jumped on the opportunity to rip his head out of Andrew's hands and roll to the side, kicking hard as he went but catching Andrew only a glancing blow.

Andrew leapt to his feet. The whites of his eyes had gone red, like he'd popped blood vessels in his overblown anger. He looked between Jared and the door as though to decide whether to finish him off or run. Jared wasn't giving him that chance. This was going to end. Now.

Jared kicked out again for the knee he'd cracked before, but Andrew jumped out of the way, roaring like he was more beast than man. Jared used the distance for the chance to roll to his feet, but his vision swam and his stomach rebelled like he was going to lose it all over the floor. He swayed on his knees, fighting back the wave of nausea that wanted to take his sight and his consciousness with it. Definite concussion.

His vision cleared just in time to see Andrew reaching behind his back, fumbling for something he had tucked away. The snick of the blade opening gave it away even before he saw it slashing toward him.

Knife! Jared dove to the side, vision and stomach twisting again, but Andrew caught him by the leg with one hand and buried the knife in his thigh with the other. Jared howled, pinned in place by the pain that exploded over him.

There was pounding now at the front door, a demand to open up, but Jared's whole world had narrowed to pain and fear. He knew there was some artery in the leg that could bleed out in moments. If Andrew had hit it—

Andrew left the knife buried in his leg and turned for the back of the house and the sliding glass door to escape as a crack split the front door, probably thinking he'd already killed his only witness. It was just a matter of time, and Jared wasn't sure how much he had.

But he was going to make it count. Andrew was *not* getting away.

It took everything he had to gather his legs under him and lunge after Andrew. He had the advantage of no longer being concerned about himself, and when he flew into a tackle, it was with everything he had. He caught Andrew around the knees, and they both came crashing down to the floor together. Andrew tried to catch himself on his hands, but they slid out from under him, and he cracked his chin hard on the sharp tile. It stunned him for half a second, but then he was flailing, thrashing, bucking, and kicking to get Jared off of him. Jared hung on as though his life depended on it.

The police crashed through the door a second later, demanding they stop right where they were.

Jared had no intention of doing anything else. He held onto Andrew until the police insisted he let go, which he did with the relief of fading strength. He heard someone call for an ambulance, watched as they cuffed Andrew, and then let his eyes close against the pain ... until he heard someone shout from outside, sounding frantic, "Is he okay? Just tell me he's okay!"

Aaliyah.

Outside, an officer tried to ma'am her, tell her to stay back, and he smiled, knowing how that would go. Maybe they could keep her back, but they'd tell her what she wanted to know first. She'd make sure of it.

"I'm okay!" he shouted from inside, hoping she'd hear him before things got heated.

"You've lost a lot of blood," one of the police officers said, squatting beside him. They hadn't cuffed him. Was it because they knew he was the good guy or because he was too hurt to be a threat? And wasn't that the same thing they'd said about Emily, "she's lost a lot of blood"?

The fear crashed in on him again. "Did he hit the artery?" Jared asked, hoping he hadn't just lied to Aaliyah. Or to Emily when he'd said he wouldn't leave her.

"I'm no medic," he said, "but I don't think so. Not enough blood. Although, I don't know what will happen when they remove the knife." He was putting pressure above the wound, using his hands like a tourniquet.

"Can I see her?" he asked, meaning Aaliyah. If he wasn't going to make it ...

The officer shook his head. "This is a crime scene. I'm sure you'll pass her when the paramedics get you to the ambulance. Want to tell me what happened here?"

"Andrew killed my mother. His mother is the one who hurt my sister, framing her for his crimes. I didn't know. I was coming to talk to her when he attacked me."

"Do you have proof?"

"How about a confession? My girlfriend—the one you won't let me see—" as if there was anyone else, "has it all recorded." Well, right up until the end.

The officer's mouth fell open in shock, and he called out to one of the other officers to get that recording. "Just hang on," he said to Jared.

There were other sirens now. Close. Jared hoped they'd put him in the same wing as Emily.

Then the paramedics arrived and started working on his leg, and his only wish was that he'd pass out.

TWENTY-NINE

Emily

EMILY CAME AWAKE SLOWLY, by degrees, floating finally just below the surface. She could open her eyes, complete the process. But then she'd have to face everything. Her father. Carla. The truth.

Someone coughed, and she became suddenly very aware she wasn't alone in the room. Her whole body tensed, and the last safety of sleep fell away. She could only hope whoever it was hadn't noticed. At least until she knew who was there and that she was safe.

She opened her eyelids just a slit, hoping to see her visitor before they knew she was awake. But she had only a limited view. Reluctantly, she lifted her head off the pillow and opened her eyes more fully. She had to know what she was up against. Her head pounded, and her vision tracked oddly, like her eyes and brain were out of sync and there was a delay between seeing and processing. So it took her a second to realize what she was seeing.

Jared, sitting there in a wheelchair, watching her. A smile

broke out across his face as she focused in on him. "Hey, sleepyhead."

She sagged with relief, then tensed back up almost immediately. Why was Jared in a wheelchair?

She went to ask, but her mouth was sandpaper dry, and it came out with a rasp he had to push himself closer to hear. His chair butted into her bed, rocking them both.

"Water?" she asked.

He looked around the room and wheeled himself over to a small sink. He had to leverage himself out of the chair to search the cabinet above it for cups, all while trying to hide the way his lips twisted in pain, compressing to keep from making a sound. She noticed he kept the pressure on his hands and unbandaged leg.

But she waited until he came back and until the room temperature water slid down her throat, soothing the dryness as it went. When she thought she could talk, she asked again and he told her. Everything.

What Andrew had done and why. What Carla had done to cover for him. The fact that the police had both in custody.

Emily closed her eyes against the onslaught of words, but it didn't help, and memories floated up, the same ones that had cried out for her attention when she was floating away, faint from blood loss and meds. Carla holding her down, her face far too close to Emily's own, stony and unmoved as she begged and thrashed, trying to escape. It had been no use; Carla's strength had been ridiculous and absolute. They said women could lift cars off infants in a crisis. Apparently, that wasn't all they could do. It was horrifying, the things Carla had done to protect her son when no one, not even their father, had done anything to protect them....

"Did Dad know?" Emily asked, opening her eyes so that she could see Jared's face when he answered, gauge his sincerity.

"Did Dad know what?"

Emily and Jared both looked to the doorway where Dad

stood, highlighted by the brighter light of the hallway. She tensed up again. For some reason, one of her arms came up defensively, only to be pulled up short by an IV tube that had gotten wrapped around the protective bedrail.

Jared turned his chair awkwardly to face his father, pushing off Emily's bed with one hand and spinning a wheel with the other.

He was only half turned away from her as he glared up at their father, so she could see the fire in his eyes, the granite set of his jaw. "Did you know that Mom was dead? That Andrew had killed her? That she was killed because of you? Did you know that Carla would do anything to protect him, even kill your own daughter?"

"Emily isn't dead," he said, stepping into the room, starting to close the door behind him.

"Don't!" It burst out of Emily with no time to analyze. But now that it was out, she realized that she did not want them to be alone with their father. Ever again. Things would never be the same. *Shouldn't* be the same. She'd always tried to keep the peace, smooth things over, but it had only covered for their problems. There was no peace to be found when Dad carried the war with him.

Her father froze, the door half closed behind him. Emily didn't want to take her eyes off of him to free her IV tube, to find the nurse call button she knew had to be somewhere close by.

"Did you know?" she repeated, glaring up at him. She hoped she looked strong like Jared. What she felt was so much more complicated than plain fear. There was burning anger. And hate. She didn't want to hate her father, but she did. It was there. Building to a boil.

"I expected this from Jared, but not from you. Bug-bear—"

He hadn't called her that since she was little, and the sound of it now made her skin crawl. It felt wrong. Manipulative. Dirty.

"Don't," she said again. More controlled this time. Completely in control, as though whatever power he'd held over her had shattered. *"I'm* asking. And you're going to answer. You owe us that."

Dad jerked his head back like she'd struck him. Was it so shocking that she was standing up to him? Had she been that docile? Well, no more. The fact that she'd tensed up at his appearance meant his threat still loomed over them, and she was done with threats. She supposed almost dying would do that to a person.

"Not at first," he said quietly. Begrudgingly. "I really thought she'd gone. It wasn't until they found the blood in her car at the train station. There was no reason to take a train when she had the car. And the blood ..." He hung his head.

"You hurt her," she said, mercilessly. "Why wouldn't there be blood?"

His head snapped up, and he looked like he was trying to keep his face neutral and failing. A muscle twitched along his jaw.

"We can talk about all of this at home," he said. "They're releasing you both today. I'm thinking we grab pizza and ice cream on the way. I've picked up a couple of new movies just out on Blu-ray, and—"

"No." Emily and Jared both said at once.

Jared glanced over his shoulder at her, and their eyes met. For once they understood each other perfectly. He nodded at what he saw and turned back around.

"I told you, we're done," Jared said, speaking for both of them. "We're not going home with you. Not now. Not ever."

"It's not your place to decide. You're under eighteen. Until then ..."

"Not going to happen," Jared said.

Her father dismissed Jared by a flick of the wrist and a quick turning away. He now looked at Emily. Just Emily, like she was the only one in the room. Dad didn't focus in often, but when he did he had that ability to make you feel like you were really seen. Special. Loved. She felt like those were the moments she'd spent her life fighting for. It hurt now, a blow to her chest, but not quite strong enough to break her heart. She was done letting him hurt her that way. Hurt *them*.

"Bug-bear, it's over. Let me make it up to you. I'm so sorry about all of this. You have no idea."

"What about Mom? Are you sorry about Mom too?"

She held her hand up to stop him. She didn't really want an answer. It would only be a lie. "Never mind, I won't believe you. I'm with Jared. We're not coming back. We'll go to Aunt Aggie. We'll go to Child Protective Services if we have to. We'll fight you tooth and nail. If Andrew and Carla's trials don't bring out your dirty laundry, we'll make sure it gets aired. But believe me when I say *we are not coming back.*"

Her father's jaw had dropped, and he looked so stunned she could almost pity him. Almost.

She got her hand free and found the button beside it to call for the nurse to show her father out.

EPILOGUE

A FEW WEEKS LATER

"THANK YOU FOR HELPING," Aunt Aggie said to Aaliyah. "Moving goes so much faster with four people, even if Jared keeps stopping for kisses and crap."

Jared glared. "Aaliyah saved my life. I think she's entitled to a few kisses."

"She also let you go through with your harebrained scheme. I'd call that a push."

Aunt Aggie didn't cut anybody slack about anything. It was one of the things he loved and hated about her, depending on whether he was the one on the receiving end. But she liked Aaliyah, and Aaliyah liked the straightforward approach.

"Wait until his next harebrained idea. You get to try stopping him," Aaliyah said.

His aunt laughed. "Challenge accepted."

He smiled at their banter, but it quickly vanished. Mom was gone. They were only moving because they could no longer live with their father and Aunt Aggie didn't have the room at her place for two kids. They'd tried it for a bit while her custody was temporary, pending confirmation, but now they were off to a new place. A new start.

Old pains were coming along for the ride. The torment of every moment he'd fought with Mom, the sharper pain of the good memories that made him miss her so much. Hiking with her at Bear Mountain State Park, the ice cream fight he and Emily had gotten into afterward that Mom didn't even scold them for, even though they got her car all sticky....

Mom's funeral had been the worst, but they'd gotten through it. He'd even given a eulogy and managed to say everything he'd meant to say to her when she was alive. He wasn't sure anyone could understand him toward the end, when the tears fell thick and ugly, but that didn't stop him. He felt wrung out afterward, but better. Like maybe she'd even heard him. And forgiven. He still didn't know what he believed, but he hoped there was a heaven and that she was in it. She deserved to be there. Mom had never wanted to hurt anyone, not even the man who'd hurt her.

"You okay?" Emily asked.

He'd stopped, apparently, in the middle of the hall, and she needed him to move out of her way.

"Yeah," he said, stepping aside. "You?"

"Getting there," she answered.

She looked good. Still pale, but not bloodless. The bandages had come off her wrists, but she still wore long sleeves to cover the scars. Maybe always would. Therapy was helping with the rest, though. For both of them. Jared still worried about becoming like Dad, but not so much anymore. When he'd had Andrew down, he could have kept pounding him. The way his father might have. The way Andrew had done to Mom, bashing out his anger, but he hadn't. What had gotten him up and moving even after he'd been stabbed was the thought of some-thing happening to others—to Emily and Aaliyah. People he loved. He was his father's son, but he was also his mother's. He was going to focus on that part of himself.

So yeah, *getting there*. It was the best they could do right now.

Healing was a work in progress. Some days were better than others. Today …

"Pizza later?" he heard Aaliyah ask his aunt.

"Of course, it's a moving tradition. Pizza and beer. Well, in your case, soda. My treat."

Today was one of the good days.

ACKNOWLEDGMENTS

There are so many people I have to thank for setting me on the right track or keeping me going with this book. No book is easy, but the important ones fight the hardest, and it was very important to me to get this one right. If I've succeeded, it's because of amazing people like retired NYPD Investigator G. Anthony Luhs, who answered a bazillion questions for me (any mistakes are likely due to questions I failed to ask), and fellow authors Amber Hart, who made an especially sharp observation that changed the whole trajectory of the book, and Amy Christine Parker, long-time friend and critique partner, whose feedback has always been invaluable. I want to thank my cousins Heather Boswell and Angela Diver Clark, who read this when I had doubts and insisted on reading more so that I had to write it for them.

Huge thanks to my husband for taking on a crazy wife and somehow finding her wonderful. (Right back atcha, hon!) To my daughter and my dogs for inspiration and occasionally giving me the time and space to write. To my parents, who are, thankfully, not the inspiration for this book, but have always been amazingly supportive.

Also, big thanks to Kevan Lyon for all her work on this, and to Kevin Anderson, Rebecca Moesta, and Marie Whittaker for believing in the book and for everything they do.

It really takes a village, and I truly do love mine.

ABOUT THE AUTHOR

Lucienne Diver is the author of the *Vamped* young adult series—think *Clueless* meets *Buffy*—and the *Latter-Day Olympians* urban fantasy series, which Long and Short Reviews calls "a clever mix of Janet Evanovich and Rick Riordan." Her favorite pull quote ever!

Her short stories have appeared in the *Kicking It* anthology edited by Faith Hunter and Kalayna Price (Roc Books), the *Strip-Mauled* and *Fangs For the Mammaries* anthologies edited by Esther Friesner (Baen Books), and Faith Hunter's *Rogue Mage* anthology, *Tribulations* (Lore Seekers Press). Her essay "Abuse" was published in *Dear Bully: 70 Authors Tell Their Stories* (Harper-Collins).

Bella Rosa Books released her first two young adult suspense novels, *Faultlines* and *The Countdown Club*.

On a personal note, Lucienne lives in Florida with her husband and daughter, the two cutest dogs in the world, and enough books to someday collapse the second floor of her home into the first. She likes living dangerously.

OTHER WORDFIRE PRESS TITLES BY LUCIENNE DIVER

Bad Blood
Crazy in the Blood
Rise of the Blood
Battle for the Blood
Blood Hunt

Our list of other WordFire Press authors and titles is always growing. To find out more and to see our selection of titles, visit us at:
wordfirepress.com

IF YOU LIKED ...

DISAPPEARED, YOU MIGHT ALSO ENJOY:

Prospero Lost
by L. Jaqi Lamplighter

Witches Protection Program
by Michael Okon

Taylor's Ark
by Jody Lynn Nye

Lightning Source UK Ltd.
Milton Keynes UK
UKHW040942240420
362180UK00003B/454